MW01140997

# ELEPHANT TEARS

For Elizabeth —

May your safari

Be a great one

Richard Stout

S. Lewu

## Mask Of The Elephant

# Richard Trout

MacGregor Family Adventures
Book 2

*Harbor Lights 2000 Series*

**LANGMARC PUBLISHING • SAN ANTONIO, TEXAS**

# *Elephant Tears*
## *Mask of the Elephant*
# Richard Trout

Adventures of the MacGregor Family—Book 2

*Harbor Lights 2000 Series*

*For Young Adults and Families*
Cover Artist: Aundrea Hernandez
Graphics: Michael Qualben
Photos: Mavis Trout

Copyright © 2000 by Richard Trout
First Printing 2000
Printed in the United States of America

All rights reserved. No part of this book may be reproduced or transmitted in any form or by any means, electronic or mechanical, including photocopying, recording, or by any information storage and retrieval system, without the written permission of the publisher, except for review. This novel is a work of fiction. Characters, names, places, and events are a product of the author's imagination. Any resemblance to actual persons, business or government establishments, events, or locations is coincidental.

Published by
**LANGMARC PUBLISHING**
*Harbor Lights 2000 Series*
**P.O. Box 33817 • San Antonio, TX 78265**

**Library in Congress Cataloging-in-Publication Data**

Trout, Richard.
  Elephant tears: mask of the elephant / Richard Trout.
    p. cm. -- (Harbor lights 2000 Series)

ISBN: 1-880292-72-6 (pbk.)

# Dedication

*for*
*Kristen Mara*

*A Lover of Elephants*

# MacGregor Family Adventure Novels

for Young Adults and Families
by Richard Trout

*Cayman Gold:*
*Lost Treasure of Devils Grotto*

*Elephant Tears:*
*Mask of the Elephant*

*Falcon of Abydos:*
*Oracle of the Nile*

Available Summer, 2000

# Contents

# Acknowledgments

A special thanks must be expressed to the following people who have been instrumental in bringing the concept of the MacGregor Family Adventure Novels to fruition. Thanks to my wife Mavis and our two daughters, Kristen and Keely, and my parents Virgil and Gwen Trout for their daily support of my dream.

Thanks to our friends Kimberli Brownlee, Donna Watson, Van Herd, Ann Hovda, Dan Threlkeld, Joe Zorger, and Steve Funk for their encouragement and technical advice for this novel and also for *Cayman Gold: Lost Treasure of Devils Grotto*.

Thank you to the Carson and Barnes Circus, who let me spend a memorable afternoon with their two African elephants Paula and Christy.

Thank you to my heroes Mark and Delia Owens of the Owens Foundation for Wildlife Conservation. Through their unselfish example and incredible courage, they have shown the world that two people can make a difference in the lives and safety of the animals of Africa.

And lastly, to Lois Qualben, President of LangMarc Publishing, and her husband, the late Dr. Jim Qualben, for their support and confidence that we too can make a difference in the lives of young people and families by bringing them quality entertainment that can enrich their lives. It was the Qualbens' dream to provide "Harbor Lights" to guide the young people of this world to a safe haven—a haven that can be found in good literature that emboldens spirits, reinforces resolve, and nourishes dreams.

To all of these wonderful people, I am truly grateful.

Richard Trout

# Introduction

During the past thirty years, wild animals of virtually every species and description have been killed illegally in Africa and around the world. Despite the efforts of many international organizations, poaching of endangered species continues and corruption within the governments of many nations allows it to happen. Breeding programs of wild animals within zoos, circuses, and private institutes have been hurried along in an effort to preserve the DNA of many of these animals before they become extinct in the wild. Some have been successful, others have not.

Scientists, zookeepers, animal trainers, and conservationists have been working frantically to save what is left of what we call "wild." And while many wild animals become domesticated in this process, it is their only hope of survival and the hope that their offspring may again return to the natural habitat that was destroyed or stolen from them.

Some nations find it profitable to protect animals and allow tourists to engage in wonderful camera safaris. Other nations attempt to combine conservation within gigantic parks with legalized big game hunting. They take the money gained from hunting and use it to protect more animals. Big game hunting, when carefully monitored and closely regulated, can provide valuable resources for conservation efforts and habitat reclamation. It is the author's opinion, however, that the hunting of elephants and endangered species should be stopped entirely. The history of some combined wildlife programs, of hunting and conservation, has not always been successful and many times corruption follows allowing more animals to be killed than necessary. Elephant ivory and other rare animal products are then smuggled into Asian nations to be made into jewelry and works of art.

This novel attempts to view wild animal conservation through the eyes of a younger generation. Through the adventures and keen insight of Chris ( age 17), Heather (age 14), and Ryan MacGregor (age 12), and their Kukuyu friend Rebecca Okere (age 14), people can learn a few lessons about saving the lives of earth's remaining endangered species and preventing other animals from ever getting on the list. After all, extinction is forever.

Richard Trout

# Prologue

## Masai Mara Wildlife Preserve
## Kenya, East Africa
### July, 1990

Six park rangers walked quietly and cautiously along the riverbank. Each step was measured to avoid walking on a branch that would crack and reveal their presence. The midday sun burned on their hot dry skin as each man eyed the coolness of the river just ten feet away. A pungent odor permeated the air. Daniel Okere, the lead wildlife ranger, stopped and held up his hand as he motioned for the other five rangers to halt. Beads of sweat rolled off his forehead and onto his cheeks. Okere then touched his callused right index finger across his lips to signal silence. The rangers knelt in the tall green grass of the riverbank and rested their rifles on the ground. The further they traveled from the river, the drier the brown grasslands became. The rains were very late this year. Only the Mara River to the northeast still provided water to this dry, parched land.

Okere gave the hand sign that there was movement ahead. He couldn't tell what it was. He leaned over and carefully pushed his old M-1 carbine out in front of him on the ground as he crawled forward. He wanted to stir up any mambas that might be sleeping. The mamba is one of Africa's deadliest snakes, and it is far better not to surprise one and risk its deadly venom. The old M-1 rifle had been in his family for years, but Okere had only fired it a few times while on patrol. Each time he had killed a mamba to save himself or one of his rangers.

The poachers, who roamed this valley illegally hunting its wild animals, carried powerful weapons that could kill the biggest elephant as well as park rangers who interfered. On the other hand, Okere and his rangers carried obsolete weapons that they affectionately referred to as their old "snake" rifles. Okere was well aware that their job was mainly reconnaissance. Find the poachers, follow them out of the valley, and report them to the government so the army could arrest them. No confrontation was expected. But to the poachers, Okere and his rangers were the enemy.

The noise became louder as the rangers approached a stand of trees. Elephants love certain fruit and will habitually follow a track through the bush and forest that includes their favorite food trees. Okere knew they were only a few yards away from the elephant trail. The noise became louder and the pungent odor became stronger. Each ranger now recognized the sounds of a baby elephant. As they peered over the top of the grass, they could see a baby elephant standing guard over the body of its mother. They crept closer to the fallen mother elephant, forgetting their own discomfort in the hot sun.

They grimaced when they saw where the large ivory tusks had been grotesquely removed from the dead mother elephant. Bullet holes marked where the mother had been shot with high-powered automatic rifles.

Okere walked over to the baby and rubbed its left ear as she turned and touched him with her little trunk. The anxiety and mourning of the baby was obvious. Okere thought he could see tears coming from her eyes. He knew elephants well. Their powerful human-like emotions and love of family were legendary in the animal world. Okere had sensed this emotion before with elephants.

Heavy thuds, accompanied by panting breaths, could be heard on the hidden path. Suddenly, all the rangers became quiet and peered nervously toward the bush. The wide-eyed men glanced at each other.

"Lions," one of them shouted as he broke into a run toward the river.

But it was too late. A large male lion, its mane of black and gold, bounded out of the bush and onto the side of the dead elephant. When he had landed, he released a monstrous growl and swiped toward the rangers with claws extended. One ranger didn't move fast enough and two claws drug across his left leg producing a bloody red stripe. The territorial male had scented the dead elephant from a mile away. With no obvious feeding noises from hyenas, jackals, or wild dogs, the lion had sensed that the carcass hadn't been claimed. The lion twirled around, jumped down from the elephant's side and then back up. He challenged the rangers to move closer, defending his claim on the dead elephant. He swung his deadly claws and raked the air ready to make any contact necessary.

Within a minute, three lionesses bounded from the same hidden pathway into the clearing. Instinctively they charged the retreating rangers. Okere dropped to one knee and took aim as a three-hundred-pound female charged him. He knew it was his life or hers; but, nonetheless, he hated this moment as he pulled the trigger. The loud boom of the rifle caused the big cats to retreat toward the bush as the female turned in a cloud of dust at his feet. The bullet ricocheted off the hard dry ground creasing her shoulder. A small stream of blood sprinkled her golden hair. She bounced violently to one side and rolled on the ground biting at the sting in her shoulder. Her attention was diverted from Okere.

Okere wanted to smile knowing that the plan he had devised in a split second had worked. But he still faced three adult lions. They were angry and hungry. Maddened from the scent of the elephant's blood and the injury of one of their own, the lions regrouped and charged again. Okere looked around only to see the last of his rangers dive into the river, risking the crocodile's jaws over the hungry lions.

Quickly taking aim, he knew he would have to shoot to kill this time, something he always avoided unless a human life was at risk. But he also realized he would not be able to kill all three lions and he would surely die.

From behind him, a twenty-foot-tall young acacia tree came crashing to the ground. A huge bull elephant charged from the bush stopping only ten feet from him. The lions retreated behind the dead elephant and postured for an attack. Their ears were pulled back and their teeth were gleaming in the sunlight. They instinctively knew they were no match for the bull elephant, which could crush them with one simple step. Slapping and biting at each other in frustration, they bounded back down the hidden pathway and were gone. The slightly injured female ran a few strides behind the retreating pride. She was more concerned about being left behind than about the scratch on her shoulder. All lions were accustomed to being poked and scratched by the "wicked" thorn trees of Africa and her wound wasn't much different.

Okere didn't move. He knew that a human couldn't outrun an angry bull elephant. If he tried, he would be overtaken in a couple of minutes and crushed to death. The bull's ears were held straight out, his head tilted back. His trunk was stretched into the air. A loud trumpeting noise bellowed from his trunk as the elephant stomped the ground, kicking up dust and breaking branches of the fallen tree.

Okere had seen this behavior before. He had to be still and pray for the bull elephant to spare him. It crossed his mind that he would much prefer the crushing foot of the elephant to the sharp claws and teeth of the lions.

Just as quickly as the bull elephant appeared, four more adult elephants maneuvered through the bush into the clearing. They formed a circle around Okere and the baby elephant. The baby elephant tried to trumpet but only squeaked out a small noise as she scurried over to one of the females surrounding Okere. The other rangers were nowhere to be found.

Okere slowly squatted on the ground and crossed his legs. He laid the old World War II vintage rifle on the ground in front of him. He couldn't see the point in taking another life. The gigantic bull elephant rocked backwards and flapped his ears in the wind. He relaxed his aggressive posture.

Okere could sense that the elephant was not going to attack. He had been a park ranger for ten years and he felt that even the elephants knew who were the good guys and who were the bad guys. It was only the mambas he hated to encounter.

The baby elephant was standing under the belly of a large female as she turned away from her dead mother. She followed the steps of her newly adopted mother into the tree island. As the elephants walked by the dead mother, each one touched her body with its trunk as if saying good-bye. The massive bull stopped and dipped his head. With his trunk he tossed a little dirt toward Okere. He then lifted his head high and trumpeted loudly. Whirling nimbly 180 degrees on his huge legs, the bull joined the last of the females as they disappeared into the bush.

Okere was glad he had resisted the temptation to run away. The elephants were almost as much his family as his own wife and four-year-old daughter. In a few minutes it was only the fallen elephant and Okere left in the clearing.

Once again the odor attacked his senses and he rose

to his feet. The smell made him nauseous. Okere kicked
the dirt out of his right sandal and walked down to the
riverbank. Crouching over the clear water, he looked
around for crocodiles. When he was convinced that an
old croc was not ready to ambush him, he dipped his
hands deep into the cool water. He noticed his men on
the other side of the river tending to the injured ranger.
He splashed water onto his face and immediately felt
refreshed.

Okere climbed the bank and took a small notepad
and pencil from the cargo pocket of his shorts. He
recorded the location of the elephant, the date, and the
time of day. He reached into his pocket and retrieved
another pencil that had a string wrapped around it. He
unrolled the string, which he had premeasured to one
meter, and measured the elephant. He recorded its
length, height, width of her feet, and the estimated
length of the ivory tusks that had been illegally har-
vested.

While recording the measurements, Okere reflected
on the events of the last ten minutes. It had been the
poachers who started the maddening chain of events
that caused the lions to attack him instead of a gazelle or
gemsbok, which would have been easy prey.

Okere would give the park scientists all of this
information. He added, "Elephant calf adopted by mature female." It was not always possible for this to
happen. Baby elephants require a lot of milk and usually a mother elephant can nurse only one calf. Most
baby elephants who lose their mothers starve to death.

It was a truly a sad day, but he felt a little better
knowing that the baby elephant would get a second
chance at freedom rather than becoming another zoo
exhibit. Okere was convinced that if things didn't change,
the baby would end up just like its mother. Okere's
sadness now turned to anger as he picked up his old
snake gun and walked quickly toward his beat-up Range

Rover. He would tell the scientists about his day, and then he would begin to track down the poachers.

As he approached the Range Rover, the other rangers were carrying their injured friend up from the riverbank. As the rangers reached their leader, they hurriedly touched him without saying anything. It was their way of saying, "We're glad you made it." One man touched his shoulder. Another man put his hand on top of his head. Another touched his forearm. It reminded Okere of the way elephants touch each other affectionately.

"Mustafa?" one of the men asked.

"Yes, it was Mustafa," Okere said.

"He must not be angry with you or you would be dead," another ranger said.

"You know Mustafa. He hurts only poachers and thieves. He came to take his baby home." Okere and the other rangers climbed inside the Range Rover that had the insignia of the Kenya Wildlife Service painted on the two front doors. It was a silhouette of a mother elephant walking next to her calf.

They drove back to camp. In the bush, the lions growled with satisfaction as they returned to feast on the dead elephant. Their entire pride of seven lions had joined them. If the lions didn't eat quickly, the hyenas would appear as darkness fell and challenge their ownership of the dead elephant. By daylight, the vultures will be circling overhead and the jackals and hyenas will be lying in wait.

But the baby elephant was safe with its new mother, for now.

# East Africa

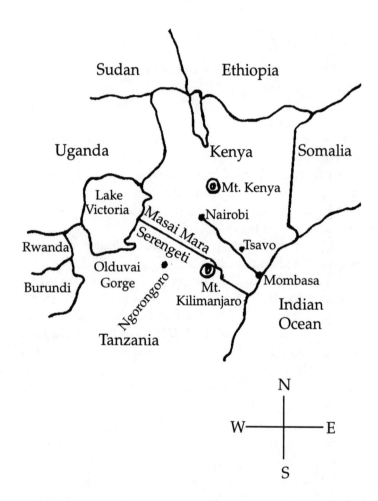

# 1

# Mambas
## Tsavo National Park, Kenya
## July, 2000

———————————◻————————————

"Christopher, watch out for those kudu," Heather yelled.

She hung on tightly to the leather strap that was attached to the roll bar of the Range Rover.

"Don't worry, they'll move before we even get close to them," Chris MacGregor replied as he squeezed the steering wheel.

"How much farther to the rail station?" Ryan shouted over the noise of the wind blowing through the open canopy of the four-wheel drive.

The Range Rover heaved to one side and then to the other as it roared across the savanna trying to follow the ruts of the old safari road.

"About thirty minutes," Daniel replied from the front passenger seat.

The Range Rover dodged another deep rut as Chris shifted to a lower gear to maintain the speed necessary for them to catch the train. In East Africa for nearly a week, the MacGregor kids had opted for a couple of days in the bush on a camera safari. The plan was to catch the Mombasa to Nairobi train at its midway point in the Tsavo National Park to return to Nairobi. As the

Range Rover pushed forward, the MacGregor teens argued about who had made them get a late start and possibly cause them to miss the train at Tsavo Station. Christopher, the oldest at seventeen, was the one his mother always put in charge. He decided to tune out his brother and sister. He gazed to his left at majestic snowcapped Mt. Kilimanjaro rising over 19,000 feet above the East African grasslands. Dodging rocks, reptiles, and an occasional termite mound, Chris drove the Range Rover along at near breakneck speed despite the constant harangue from his sister to slow down.

"Chris, slow down! We've got plenty of time to make it," Heather said.

She was still holding fast to the leather strap in the backseat. Ryan, her twelve-year-old brother, sat next to her. Topping a hill, Chris noticed a shallow river at the bottom. He shifted to a lower gear to slow down the vehicle so he could pick the best spot to cross.

"There!" Daniel said as he pointed to the rock bed that had been pressed flat from safari traffic. "Stay in tight or you will sink in the mud."

"Be careful, Chris," Heather said.

"I've got it, Heather. No sweat. Just lift up your feet when we cross the river."

"Whatever," Heather snapped back.

"Looks like we're about five miles from Tsavo and the train station. The safari company said to leave the Range Rover there and they would pick it up around noon." Daniel spoke with such confidence that no one doubted him. No one knew he was quite lost.

Daniel Okere had been a blessing to the MacGregors ever since they landed in Nairobi. Serving as an officer with the Kenya Wildlife Service, Daniel had been loaned as a personal guide and attache' for the three MacGregor kids. He welcomed the break from the desk and paperwork that accompanied his government job in the capitol. So he jumped at the chance of getting back into the bush, his first love.

As Chris steered the vehicle out of the stream and into the steep climb of the riverbank, Heather suddenly screamed. Frantically she started crawling toward the back of the Range Rover, climbing over her seat into the cargo area.

"A mamba," shouted Ryan as he pointed toward the snake that was now peering over the door and into the Range Rover.

Chris looked to his right and tried to accelerate, but the muddy slope caused his wheels to spin and the massive nine-foot mamba easily kept up speed with the Range Rover. The inside of the vehicle was in turmoil. Heather was climbing on top of Ryan. Ryan was shouting how cool it was while Chris worked feverishly to find traction for the Range Rover so he could drive up the slope and away from the venomous snake.

"I'll get him," Daniel shouted.

He reached to his side where his .375 double rifle was propped against the door, the barrel pointing toward the floor. The .375 double rifle was indeed a great advancement from the old M-1 carbine that he had carried in the field for fifteen years. Reacting quickly, he leaned out the window to shoot the snake. But in the panic and hysteria of the moment, he released the safety too soon and accidentally pulled the trigger. The gun discharged sending a round through the floor of the vehicle and into the right tire. The tire was destroyed. The Range Rover bounced to a stop in the muddy quagmire of the riverbank.

"Here he comes," Ryan shouted.

The mamba, seizing the opportunity as predators always do, now started moving through the window and inside the Range Rover. Ryan was preparing to dive out the window on the opposite side. Heather was burrowing under layers of sleeping bags and camping equipment.

Suddenly, diving from the sky above, an African secretary bird, with its sharp talons, swooped down and snatched the snake from the side of the Range Rover and began to fly away. The secretary's seven-foot wingspan would have been enough for most of the animals it preyed upon. But the weight of the long heavy snake immediately pulled it to the ground before it had flown ten feet. As the mamba recoiled to strike, the three-foot-tall bird of prey spread its beautiful black and white wings to distract the venomous snake. It danced in the dry dirt with its heavily scaled legs to out maneuver the dangerous serpent. As the mamba struck, the secretary caught the head of the snake in mid-air with its large talons. The bird's head quickly dipped down to the snake, its exquisite long comb of feathers jutted from the back of its head, and ripped the neck of the snake open with its sharp beak. The secretary bird then began to flap its mighty wings until it had lifted nearly half of the mamba off the ground. Catching a gust of wind, it became airborne with its prey and sailed through the air to a grove of trees near the river. Once high off the ground, away from "big cat" reach, it draped the now dead snake across a branch next to its nest. The nest was at least five feet in diameter and had two young secretary birds waiting. Dinner had arrived!

"Wow, that was so cool," Ryan exclaimed as he climbed into the backseat from the rear cargo area. "Did you guys see the dance that bird did? Like, I mean he was so fast the snake couldn't guess where he was going to jump next."

Ryan found Heather curled up in a ball on the floor under a bedroll with her hands over her face.

"Heather!" Chris leaned over the seat next to Ryan and touched her arm. She jumped. "He's gone. This giant bird got him. We're safe now."

Heather moved her hands off her face. She sat up slowly, pushing the navy and orange bedroll to the side.

"You really missed a great show, Heather," Ryan boasted. He followed Daniel out the door onto the muddy riverbank. "Wow. I thought that snake was going to bite Daniel in the neck. But that giant bird swooped down from the sky and just plucked him off the earth. It was awesome!"

"OK, R.O. I'm sure Heather regrets that she missed watching a poisonous snake almost bite Daniel and then almost crawl through the Rover killing all of us." Chris was laughing as he got out of the Rover.

"You guys make me sick. This is not funny." Heather crossed her arms to pout. But the mood swing didn't last long.

In a few minutes all three kids and Daniel were standing ankle deep in mud and scrutinizing the ruined tire. Chris checked his watch and shook his head.

"It looks like we're going to miss the train. Boy, mom will be mad," Chris said.

"OK. Let's unload the truck. Take only your cameras and packs. Chris and I will carry the two rifles for protection," Daniel said.

"Protection from what?" Heather asked.

"Well, it's like this, Miss Heather. Since we are on foot, we will resemble prey or pests for the big cats, a few snakes, and cape buffalo. And we also resemble predators so any large female animal that is protecting her young might get excited if she sees or smells us. We need to be alert, but I am sure we'll be just fine," Daniel said as he reached inside the Range Rover.

"Why don't we just change the tire?" Ryan asked the obvious question.

"The truck is sitting at a forty-five-degree angle on a muddy bank. There is no way we can change the tire. It would fall off the jack. There are no trees close enough for us to use the winch to pull the Rover to the top of the riverbank. We have only one choice. Walk to Tsavo," Daniel said resolutely.

Heather and Ryan packed their cameras in two packs and each grabbed a bottle of water. Chris threw a water bottle in a netted sling over one shoulder and his 7mm rifle over the other. The 7mm was strictly a large game hunting rifle he used for deer back home in the Big Bend country of Texas. It had been a gift from his dad. Chris had been told by his dad that he should carry the rifle in Africa and other stops on their global journey strictly for protection. This could be one of those occasions.

Daniel swung the .375 double rifle over his shoulder and retrieved a bottle of water. Trudging through the mud he led them up the riverbank. In unison, they put on their canvas safari hats for protection from the sun. Once on top of the riverbank, they could see across the flat grassland for about three miles. Tsavo was nowhere in sight. The three kids looked at Daniel.

"How far to Tsavo, Daniel?" Heather asked politely.

"Well, I guess I was mistaken. It looks like it's about ten miles. I know this country well. A Kikuyu never forgets his homeland." Daniel spoke with pride, but he was beginning to have doubts about their exact location. "We better get moving before the sun does some damage to us." He started walking northward.

Heather and Ryan, with Chris bringing up the rear, followed along. In the distance they could hear a pack of African wild dogs chasing a warthog piglet. About the size of a German shepherd, the wild dogs are considered to be "real" dogs. Their tall rounded ears provide them exceptional hearing. Camouflaged with their black and tan hair, they can lie in wait and easily ambush unwitting prey. But their primary means of attack is simply running as a pack and bringing down the antelope, the gemsbok, the wildebeest, or the unfortunate warthog piglet that strays from its den.

In a couple of minutes the barking stopped. The growling and fussing of the dogs over the puny little pig soon came to an end. Daniel turned westward to look their direction. All the kids stopped walking and stood perfectly still.

Daniel turned quickly to the kids.

"We've got to get moving, I mean like right now, kids. There's a baobab tree." Daniel pointed to the ancient tree that was about two hundred yards away. "Run. Now! And don't look back!"

Chris knew that in a few minutes the wild dogs would be headed in their direction.

"I've seen wild dogs take down five big gazelles in less than an hour. They're efficient killers," Daniel said. His face was creased with worry.

"Let's go," Chris said firmly and started an easy run toward the huge baobab. Heather and Ryan started behind him but suddenly Ryan stopped.

"R.O., let's go," Chris yelled again, this time making eye contact. R.O. was the nickname that he preferred. It was short for Ryan O'Keef MacGregor.

Ryan started running to catch up with them. Daniel moved quickly behind them, turning toward the west and scanning the grass for any movement. Then he spotted it. The tall grass started moving as if someone were rolling boulders through its tall blades.

"Go, go! They're coming," Daniel hollered. He ran as fast as he could behind the kids.

Chris reached the baobab first. He turned and brought the 7mm rifle to his shoulder to cover the others. Heather and R.O. touched the thick bark of the baobab at the same time and stopped, gasping for breath.

All three watched Daniel running across the grassy plain toward them. He was out of shape and breathing hard. Suddenly like a swarm of bees, the wild dogs emerged from the tall grass barely fifty yards behind Daniel.

"Climb, start climbing," Chris yelled.

R.O. jumped high and grabbed a lower branch and

pulled himself up. Heather was next.

"Come on, Chris," Heather yelled.

Chris hesitated. He looked back at Daniel. He switched on the safety and handed the rifle up to Heather. He then jumped and grabbed the lower branch and pulled himself up. R. O. had already climbed up another ten feet. Sitting on the lower branch, just seven feet off the ground, Chris looked back toward Daniel. He was fifty yards away. The wild dogs were gaining ground. Their teeth revealed the excitement of chasing this two-legged prey. The wild dogs were accustomed to the centuries of competition among the lions, hyenas, and jackals. Chasing a human was sheer joy and their nostrils flared from the energy of the chase. Pulling down a 150-pound gazelle was not much of a challenge. The human would be easy prey.

Daniel could hear the panting, barking, and snarling of the predators closing in on him. He knew if he stopped to shoot, he would kill one or two but the others would not stop. They would be on him in an instant, tearing at his flesh with their sharp canines. As a bush ranger in his younger days, he had seen the remains of travelers who wandered too far into the bush and met with a pack of wild dogs. These dogs were bred through centuries of competition in the harshest of African environments. They were fierce enough to battle the brown hyenas. Their large canine teeth were designed to rip flesh. The wild dogs were a selectively tough breed. They were survivors.

Suddenly there was a loud pop followed by the whizzing noise of a bullet ricocheting off a rock. Chris took aim a second time, trying not to kill the lead dog. He only wanted to kick up some dirt and scare them. But Chris knew he wouldn't hesitate to kill the dog if it meant saving Daniel's life.

Daniel saw the light from the barrel as the powder flashed from the rifle. From his perch in the baobab tree,

Chris fired a second round. Daniel felt the whiz of the bullet go by as the dirt kicked up in front of the pack. But the dogs never missed a stride and Daniel could feel them getting closer. His out-of-shape heart was pounding in his chest. He reversed the .375 double rifle under his arm while running and, without looking back, he fumbled with the safety and almost dropped it. Finally his finger found the trigger. There was a loud pop and the recoil of the rifle jerked the gun from his hand nearly dislocating his trigger finger. The rifle fell to the ground and before it hit the dirt, he heard a yelp as the bullet clipped the right ear of one of the dogs. But he knew from the barking and sounds of their feet digging in the dried grass, they were still in hot pursuit of their human prey.

Safely up in the tree, Chris checked the clip and switched the 7mm to semiautomatic. He took careful aim but Daniel was blocking the shot to the lead dog. Chris held perfectly still.

At exactly twenty yards from the massive tree, Daniel made eye contact with Christopher and realized his only hope. Suddenly, as if sliding into home base, Daniel dove to the ground in a cloud of dirt. Chris pulled the trigger sending five rounds toward the wild dogs while Daniel hugged the ground.

The sudden barrage of noise and whizzing of bullets kicking up a line of dirt was enough to turn the pack. They came to a dead stop just a few feet away from Daniel. Daniel jumped to his feet and ran the final yards as Chris loaded another 7-shot clip and fired a second volley of bullets toward the still-startled pack. Daniel, his legs feeling like tree trunks, reached the lower limb and pulled his body up into the ancient baobab.

"Thanks, Chris," Daniel said panting heavily.

"You're welcome," Chris rested the gun on the huge limb he had made his perch. From above, R.O. yelled down to Chris.

"Why didn't you just shoot the dogs the first time?"

"I didn't think I'd have to. Besides, that's not why we're in Africa," Chris said. "But I wouldn't have let them get Daniel anyway. Daniel's life is more important than any hundreds of animals, or even thousands!"

"I'm glad you feel that way. For a moment out there I wasn't sure. Look, here they come again." Daniel looked down as the wild dogs reappeared out of the tall grass and ran to the baobab tree.

Yelping, barking, and biting at each other in frustration, the wild dogs pranced and ran around the tree. Some tried to jump up to their presumed prey, four humans. But each jumping wild dog met with defeat rather quickly and settled for running about barking and biting at each other.

"Ouch," R.O. yelled out.

Chris, Daniel, and Heather looked up to see a troop of vervet monkeys, about twenty in all, perched around R.O. One of them had tugged at his hair and yanked his ear.

"Come here, Mr. Monkey." R.O. tried to entice them with a candy bar he had taken out of his pack.

"Be careful, they have sharp teeth," Daniel warned.

"I'm always careful," R.O. boasted as two of the monkeys made a fast movement toward the candy bar. One of them nabbed it and escaped up the tree while four monkeys trailed close enough to the thief to be his shadow. R.O. laughed as he jokingly counted his fingers.

"How long before the dogs leave?" Chris asked as he repositioned himself and the rifle on the limb.

"They won't stay long." Daniel moved on the wide limb to find a more comfortable spot.

Some of the ancient tree's limbs were as much as two feet in diameter. The bark had been worn smooth by the dozens of monkeys that called it home. Heather, Chris, and Daniel shifted from place to place trying to get comfortable. Daniel told them about how early Portuguese explorers would always bury their dead with a baobab seed pod. The story, fact or fable, was that every baobab on the grasslands represented a memorial to the early settlers. East Africa, he explained, was a combination of tribes that migrated from the north about the time Columbus was landing in the New World. There were also European settlers, Arab merchants, and a few native tribes. It was a true melting pot of tribes and cultures.

Chris and Heather listened intently fully expecting to hear it again from their mother in their weekly homework assignment. R.O., on the other hand, continued to bond with the wild monkeys in the baobab tree. What he didn't know was that he entertained them as much as they did him!

Soon the wild dogs became bored with their intended prey and left in a cloud of dust. Before the day would end they would search out more mischief and more prey to kill. It is after all, the way of Africa!

# 2

# Samburu Warriors

R.O. was the last of the four humans to climb down from the baobab tree. A troop of monkeys followed him all the way to the bottom. The monkeys appreciated these entertaining humans and immediately swarmed on Chris, Heather, and Daniel.

"Ouch," Heather shouted as one of the monkeys pulled at her blond hair while a second one yanked at the zipper pull on her yellow and green pack.

Meanwhile Chris gently brushed two of the black-faced monkeys off his shoulders. He leaned over and picked up his camouflage backpack and 7mm rifle. The dozen or so monkeys that had been prancing around them suddenly began screaming. They jumped off their newfound friends and scampered up the ancient baobab.

"That's strange," Daniel said as he watched them scurry as far up the tree as possible.

"Guess they knew I didn't have any more candy bars," R.O. said.

Heather was kneeling on the ground tying the lace on her left boot. She was facing the tall grass of the bush when something caught her eye. Not thirty feet away, concealed in the heavy grass, was a female lion. The lioness's face was blood stained from a recent kill. She crouched in a stance ready to charge, her ears laid back. But having a full belly, she didn't seem committed to the moment. Her tail was still twitching. Heather froze, barely able to speak. Somehow she forced out a few words.

"Lion. Chris. Lion," she said softly.

"Heather, did you say something?" Chris asked as he adjusted the sling of the rifle over his shoulder to be more comfortable.

"Lion. There's a lion," Heather said again, her throat somehow regurgitating the words.

"Speak up, Heather. I can't hear you," Chris replied as he walked toward her. She remained perfectly still.

"Chris, I think she said lion," R.O. shouted as he rearranged his gear after it had been shuffled about by the monkeys.

"Lion? What about a lion?" Daniel said as he leaned over to pick up his rifle out of the dirt.

Not being able to take the anxiety any longer, Heather stood up and rotated on her left boot. She set off in a run toward the tree. Daniel, Chris , and R.O. froze in their tracks when she ran by them. As she reached the tree she finally yelled.

"Lion in the bush."

Chris, R.O. and Daniel stood in shock as the female lion bounded from her hiding place and loped toward them. In less than a minute, all four adventurers were again perched in the baobab. It was as if they, too, had an instinct like the monkeys. An instinct that told them just how far they could venture from the tree and still get back in time before a predator's claws could tear them apart. But much to their surprise the lioness had plopped down on loose dirt around the tree and rolled on her back.

Still breathing hard Daniel spoke. "She was too full to chase and kill us. She must have just finished her kill when the barking of the wild dogs alerted her to the possibility of more prey."

"Look," R.O. said. He pointed to the edge of the clearing around the tree. Three lion cubs bounced along toward their mother who was now relaxing at the base of the baobab.

"How cute," Heather said as she began to recover from her fright.

"Cute now, but lethal predators in a few months," Chris replied.

All three cubs were now cuddled up to their mother to nurse. It was obvious from their blood-soaked hair that they too had enjoyed the kill. The mother slapped one of the cubs when it bit a little too hard. Although her claws were retracted, the love tap sent the cub rolling and snarling. It jumped back up and leapt on the back of another cub who then engaged it in a playful battle. They were imitating their mother killing her prey by biting at each other's necks.

Everyone was securely perched in the trees as the lioness and her cubs claimed the baobab as their new afternoon shade tree. At first no one spoke. After awhile Daniel broke the silence.

"She's not going anywhere today."

"No kidding," Chris responded and shifted his position on the tree limb.

"Secure your rifle, Chris. Pull the clip and eject the cartridge in the chamber. Then snap the clip back in. We don't want any accidents up here today," Daniel instructed.

Chris did so quickly. When he was younger, he had been trained in gun safety by his adventurer father. Daniel's rifle was still lying under the tree in the dirt. The monkeys climbed down from the upper canopy of the tree, hopped around and begged from R.O. again. Heather was four feet higher than Chris and Daniel and was busy flipping bugs off her boots and legs.

"Wow, I've never seen so many living things in one spot," she said as she brushed off another orange and green bug.

The four carried on a rather normal conversation fully aware of the three-hundred-pound lioness and her three cubs lounging below. Not once did they pretend that the lioness was not aware of their presence. An occasional shift of her head and furtive eye contact with the four humans was all that was needed for both man and wild beast to respect the others' presence. Neither had the desire to kill the other. At least not for now.

"Chris, do lions climb trees?" Heather asked warily.

"No, not usually."

"But she could if she had to, or if we were the only food around," Daniel said.

"That's comforting," Heather commented. She then adjusted her now sore bottom on the hard limb.

Suddenly the cracking noise of a breaking limb and the scream of the monkeys pierced the air as R.O. lost his balance while playing with his new friends. The smaller limb he had reached for was rotted through and had snapped under his weight. The black-faced monkeys scrambled to clear the way as the hundred-twenty-pound twelve year old became an object of gravity's curse. He tumbled from one branch to the next.

Chris and Heather reached out to steady themselves while at the same time trying to grab a piece of R.O. It didn't matter what they connected with—they just wanted to connect. Their hands flailed at R.O.'s body, clothing, and pack. But R.O. had ventured too far out on the periphery of the huge baobab.

Literally bouncing from one limb to another, frantically stripping small branches of their leaves, R.O. broke through the lower canopy and was firmly earthbound like a large cannonball. Then mysteriously a small branch reached out and snagged the shoulder strap of his emerald green backpack. As his fall came to a sudden halt, he let out a big yell and gulped air.

"Ow!"

Daniel, Chris, and Heather sat in stunned silence. Even the monkeys were quiet. The lioness, startled by all the commotion, was now sitting up and looking at R.O. He was dangling from the baobab just four feet above her head.

"Oh my gosh," Heather said. She put both hands over her mouth.

Chris rapidly loaded a round into the chamber of the 7mm rifle and took aim on the lioness. Fear and anxiety engulfed his body. The three cubs ran over out of curiosity and started jumping in the air swatting at R.O. The largest cub was still two feet from R.O. with each jump. But it didn't stop their playfulness or pretension at hunting prey.

The mother lion stood on her back legs and reached up with her right paw. Her claws were retracted. Chris flipped off the safety and was prepared to shoot.

"Hold it, boy," Daniel said calmly. "She may just be curious. No need to kill her if she's not going to hurt your brother."

The lioness gently tapped R.O.'s boot a couple of times and then sat down. She sniffed her paw and gently swatted one of the cubs who had gotten a bit rough and decided to bite her tail. Noise from the bush caused all four humans and four lions to turn their attention to the outside rim of the clearing around the baobab.

As though they were an eery apparition appearing from another world, four men entered the clearing. Their bodies were painted red from the chest up, and they were carrying spears and netted bags over their shoulders. The red paint came to a point in the middle of their chests, "v" shaped from the shoulders downward. The dark red paint extended upward, crawling up their necks until it engulfed their lower jaw. Their thinly braided hair was also painted red and had been neatly twisted and formed with rows of colorful beads making an artificial shade over their eyes like the bill of a ball cap. Ornate and functional easily described their hairstyles. Their earlobes were elongated and held a circular cut piece of ivory. Their necklaces were beaded chokers that were two inches wide with varying designs of black, red, white, and yellow. Each row of beads and the order of the color told a story.

The lioness quickly rounded up her cubs, which had instinctively run behind their mother. She crouched ready to charge. With her ears laid back, her soft guttural purr was now a distinctive growl.

"Samburu warriors," Daniel whispered.

Heather still held one hand over her mouth and tightly gripped the tree with the other. Chris, his rifle trained on the lioness, looked at the four brightly painted men who were now standing in the clearing.

"Don't move," Daniel whispered to Chris and Heather.

R.O., who was now completely still, stared wide eyed at the mother lion and then across to the Samburu. He held his legs as high as he could.

The lioness's tail had noticeably stopped twitching, a sign she was preparing to charge. Every muscle in her shoulders and legs was tight and bulging. The Samburu gently moved apart from each other. They were making themselves a much bigger target trying to confuse the lioness as to who she wanted to attack first. A couple of minutes had passed before it was obvious that the challenge had reached a stalemate.

The Samburu now crouched low to the ground with their spears pointed directly at the lioness. A clicking sound could be heard from their mouths. First one, then another, then all four, completely out of synch and very distracting. Then as if each had been led by a conductor, they stepped forward with their right foot then back quickly. Then they were perfectly still. The clicking now began to match their steps. Several movements forward then back and then they touched their spearheads to the ground.

The mother lion now rose out of her crouch and paced sideways, always aware where her cubs were sitting. Suddenly she turned toward them and let out a large growl. The cubs scurried behind the baobab tree and into the bush on the opposite side of the clearing. Turning quickly, she charged four feet then stopped and retreated. Then she charged again. The Samburu never stopped their rhythmic motion or the annoying clicking. They began to move closer toward the lioness.

With each charge and with each Samburu advancement, the lioness would withdraw a little closer to the baobab tree. Soon she was behind the tree. Then suddenly with one large growl, she pivoted on her hind legs and took off in a run into the bush where her cubs were now hiding. The Samburu stopped their movement and the clicking noise.

Daniel bounded out of the tree, while Chris crawled out on the limb and reached down and grabbed R.O.'s shoulder strap. He pulled with all his strength to unhook the shoulder strap. Daniel steadied R.O. from below as he fell to the ground landing on both feet. Heather was the last to reach the lower branch.

"Are they gone?" she asked Chris before she jumped to the ground, the second time that day.

"Yep. I don't think they'll be back. Will they, Daniel?" Chris said and then deferred the question to Daniel.

"No, they're gone. But what do we have here?" Daniel turned to the Samburu who were now only a few feet away.

"I have never seen Samburu this far south. I wonder why they are in southern Kenya. They must be three hundred miles from their homeland," Daniel said to Chris.

"I believe I can answer that," one of the Samburu spoke in a clearly British accent with perfect English.

Daniel, Chris, Heather, and R.O. raised their eyebrows in astonishment at this beautiful 18th-century specimen of an African warrior. A warrior who, using ancient hunting methods, had just stared down a three-hundred-pound lion but, nonetheless, spoke the Queen's English perfectly.

"You have good English," Daniel said politely.

"Thank you. Christ's College, Oxford, class of 92," the Samburu warrior replied. He grinned a big toothy smile.

"Wow," R.O. said.

"Wow is right," Heather echoed from behind them. She was still surveying the bush for lions and wild dogs.

"What's an Oxford graduate, well you know. I bet you've been asked before." Chris wanted his curiosity satisfied.

"Yes, I have been asked before. It's a long story. But since the sun is getting low in the sky, it will be dark before you reach Tsavo. We will have time to talk about it tonight," the warrior said.

"How did you know we were going to Tsavo?" Chris said.

"All white men in this area go to Tsavo before dark," the warrior said. "That is unless you have camping gear. It's obvious to me you don't."

"We're sleeping here tonight?" Heather said with anxiety in her voice.

"Yes. He's right. It's still too far to make it to Tsavo. If we start fresh in the morning, we can walk there in a two or three hours," Daniel said.

"When we don't arrive in Nairobi by dark on the train, our mom will go ballistic," Heather said.

"I know. But she knows you're with me. So I bet she won't worry," Daniel replied. "And now that I think about it, we have four strong men who can help us go back and get the Range Rover out of the mud. Then we can drive to Tsavo or all the way into Nairobi."

"This tree island will make a good camp tonight," the Samburu said.

"I agree," Daniel replied. "Let's gather some firewood and dig out what food we have in our packs."

"No need for food," the Samburu said. He then turned and spoke in Swahili to his three friends. Each one opened their net bags revealing three large guinea fowl and a couple of birds they had trapped. "Dinner!" The Samburu had a big smile on his face.

"Can we at least pluck the feathers first?" Heather said as she sat down on the ground letting out a big sigh.

Soon the sun was dipping behind the mountains around Mt. Kilimanjaro and the cool African night crept across the plains. Campfires lit up where there were travelers, safaris, and small villages. At night, only the hyenas, owls, and rodents arose to mingle and play their part in this exotic ecosystem. For the large beasts, mammals and humans, it was time to rest so that tomorrow they would not become someone's prey.

# 3

# "Roger"

———————◼———————

The African darkness raced across Tsavo National Park chasing the last long shadows of the evening sun. Without clouds to capture earth's radiant heat from the heart of Africa's wild country, the cold quickly fell upon the animals that crawled into their dens and nests. The fire that Daniel had built was beginning to generate a substantial amount of heat when two of the Samburu arrived with the bedrolls they had retrieved from the Range Rover barely a quarter mile away. As two guinea fowl began to roast on the open flame, Heather slipped inside her soft bag and pulled the zipper high up to her chin. It made her feel safe.

"Why are four Samburu warriors three hundred miles from home?" Daniel asked as he poked a stick in the fire to get some oxygen to the now red coals. "And by the way, we don't know your names."

The oldest of the Samburu, about the age of thirty, sat next to the fire with his bottom resting on the back of his heels in a crouching position. His long hair, dyed red with ochre, was finely beaded with at least fifty strands of hair dangling down his back where they touched the scabbard of the lalemma (long knife) he carried at his

side. The two layers of red and white fabric that hung
from his waist were now bunched around his knees.
Chris stared at the dozens of scars on his legs and feet.
His feet were protected by traditional giraffe skin sandals with two crisscross straps on top. The fire flickered
and reflected off the jewelry that adorned both his hair
and choker necklace.

Heather stared from the confines and presumed
safety of her sleeping bag.

"Our names are important only to our mothers. We
do not even know each others' names. A name is sacred
and intimate. It must be protected. We are known as the
sons of our mother. As Samburu, we are one." The
Samburu rotated the guinea fowl on the fire with his
callused hands.

"You said something about Christ's College, Oxford, Class of 92," Daniel said.

"Yes, I did," the warrior said. He looked across at
R.O. who was sitting next to Chris. He was spellbound
by the presence of the exotic and colorful warriors.

"When I was that boy's age, my mother and father
were killed by a cape buffalo on the road to Nairobi. A
missionary found me and took me into the city. They
adopted me and returned to England where I learned
the ways of the English. I attended prep school and then
went on to Oxford. There I studied, well the obvious!
African languages and culture. It was a rebirth. I became
Samburu again. It was only then that I discovered who
I really was. Who my people are. I knew that I had to
come home." The Samburu again rotated the roasting
guinea fowl with his bare hand.

"What did you find?" Chris did not want the moment to escape.

"I found my people loved life. Even though the
colonialists labeled us as living in poverty, we didn't
know we were poor or primitive. I found uncles and
cousins who loved me from the moment I returned. It

was as if I had never left. I found a people at peace with
Africa, at peace with the earth."

"That's beautiful," Heather whispered, the firelight
dancing off her face. Chris and R.O. turned to smile at
her.

"My British name is Harrison Cleveland Wells. I
thank my English parents for the life they gave me. I can
never repay them. But I am Samburu and I am called son
of my mother."

"Hey, that's the same name as the guy who wrote
*The Time Machine,* H.C. Wells." R.O. jumped into the
conversation and smiled at his own observation.

"No, R.O., that was H.G. Wells. Not H.C. Wells."
Chris corrected him without much expression so he
wouldn't embarrass him.

"Whatever. They sound the same to me," R.O. tossed
back. "Anyway, I liked it. I would like to build a machine like that someday."

R.O. reached into his pack to retrieve one of the
dozens of mechanical contraptions he was constantly
building and destroying. With a vivid imagination, one
could see the little machine he slipped out of the pack
resembled the shape of a boat, or maybe it was a car. No,
it was a box. Only R.O. knew for sure what the little
machine was. It required two nine-volt batteries and the
flip of a small switch brought the machine to life. It had
gears and wheels that moved, red and green lights that
flashed alternately, and a small lever that rhythmically
popped up and down.

The three Samburu sitting next to Harrison C. Wells
moved closer and watched in awe. It was hard for them
to understand something smaller than the palm of their
hands that could do so many wonderful things and also
purr like a kitten. R.O. noticed their interest. He handed
the machine to Harrison, who turned to the other three
and in Swahili tried to explain it to them. But without an
understanding of light, the motion of wheels, and the

stored energy in the batteries, it might as well have been magic. And to them it was.

"What do you call it?" Harrison asked.

Chris and Heather laughed. They already knew the answer that was coming. R.O. looked at them and squinted a mean face. Giving each other "the face" was expected between these brothers and sister.

"That's Roger," R.O. finally said.

"Who is Roger?" Harrison asked.

"That is Roger. That's its name," R.O. said.

"What does Roger do?" Harrison asked.

"Well, Roger makes a noise. He also flashes red and green. Roger can speed up and slow down, depending on whether the batteries are fresh. Roger's Roger," R.O. said. He was a little put out with the adult. He hated having to explain himself.

"I see," Harrison the Samburu warrior said. He touched his dark hand to his red chin, reflecting on the answer. "Roger is a good spirit. Roger hurts no one. Roger doesn't take from anyone. Roger makes me smile. I smile at Roger's colors as they flash. They are Samburu colors. I am relaxed by the sound of the tiny wheels turning, much like a mother humming to her baby in our huts to the north. Roger pushes the little lever out and pulls it in, much like I do with my rungu (club) when I dance."

Without warning, one of the batteries failed and the little machine started to slow down. R.O. rummaged around in his pack and found another battery and traded it out quickly. Roger began to speed up again. The humming noise became louder, the flashing lights quickly turned on and off. The lever popped up and down in time with everything else on the little machine. Harrison held it in cupped hands.

"Roger is beautiful and strong. But Roger works better when someone else helps him. Someone who gives him more strength and power. Roger is better if not alone." Harrison turned and looked R.O. in the eyes. "Roger is Samburu!"

Everyone was quiet. Chris's bottom jaw was hanging free at the wisdom that had come from Harrison C. Wells, Oxford graduate, Samburu warrior.

"That's really cool, Mr. Wells," R.O. replied politely.

"When I named Roger, I didn't really know why. I name all of my machines. It makes them seem real to me. I then think of them as friends. If they stop working, I try really hard to save them, to rebuild them. Sometimes I accidentally burn them up with too much power or they quit working and I can't figure out why. So I take the parts and build something else. And I give it a new name."

"Do you ever use the name again?" Wells asked in his English accent.

"No. No I don't. Because what I make is always something new, something different," R.O. replied rather solemnly.

Chris and Heather both had curious looks on their faces. They were realizing for the first time what these machines really meant to R.O. For the past two years, they simply thought he was going through a phase, a phase that included building mechanical gizmos. Now they realized that the phase was more than that. They glanced at each other at this new revelation about their brother. Inside, they were both sorry they had laughed at the naming of his machines.

"When I build a new machine, I learn from the old one. It always stays inside me."

"In my village, the elders teach us the ways of a warrior," Harrison said. "When I was studying in England, I learned about another tribe in Africa. The tribe is located on the west side of the great rift valley, a thousand miles from here. When the young boys reach twelve, they are sent into the forest to conquer their fears and the forest itself. And when they have succeeded, they must return to the village and carve a mask. The mask must be like the animal they have come to understand and respect. And then they must explain what the mask and the animal mean to them."

"If you were from that tribe, what mask would you make?" R.O. asked.

"R.O. I would carve the mask of the cheetah, an animal that is swift, very smart, and takes no risks. A cheetah always knows the consequences of each of its choices before it acts. There are no surprising outcomes for a cheetah. That is why cheetahs live long lives," the Samburu replied.

"That's really cool. I like all the animals so I don't know which one I would pick," R.O. said.

"You don't have to pick one," Wells said as he turned the switch on the side of Roger to the off position. The red and green lights stopped flashing. The lever came to a halt when the little wheels stopped moving. The machine was silent. He handed Roger back to R.O.

"I get it," R.O. said. "Roger and all of my machines are my mask. They bring me the greatest happiness, fun, whatever. I play with them and remake them every day."

"And by doing so," Wells interrupted, "you are conquering the unknown. Directing your thoughts toward something good. You are challenging the laws of nature with each new wheel, light, or wire you place on the machine. By doing so, you prepare yourself for even greater challenges to come. Like a Samburu, you choose not to sit around and waste the light of the sun, but to use it for the warmth it provides. We can't capture a wind that has already touched our face."

"R.O.," Chris said, "I'm sorry I laughed at Roger's name."

"Me, too," piped in Heather.

"That's OK. It never bothered me. Roger understood." R.O. chuckled.

They all laughed, including the three Samburu who didn't have a clue what was just said. Laughter is always contagious. Soon the guinea fowl were completely cooked, torn apart, and passed around. All began eating except the Samburu who opened a round container called a *nkarau* and began to drink from it. First one, then the second, then another until all four had consumed a substantial amount.

"What is it?" Chris asked Daniel whose mouth was bulging with cooked guinea fowl. After he swallowed he answered.

"It is a mixture of goat's milk and cow's blood," he said before he took another bite.

Immediately Chris, Heather, and R.O. pulled the cooked fowl away from their mouths and looked at each other. The firelight flickered off their faces giving them the appearance that they too were wearing paint.

"I don't think I'm hungry anymore," Heather said.

She slowly set the guinea fowl leg on the makeshift plate, which was simply a large piece of tree bark. Rolling over in her sleeping bag, she went to sleep dreaming of ham with pineapple slices, scalloped potatoes, and hot rolls with real creamy butter. She worked hard to push the guinea fowl, the goat's milk, and cow's blood from her mind. R.O. reached in front of Chris and picked up Heather's guinea fowl leg and decided he was more hungry than sickened by the ancient tribal tradition.

"Is that all you ever eat?" R.O. asked as he took another bite.

"No. We eat almost all kinds of antelope. We also like cape buffalo and giraffe and lion fat. Many animals have a foul odor and we stay away from them. We never eat elephant. Elephants are too much like a man. They think like men. Their families resemble our families. Elephants are sacred."

After awhile only the bones of the guinea fowl

remained. They were tossed into the fire so wild animals would not pick up their scent during the night. Daniel placed the remainder of the wood they had collected on the fire. Within a few minutes, everyone was asleep. The stress and excitement of the day had taken its toll. In fact, they were all so tired they never noticed the spotted hyena that wandered through their camp two hours later and then quietly left. And Heather didn't even roll over when the "furry" African hunting spider, measuring eight inches across, dragged its freshly-killed prey, a small mouse, across the foot of her bedroll. But then it was better she was dreaming about Thanksgiving dinner at her grandmother's house back in Texas. The night passed quickly.

The morning sun peeked over the horizon and into Daniel's half-opened eyes. He glanced around and counted three MacGregors and zero Samburu. He noticed fresh wood on the fire that helped break the morning chill. The breaking noise of a small twig caused him to sit up quickly only to see Harrison C. Wells, a sweating Samburu warrior standing six feet tall. The scene of the cool morning wind and Harrison's sweat just didn't match.

"The Range Rover is at the top of the riverbank. I taught my friends how to change a flat tire. They enjoyed it," he said as he crouched next to Daniel. "We will be going."

"You never told us why you are so far away from home," Daniel said. He crawled out of the sleeping bag and started putting on his boots.

"We are looking for my sister. She no longer lives with the tribe. She works for the government counting animals. She wrote to us and asked us to come see her in Tsavo. We did not find her at Tsavo, so we came to this area where she has been counting animals. We have yet to meet her." The Samburu showed no emotion.

"Is she in danger?" Daniel asked.

"We do not know. She sent for us, so we came," Wells said with his stoic reply.

"Where will you go now?" Daniel asked.

"We will look next at Amboseli. She has written from there before," Wells said.

"Amboseli is a big park. It would take you days, maybe even weeks, to travel all of it." Daniel stood up.

"What is time to Samburu?" Wells turned around to walk away.

"Thanks for what you have done for us," Daniel said. The kids began to wake up and crawl out of their bags into the morning chill.

"Saying thanks is an English custom. To Samburu, if something needs to be done, it is done. No thanks is needed. But you are welcome," Wells said. He smiled, turned and walked into the bush and was gone.

Everyone was hungry and cold. It took them just a few minutes to clean up their camp, burying the hot coals in the dirt. Before long they were back in the Range Rover and motoring across the grasslands. They were looking for a track that would lead them back to Tsavo. Chris was still driving.

"See that kopje?" Daniel pointed to the rock formation that rose thirty feet above the plains. "Drive us there and we'll climb to the top. We should be able to see if we can find the track that runs northeast to Tsavo."

"Gotcha," Chris said.

He steered the Range Rover through some tall dry grass. Fifteen minutes later they were parked next to the kopje, an ancient rock formation. Chris and Daniel loaded their rifles and led the foursome up the steep incline. Once on top they found a smooth flat surface that had been worn clean from centuries of winds that had rushed from 17,000-foot Mt. Kenya in the north to 19,000-foot Mt. Kilimanjaro in the south. And then, of course, there were the trade winds that blew in from the Indian Ocean to the east.

"There's a track." Heather pointed at a track toward the north.

"There's another." R.O. pointed to the east.

"I think the one you are pointing to, R.O., is an animal track that the wild animals follow from one water hole to the next. Miss Heather's is probably the one that will take us to Tsavo Station."

"Look. To the west!" Chris shouted.

As they all turned to look, about twenty-five zebras were running and prancing across the plains about a quarter mile away.

"Those are Grevy's zebras. They are pretty rare in these parts," Daniel said.

"What makes them so rare?" R.O. asked.

"Years ago their hide was prized for their thin stripes. Most zebras are of the common variety and have wider stripes. Since hunting is not allowed in Kenya any longer, all animals including the zebras are growing in numbers. Wait. Look at that," Daniel said, interrupting himself and walking over to the edge on the north end of the kopje.

"What is it?" Chris asked in a concerned tone. He remembered their close encounters with the wild dogs and the lioness.

"It's a meat-drying rack. Hidden between two thorn trees. See, there!" Daniel leaned over and pointed so everyone could line up his arm and hand with the target.

"I see it," Heather said. "What is it? A meat-drying rack?"

"Poachers kill the wild game and then butcher it on the spot. They build a meat-drying rack in a secluded area and come back in a couple of days and haul out the meat. They take out the hides and ivory on the first run."

In a few minutes they were all back down on the ground and in the Range Rover and headed toward the track.

"We better keep moving toward Tsavo and get away from this part of the park. If we were to run into poachers, our lives would mean very little." Daniel drove them down the track with his fingers taped up tight. It throbbed a little from the slight dislocation he had experienced when the rifle recoiled in his hand. He thought it was better to have a slightly painful hand than wild dog teeth marks on his legs.

Everyone was quiet but their thoughts were all the same. Wild Africa was a dynamic and bold environment that ran efficiently like a fine-tuned machine. Just like Roger. They all agreed on one thing. When man interfered, there could be tragic consequences for both man and wild animal. A hornbill flew across the front of the Range Rover and landed in a thorn tree. Daniel downshifted and swerved around a large rock.

In two hours they could see Tsavo Station on the horizon. They were all relieved.

# 4

# Tsavo Station

———————————⬭———————————

Mavis MacGregor was standing with her hands on her hips looking southward from Tsavo Station when she spotted the Range Rover bouncing across the old dirt track. When her three kids had not arrived in Nairobi by dark the day before, she bought a ticket on the returning train to Mombasa. Her goal was to disembark at Tsavo and track them down. While she trusted Daniel, she still felt that events were out of her control when she was absent. The adventure to find Christopher just a month before in the Cayman Islands was fresh on her mind. It didn't take much coaxing from her husband Jack for her to catch the train. She needed to know for sure her kids were safe.

The Range Rover came to a stop amidst the collection of rusting vehicles and sharp new safari buses with exotic paint designs. There was one painted like a zebra and another one mimicked the spots of a leopard. The wild animals didn't notice the patterns the buses sported, but the tourists loved them. Mavis marched down the long wooden steps to the parking area.

Old Tsavo Station had remained in this same spot for over a hundred years. Its original wooden structure resembled a train station that could have been found in London or Edinburgh. But the station had begun to deteriorate because of time and weather. In recent years it had once again become a vital crossroads.

The Nairobi to Mombasa railway traveled east and west through the station. The north-south track guided citizens between Kenya and Tanzania. The station served as the halfway point between the capitol city of Nairobi and Kenya's major seaport Mombasa. The Portuguese built the railroad to carry supplies to countries such as Uganda and Rwanda in the heart of Africa. It had become the only trade route with the outside world since there were no large navigable rivers from the heart of Africa to either the Indian Ocean or the Atlantic.

History had been made and many great safaris had originated at Tsavo Station. After all, the Swahili word *safari* had been adapted by the colonialists to refer to a hunting expedition. But in the language of the Masai and Samburu, it meant embarking on a great journey. The MacGregor teens didn't know it yet, but they had just embarked on the greatest journey of their young lives.

"Mom! Hi, Mom!" Heather yelled as she waved from the Range Rover.

When the Range Rover had come to a complete stop, she bounded out of the SUV and ran up to her mother, who gave her a big squeeze.

"What are you doing here?" Heather asked as she stepped back.

"Your clothes are a mess, young lady," Mavis said in her British accent, which remained from her London upbringing. She tried very hard to restrain her curiosity and not seem like a doting parent. But her mere presence guaranteed she would appear as one.

"Hi Mom." R.O. walked over to her and sat down on the steps. He was glad to be on a platform that wasn't bumping up and down and swaying sideways. The old safari tracks weren't much more than ancient ruts.

Chris and Daniel unloaded the gear and the two hunting rifles from the rear of the vehicle. Without help from the others, they carried all of it up to the steps.

"Hi Mom," came the greeting from the third and eldest of the MacGregor kids. "I would have called but I was fresh out of change," Chris said with a slight smirk on his face. He knew he would draw his mother's ire, but he risked it just the same. Most teenagers do.

"No change? That's good. I'll have to remember to give you some coins next time you go into the bush. Would you also like for me to include a telephone as well. Maybe even a GPS receiver to hook to your belt. Or possibly I could include a video phone so we can see each others' pretty faces," Mavis MacGregor shot back, not appreciating the humor amidst her motherly worries.

Chris set down the gear that was in his hands and pulled the rifle from his shoulder. He walked over to his mother and kissed her on the cheek.

"Good to see you, Mom," Chris said as he looked her in the eyes.

Her normally powder blue eyes were steel gray—a color they changed to when Mavis MacGregor was stressed out.

"Good to see you, too." Her face softened from the affection her oldest had given to her. "Why are you so late?"

"Daniel shot a hole in a tire," R.O. blurted out from his resting place.

"Shot a hole in a tire?" Mavis looked alarmed.

"Yes ma'am. I was trying to kill a mamba and the gun discharged through the floor of the Range Rover. The bullet ripped through the tire. I know your next question, so let me answer it first. No, we couldn't change it because we were on a muddy slope of a riverbank," Daniel said.

"The Samburu warriors pushed the Rover up the bank this morning. But that was after they drank more blood," R.O. said.

"What? Drank blood. Samboro warriors?"

"No, Sam...bu...ru warriors," Heather said. "And the cow's blood was mixed with goat's milk. It made me sick. I couldn't eat last night or this morning. You wouldn't have anything to eat, would you Mom? Please, Mom?" Heather tossed her safari hat on top of her bedroll.

"You drank it, too?" Mavis had a shocked look on her face.

"No, Mom, nobody drank it but the Samburu." Chris needed to clear up the confusion. "Heather, there's a canteen in the train station. Take this Kenyan money." Chris handed Heather three pieces of bright red and blue paper money. "Go see if they sell anything you can eat." Chris took control of the confusing moment. "R.O., go with her and stay close."

The two MacGregor teens bounded up the stairs into Tsavo Station. As Heather and R.O. walked through the crowded station, a fine mist of dust hung in the air causing Heather to cough. The afternoon sun had yet to turn the old station into the sweltering sauna that it would be by 4:00. Despite the stories they had heard about the primitive conditions of the railroad and the old train cars, Heather and R.O. spotted only three chickens in cages and one goat. The native passengers carried brightly colored fabric bags and totes. No English or European style suitcases were to be found.

Chris and Daniel explained the exciting events to Mavis MacGregor as she sat down on the steps of the station. They did hold back some vital details.

"They were never in real danger, Mrs. MacGregor," Daniel explained.

"I know. I trust Chris and he said he trusted you. So I'm OK with that. Let's go find Heather and Ryan and get your gear up on the platform for the next train to Nairobi. We've got some things to do when we get back to the city. Maybe we can get back out here in a few days." Her motherly needs having been met, Mavis stood up and started carrying bags inside the station.

"That would be good. Tsavo National Park is a jewel with many large animals and beautiful landscapes. Or you could visit Amboseli or even Masai Mara, which is my favorite in all of Africa," Daniel said.

"We have about two weeks while my husband meets with wildlife and government officials about the state of wildlife poaching in East Africa. After that we are scheduled to fly to Cairo for an international summit on the environment. Jack is also going to talk to resident scientists about the accumulation of silt in the Nile River. What about the Range Rover?"

"I am supposed to leave the keys with the station master and the safari company will pick it up this afternoon," Daniel said.

"Thanks Daniel," Chris said. Instead of shaking the outreached hand that Daniel offered, he leaned forward and gave him a hug. They looked at each other and knew the bond they had created. Some details about the wild dogs would be better left untold until Dr. Jack MacGregor, zoologist, could be present to buffer it. Then Chris could mention R.O. hanging from the tree and the Samburu lion ritual. There would be lots to share later!

Walking through Tsavo Station was like taking a walk in 18th-century Africa. The colorful robes of the people represented their pride in the culture and traditions of their tribes. Many people were dressed in 60s, 70s, and 80s fashions as well. Sometimes it would take years for the clothes to filter into the continent from some of the relief agencies.

Heather and R.O. were camped out on a picnic-style table and bench in front of the open air canteen that overlooked the railroad tracks. They were hungrily munching on little sausages they pried out of a can with their fingers. An empty can lay nearby as evidence of their famished condition.

"What is that?" Chris asked as he picked up one of the cans. "I can't read it. It's in German." He handed it to his mother.

Mavis took the empty can and spun it around in her hands until she had read the label completely. She could speak and read five languages. She leaned over to Chris and whispered in his ear.

"From lamb kidneys."

"What is it, Mom?" Heather said. She stopped eating with half a sausage in her mouth.

"Are they good, sweetie?" Mavis took one from the opened can that R.O. was digging into. She quickly popped a little sausage into her mouth and smiled while she munched away on it.

"As a girl, I used to eat these by the dozens."

"I'll see if they have some bottled water," Chris said. He grimaced as he walked away.

Heather sensed that the sausage was OK and continued chewing while reaching for another. Chris came back with four bottles of water and some beef jerky that he began to chew. Actually he was wrestling with it more than chewing it. Before long, they heard a train whistle from the east. The Nairobi-bound train was entering Tsavo Station but didn't stop. The beautiful silver and white passenger cars whizzed by at breakneck speed with the air horns blaring. It was a fair warning for all to stay clear of the tracks.

"Mom, it didn't stop," R.O. shouted over the noise.

"No, honey. That's the nonstop passenger service between Mombasa and Nairobi. It goes on to Kampala, Uganda. Here's our train," Mavis said.

When the last of the beautiful silver cars had passed, the "other" train could be seen lumbering into Tsavo

Station on a second track. All three kids looked at each other in disbelief as the vintage train chugged to a stop.

"We're riding this?" Heather was offended.

"Yes dear. This is the only train that stops at Tsavo and three other places. All aboard." Mavis MacGregor smiled as she motioned to the teens and picked up two bedrolls.

Chris turned around to pick up their packs when two armed soldiers stepped up to him, not two feet away. One of the solders lowered his M-16 automatic rifle but didn't point it at him.

"Do you have a permit to carry that rifle?" one of the soldiers asked in English.

"Yes, he does." Mavis MacGregor stepped into the conversation.

"Excuse me madam. I am not addressing you. I am talking to this man," the soldier replied.

"I am his mother. He's just a boy!"

"Being his mother is irrelevant. It is not a boy standing in front of me with a rifle slung over his shoulder. He is old enough to make his own decisions and right now he has only one to make—to answer my question or not." The soldier stood perfectly still.

"Yes, I have the papers in my pack," Chris replied.

The soldier nodded for him to get them and in just a minute Chris handed him the burgundy leather folder that contained his U.S. passport, his immunization records, a visitor's visa, and "sporting rifle" permit. They were scrutinized carefully. When the soldier noticed the permit had been personally issued by the Chairman of the Kenya Wildlife Service, he folded them neatly and put them back into the leather pouch secured with a Velcro latch.

"Sorry to detain you, Mr. MacGregor, and you as well, Mrs. MacGregor. We can't be too careful these days after the terrorist bombing in Nairobi last year. We have also experienced an increase in wild animal poach-

ing lately. The 7mm rifle could easily be used for both
purposes. Your papers are in order and we are very
pleased that you chose to visit Kenya. Have a pleasant
and safe stay. But remember to keep your rifle unloaded
while you are not in the bush and never leave it unat-
tended. Our laws against hunting are strictly enforced.
You may only use your rifle for protection of your life
and not for sport." The soldier tipped his hat and turned
abruptly.

"What was that all about?" Heather asked as she
stood next to Chris.

"Just checking weapons, I guess," Chris said.

"I suspect that you were a little young to be standing
here with a rifle slung over your shoulder and no older
male present, like a father or safari guide. I wonder if
your father has learned about the poaching yet." Mavis
had a puzzled look on her face.

"Maybe they just wanted to talk to us, to see if we
were smugglers or something," R.O. said.

"No, Ryan," Mavis said. "They were just doing their
job. The bombing at the Nairobi embassy killed over
two hundred people. It was as bad, if not worse, than the
Oklahoma City bombing a few years ago. That would
make anyone nervous. Of course security is going to be
tighter."

"Mom, look at this." Ryan was standing by a window and looking out on the dirt and gravel parking
area.

As the MacGregors crowded against the window,
they could see the two soldiers, now joined by six
others. Sitting on the ground next them were seven men
with bare feet and wearing shabby shirts. They were
shackled together with heavy chains that were manacled
to their ankles and wrists.

"Wow," Chris said.

"Double wow," R.O. said.

"Looks like they found some of those terrorists or

poachers," Mavis said.

"Tsavo to Nairobi now loading on platform two," came the voice over the intercom in English, then Swahili, then Arabic.

"Let's go," Mavis said to her brood as they all grabbed bedrolls, backpacks, and camera gear. Chris held on tightly to his rifle.

Within a few minutes, the old noisy train was chugging down the tracks. These tracks had been the source of life to the interior of this region of Africa for over a hundred years. The kids sat down in the dusty compartment amidst the masses of Africa. With their gear piled all around them, Heather and Ryan fell asleep. The ground under the ancient baobab hadn't been the best bed, especially accompanied by the fear of returning wild dogs and lions.

Chris and his mother talked for a few minutes. Then he leaned his head on her shoulder and closed his eyes. In a minute he was asleep. She touched his cheek as she had for his nearly eighteen years and felt good her kids were safe and sound.

Suddenly the train applied its emergency brakes. It started sliding down the track making a screeching noise. Heather, Chris, and R.O. all jumped up and looked out the window. Mavis reached out to grab them but all three bounded down the aisle toward the end of the car. Chris jerked the door open just as the three Kenyan soldiers raced out the door of the opposite car and leaped to the ground below.

A rumbling noise could be heard nearby when a mad bull elephant charged toward the train only to reverse himself on two feet, as nimble as a gazelle, and dart back into the bush. The three soldiers, clad in their camouflage uniforms, chased after him. Heather jumped from the train and followed after them. Chris grabbed R.O. and held on tight while the train finally came to a halt.

As the soldiers ducked into the bush, Heather, now at full speed, kept up with them. She was no more than ten yards behind them. The bellowing and trumpeting of a herd of elephants could be heard dead ahead. Three quick bursts of an automatic rifle deafened everyone's ears, but the soldiers and Heather kept on racing. The heat of the sun bore down on them and sweat dripped into Heather's eyes. Her shirt was now sopping wet. She kept pace with the soldiers.

When suddenly, out of nowhere, a young girl about ten years old stepped into the pathway. She was adorned with the colorful beads and necklaces of the Samburu.

"Stop," she said to Heather softly.

"No," Heather shouted back. "I've got to stop the killing. They're killing the elephants."

Heather brushed her aside and ran onward trying to catch the soldiers now fifty feet ahead. But she came to a halt when limbs began to break and small trees began to fall. The bull elephant had turned and was now charging toward them. The Samburu girl reached out and touched Heather and she stopped.

The soldiers were gone and she realized she was standing in a clearing next to a meat-drying rack. Parts of elephants lay all around her.

"I've got to stop this," Heather said to the Samburu girl.

"Yes, I know. And we can," the girl replied.

A puzzled look came over Heather as she glanced around at the raw elephant meat complete with millions of flies and a horrible odor that penetrated her nostrils.

"But what can I do?" Heather asked the girl.

"You will see. It won't be easy. But you'll know what to do when the time is right." The Samburu girl turned to walk away.

The giant bull elephant returned to the killing place and stomped his feet. He trumpeted toward the sky, wishing it was a poacher standing there instead of two young girls. Heather grabbed her head. It ached.

"Heather, Heather," Chris shouted.

"Sweetie. Wake up, Sweetie. You're having a bad dream," Mavis said as she cradled her in her arms on the hard oak bench of the train.

"What? Where did she go?" Heather sat up. Sweat was running down her neck on to her damp safari shirt.

"You were having a bad dream, honey," Mavis said again and brushed her hair out of her face.

"I'm still on the train," Heather said with a bewildered look on her face.

"That was too weird, Heather," R.O. said. "I thought you were going to jump up and run around the train or spin your head or something." R.O. took a drink of bottled water.

"You'll be fine, Sweetie. We're almost to Nairobi." Mavis pulled Heather back against her chest.

Heather leaned into her mother and thought about what she had just dreamed. The mad bull elephant, the killing field, the Samburu girl. She didn't know what it meant. But for now it didn't matter. She closed her eyes again, but she didn't sleep. She thought about the elephants and felt a great sadness.

The rusty, rickety old train chugged to a halt in downtown Nairobi. It stopped next to the beautiful silver passenger train that had already been unloaded two hours earlier. Mavis herded her exhausted silent brood through the car and out onto the platform. Everyone did a quick baggage check. A uniformed steward, smiling from ear to ear, greeted them, reached into his pocket and handed Chris a card. On the card was printed the train depot's regulations about weapons, since big game hunting is not allowed in Kenya. Chris nodded. He got the point!

"Do you need a case, sir, for your rifle?"

"Thanks, but I have a cloth sock covering in my bag." Chris retrieved the long green rifle "sock" that he slid smoothly from the barrel to the butt.

The steward grabbed the bags and packs. Ordinarily Mavis MacGregor would have insisted that everyone carry their own gear, but on this day all the arms and legs were quite tired. They were loaded into a taxi and headed for the Ngong Hills, a suburb of Nairobi. The taxi followed a long route through Nairobi taking them through downtown.

"Look everybody." R.O. pointed through the back window.

"I didn't notice that the other day. This is awful," Heather said.

"Probably because it was too early in the morning and you were sleeping," Chris said.

"It is one of the great tragedies of humanity," Mavis said. They all gawked at the largest slum in Africa, home to thousands of poverty-stricken people. "To live in a land with so many wonderful resources, but yet these people might as well have been born on Mars."

"Across the street are high-rises, office buildings, churches. But that is, is, well, the most awful sight I've ever seen," Heather said.

For these tired kids, this had been an eye opener. In all of their travels they had not seen such poverty. They were solemn during the thirty minute ride to the government V.I.P. estate in the suburbs.

As the sun dipped behind the mountains to the west, they arrived at the large estate loaned to them by the Kenya Wildlife Service. Thousands of lights could be seen across the foothills. They weren't electric lights, but fires built to cook food and keep families warm during the cool nights of Africa.

The hills of southwest Kenya were at a higher altitude than much of equatorial Africa. This accounted for the cooler nights. Closer to the flatlands of the coast and further to the south, the temperatures were more in line with the hot and steamy Africa depicted by the media.

The MacGregor kids dutifully carried all their gear inside and unpacked like robots performing routine tasks. A large pile of dirty clothes grew quickly on the large square tiles in the middle hallway. Chris opened a cleaning kit and performed a fast cleaning job on his rifle and stored it away in the closet. Heather was first in the shower. When Chris and R.O. started complaining that no hot water would be left, she exited wearing a towel wrapped around her head and a yellow terry-cloth robe. Yellow was her favorite color. Her still wet feet left prints along the tile to her room.

In less than thirty minutes, each MacGregor ate a sandwich, drank a big glass of fresh milk and headed off to bed. As Mavis went from room to room, she leaned over to kiss each of her youngsters on the cheek or forehead, whichever was available.

The clean soft sheets, the weight of the comforter over her feet, and the down pillow that crept up around her face set the mood for a good night of rest.

Mavis MacGregor drifted off to sleep without knowing that this would be her last good night's rest for the next four days.

# 5

# Game Wars

The Aerospatiale helicopter swung low through the valley just barely missing the tops of trees. The large French-made helicopter could haul heavy loads as well as maneuver like a military aircraft. With its retractable landing gear, it was perfect for Africa.

As the broad expanse of the escarpment loomed ahead, the pilot made a decision to drop below the tree line and follow the river. The whipping of the rotor blades created air waves that creased the surface of the smoothly flowing water. Two large hippos lunged from a sandbar and dove into the deep channel near the middle of the river. A solitary crocodile never moved. If he even noticed the strange and loud bird overhead, he didn't show it. His mouth was propped open waiting for an unwary or careless creature to hop or land nearby. Then with dagger-like teeth he would snag it and swim for the deep channel to drown his prey. When it was dead, he would stuff it into a root bank to rot. Only when the victim was good and tender would he return for the feast.

"Safari 1 to Safari 2, do you copy?" The pilot of the Aerospatiale radioed the truck driver as he continued to follow the flowing river below. The long rains of summer had not arrived as they should have by now. With a minimal amount of water, the river lumbered along slowly.

"Safari 2, we read you, go ahead," came the response from the driver of a truck waiting on the bank ten miles down river.

"We're about five minutes from your '20.' Is there a landing spot nearby?" The pilot adjusted the controls of the Aerospatiale. He followed the bend in the river like it was a high-speed Nascar racetrack.

"That's a roger," the truck driver said into his handheld radio. He noticed a large crocodile slide into the water on the opposite side of the river.

"Safari 1, out."

In exactly four minutes and thirty-six seconds the long, sleek blue and white helicopter was hovering over a clearing about a hundred yards away from the truck. After he touched down, the pilot switched off all of its power. The rotor blades began drifting to a stop, making one last rotation. The truck full of men arrived in the clearing. A Range Rover with three more men suddenly appeared from the bush. As the Range Rover came to a stop, a large obese man climbed out of the passenger seat. He was greeted by the helicopter pilot and truck driver.

"Well, chaps, I made it just in time, it seems." He spoke with a colonial British accent. "Such a fine machine you have there, son. What's an Aerospatiale cost these days? Three million? Four million?"

"Not that much, sir, but she isn't cheap either," the young sandy-haired pilot said.

"Don't recognize your accent, young man." The big man started walking toward the riverbank.

"Billy is from Zimbabwe. It's the old Rhodesian slang that gets you. Not British, not Australian, not South African, and not even colonial. But he's a darn good pilot and can flush out a pride of lions or run down a cheetah without so much as a thank you ma'am," the burly truck driver said.

They were now standing on the bank of the river. The large crocodile had finally made it across the river and was floating near the bank keeping a keen eye on the three men. The truck driver turned toward the truck and shouted a long string of words and phrases in Swahili. Five men, dressed only in cotton pants and sandals, bounded out of the truck. Each man carried an AK-47 assault rifle, a gun easily acquired on the black market. The ammunition was either Russian or Chinese. As the men lined up on the bank and took aim at the crocodile, the big obese man stepped in front of them and raised up his right hand.

"Hold your fire, gentleman," he said and looked at the truck driver. "Mr. Hanes, I suggest you translate the request to these fine men."

Hanes spoke the words quickly and all five men lowered their guns and stepped back.

"Thank you, Mr. Hanes. I think it would be a waste of good ammunition to retire that old croc down there. We aren't poor, but buying the caliber of ammunition your rifles require gets more and more difficult. It's time to talk."

Mr. Hanes gave new instructions to the men. In about fifteen minutes a canopy tent that was open on all sides, a stylish mahogany table, and three wicker chairs had been set up. As the big man, Billy, and Mr. Hanes sat down, one of the men laid a clean white tablecloth across the small round mahogany table. Two other men brought over a tray with a teapot and cups. Another tray was delivered with an assortment of fruit and cheese. Billy didn't wait for the social amenities to take place; he grabbed for a piece of cheese. With a wad of cheese in his mouth, he turned toward the big man and spoke.

"Sir, Charles here never told me your name," Billy

said and swallowed. He picked up the cup of tea that the
big man had poured and drank it like water. It must
have burned his tongue and mouth, but he never blinked,
flinched, or said a word. He set down the cup and
pointed with his index finger on his right hand that he
wanted more. After the cup was refilled, the big man
put down the pitcher and reached into the front but-
toned pocket of his safari jacket.

"Billy, names aren't important," he said as he laid a
wad of hundred dollar bills on the white tablecloth. "I
have been in Africa for nearly forty years. I came here as
a lad with my parents from England. I have owned
several businesses, a coffee plantation, tourist lodges,
and many more successful ventures. But the population
keeps growing and as the population grows the habitat
for all of these wild creatures gets choked out. Soon,
Billy, there won't be any more safe rivers for old crocs
like that one down there. And there won't be any more
open grasslands for lions and gazelles. They'll be fenced
off for cattle. The elephant will be shot on site for the
destruction they cause to life and property. They will all
die sooner or later." The big man took a sip of his tea,
then added two cubes of sugar. "It really is good tea. Mr.
Hanes knows exactly how I like it served, don't you,
Charles?"

"Yes, sir. Exactly 122 degrees." Charles took a sip of
his tea.

"Billy, what I am offering you is freedom from
flying grumpy and greedy old tourists around ever
again. This stack of bills comes to $20,000. You will get
$80,000 more when the job is done. Is that clear?"

"Very. What do I have to do to get it?" Billy shifted
his weight on the small chair.

"Mr. Hanes and I have an enterprise here in Tanzania, just across the border from Kenya, that involves
liberating these poor dying animals. These beautiful
specimens of nature will die horrible deaths through

starvation, traps, and at the hands of ignorant people. By helping them go in peace, we can preserve part of their existence for posterity."

"And what are you preserving?" Billy asked. He took another big swig of tea.

"Their skins, their bones, their ivory. Billy, a lion's skull is worth over $800 to science teachers. The beautiful skins of the big cats are worth thousands to fashion designers and furriers. Ivory tusks from elephants can bring hundreds of thousands of dollars in the Far East. Ivory dropped from $400 per pound to less than $2 per pound after the international agreement to stop shipping ivory that was being collected by nations from culling elephant herds. But Billy, I know for a fact that after the embargo, there were several countries that continued to sell their ivory. Oh, yes, they made a big show by burning tusks in giant bonfires. But let me tell you, the ivory market never went dry. And now that there is a shortage of quality African ivory, the prices on the black market are creeping up. What Mr. Hansen and I have set aside will keep us in, shall we say, fine linen and exquisite tea for years to come." The extremely huge man put the dainty china cup to his mouth and slurped some tea. The steam filled his nostrils.

"And you're offering me $100,000 to fly around and guide Mr. Hanes and his sharpshooters to African wildlife. Look, Mr., well, what do I call you?" Billy asked.

"Call me whatever you want, Billy. Names are simply a trivial label we assign to our human forms. It is our wealth and accomplishments that truly separate us from the common man." The big man took another sip.

"How about," Billy paused, "Mr. Big?"

Everyone was silent. Then the big man started laughing hard, his fat tummy wiggled like jello. He was cautiously followed by Mr. Hanes and then Billy.

"Mr. Big will do just fine," the big man said in a jovial tone. But just as quickly as he started laughing, he stopped and a serious look crossed his face. "Billy, is $100,000 really not enough?"

Billy sat quietly and looked into the faces of Mr. Hanes and Mr. Big. He looked around the makeshift camp and the five young men seated outside the tent sipping Evian bottled water. The oil on the barrels of their AK-47 rifles was glistening in the sun. Their sweaty dark skins shined. It was time for Billy to speak.

"I know the cost of all those things you mentioned. I also know that the international market is very tight right now. Whatever skins or ivory move into the market must first go through many hands. Much greed creates much graft. No, I think $100,000 is not enough. The Aerospatiale is at risk from gunfire every time I fly. Storms dropping off the top of Mt. Kilimanjaro or Mt. Kenya can catch even a veteran pilot off guard. My father and grandfather fought the wars in Rhodesia. They lost everything. I want $100,000 now and $400,000 more when the job is done in sixty days." Billy stood up and stepped away from the table.

Mr. Big casually took another sip of tea.

"Mr. Hanes, would you go to the Range Rover and bring me my briefcase, please?"

"Yes, sir." Mr. Hanes hurried over to the vehicle and came back with a crocodile skin briefcase. He laid it on the small mahogany table covered by the white linen cloth.

Mr. Big snapped open the brass latches and lifted one side up where Billy couldn't peer into it. Slowly he reached in and picked up a very old Colt .45 revolver with ivory handled grips. It appeared to be made of chrome because the bluing of the steel had rubbed off. He slowly cocked the trigger and pulled it out. Billy saw it and stood up.

"Don't worry, Billy. If I were going to shoot you, you would have never seen the gun my father gave me. It is one that he had brought with him from England." Mr.

Big laid the gun on the table. The hammer was still cocked back ready to fire. He then reached back into the briefcase and returned with a handful of money. Fresh bank bands were wrapped around the bills.

"Here is the rest of your $100,000. When I have bagged enough game to retire, you will receive the other $400,000. If we can do it in two weeks, it will be one million." Mr. Big handed him the money.

Billy reached out for it and at the last moment, Mr. Big picked up the gun and slowly lowered the hammer.

"In another moment you could have died, Billy. Don't ever give me a reason not to trust you," Mr. Big said.

Billy slowly took the money and stuffed it into the cargo pocket of his pants.

"I understand. I just need enough notice so the safari company doesn't suspect I'm using their chopper to track down elephants and lions. I also need some fuel so that the office doesn't suspect something is wrong if I fill her up too often."

"The fuel can be arranged through my contacts in Nairobi. The Kenya Wildlife Service subcontracts with helicopter rentals from time to time. What's another Aerospatiale to fill up." Mr. Big took a sip of his tea.

"Ready for a trial run?" Mr. Hanes asked.

"Sure," Billy replied and stepped out from under the canvas canopy into the hot African sun.

"I will expect a report this evening. Call me at my farm. Here's my number." Mr. Big wiped his mouth with an expensive linen napkin and stood up. He handed Billy a card. Taking a bright red apple from the tray on middle of the table, he turned to leave. He then stopped and took a big bite out of the apple.

"Billy," he said with a full mouth.

"Yes, sir?" Billy stopped to look toward Mr. Big.

"How old are you?" Mr. Big asked. He chewed the apple.

"Twenty-three, sir."

"If you mess this up, you will never see twenty-four," Mr. Big said. It was the second threat in five minutes. He took another big bite of the apple. The crunch echoed throughout the tent.

"I understand completely, sir," Billy replied.

"That's good. I thought you were a bright boy. There are forty-seven privately-owned helicopters within five hundred miles of this spot. You can be replaced overnight."

"That's very clear...Mr. Big," Billy said.

"That's good, Billy. I like people who push the edge. Excitement is not enough. People like you need 'extreme' excitement. You will be a worthy millionaire in a couple of months." Mr. Big turned and walked through the grass to the waiting Range Rover.

In just a few minutes he was gone. Billy was starting up the Aerospatiale and Mr. Hanes and his men were in the truck. The helicopter lifted off, flew down the riverbed, and began to gain altitude.

"Proceed southwest along the escarpment." Billy spoke into the radio microphone attached to his headset.

"That's a roger. We'll be right behind you," Charles Hanes replied over the wind noise and the whine of the Brazilian-made truck.

In about fifteen minutes, Mr. Hanes' radio crackled with the noise from the helicopter's radio.

"Safari 2, do you read me?" Billy asked.

"Go ahead," Mr. Hanes said.

"We have our first clients. Proceed down your current track south-southwest. When you reach the west bend of the river, turn due west for one mile."

"That's a roger," Mr. Hanes replied.

Billy flew around the area for the forty-five minutes it took the truck to travel the four miles through the heavy bush. Suddenly the truck broke into a clearing where a pride of lions were sleeping under the shade of an umbrella tree in the heat of the afternoon. There were a large male with a beautiful black mane, five females, and three cubs. As Billy banked the large helicopter against the clear blue sky, he could see the flashes of light coming from the rifles of Mr. Hanes' men. The male lion dropped quickly. Not wanting to watch the slaughter, Billy turned northeast toward Nairobi and the Kenya border. Somehow, being separated by wind, space, and sky, he didn't feel the emotion that he knew he would feel if he were there. He put a rock CD into the player on the console and got lost in the music. Billy felt better.

In the blink of an eye, from out of nowhere, a twin engine Cessna 310 Sky Knight dove in front of him. Jerking back hard on the collective with his left hand and pushing forward on the cyclic with his right hand, the helicopter dropped into a deep dive. Looking around the sky Billy couldn't see where the plane had flown. Then suddenly the Cessna was there again, nearly clipping his main rotors. Billy pulled back on the cyclic attempting to bring the Aerospatiale into a hovering position. But the momentum of his air speed forced the helicopter along at a speed of sixty knots before he finally slowed his forward motion. Rotating quickly from one direction to another, he couldn't find the Cessna.

Then a loud roar shook the helicopter as the Cessna 310 dove down from above him creating enough turbulence to bounce the big helicopter up and down. Billy attempted to provide forward thrust and regain control.

"Yee ha, ride em cowboy. Take that, Frenchie. A French-made helicopter is no match for a Kansas-made airplane," came the exclamation of the bearded old man behind the controls of the Cessna. He was chewing on a piece of red licorice that hung from the corner of his mouth, which was surrounded by a grizzled white

beard and very tan skin. His old, stained Resistol cowboy hat was a triple X beaver with a snakeskin hat band.
He wore a khaki safari shirt and denim pants. His dusty
brown Rios boots were pressed firmly on the foot controls. On the front left pocket of his shirt was pinned the
Silver Star of the US Army Air Corps for World War II
heroism. Next to it were medals from Korea and Vietnam.

"Just sit there long enough and I'll suck your rotor
blades right off, just like I did those little Messersmitz in
1944." The crusty old pilot banked around again only to
find the Aerospatiale dropping to treetop level flying
full speed toward the Kenya border.

"Heading home, are we? Well, I'll give you a going
away present."

He pushed the Cessna to full throttle. A red light
immediately appeared on the console.

"Just hold together, Betsy. We're going to repaint
this chopper."

The Cessna dove hard and straight, catching the
helicopter in about forty-five seconds. As the airplane
overtook the helicopter, the grizzled old pilot flew the
Cessna 310 hard and fast, a steely-eyed determined look
on his face. At the exact moment when the Cessna was
only five feet over the helicopter, the airplane reached
an air speed of nearly three hundred miles per hour,
exploding past the Aerospatiale. The delicately tuned
rotor blades of the Aerospatiale were violently pounded
by the excessive turbulence of the Cessna. Billy pushed
and pulled with both hands and feet and fought to keep
the helicopter from spinning wildly out of control. He
was now below treetop level. Frantically maneuvering
right and left, he was able to dodge the large branches
and groves of small trees.

He jerked back hard on the cyclic and pushed forward on the collective, attempting to lift the Aerospatiale
up over the trees in a hovering position. He could see the

Cessna turning to the east. It worked. He had learned to be a good pilot in the civil wars of Africa. But the attack had left its mark.

"Well, Betsy, nice job. He'll be lookin for us the next time he comes back to our neck of the woods. You can bank on that. He'll learn that I watch out for the animals that live down here," the Cessna pilot said to the imagined persona of the airplane. "I won't be late next time!"

He pulled the Cessna up to about 5,000 feet and pointed her east toward the Indian Ocean.

Billy looked out the right window of the helicopter and noticed the Cessna disappear into the blue sky. His hands were sweaty, but he felt a huge sense of relief. He had never before been assaulted in the sky quite like that. He wouldn't soon forget it.

In the clearing below, Mr. Hanes and his men loaded the bodies of the dead lions into the back of the truck. It took all five men to carry the big male.

# 6

# Tastes Like Kudu

It was nearly noon before Heather woke up to the noise of a steam kettle whistling in the kitchen. Pulling on a robe over her flannel pajamas, she wandered down the hall, her feet patting noisily on the ceramic tile floor. As she turned the corner into the large kitchen, the stainless steel doors on the double wide refrigerator, dishwasher, and oven reflected more light than she wanted. Before her eyes could adjust to the light, she was met with a staccato whistle. It was so annoying that it forced her to put her hands over her ears.

"What are you doing?" she shouted at R.O.

"What? I can't hear you," R.O. shouted back. He leaned forward and adjusted a makeshift valve he had fixed over the teakettle spout. The valve consisted of a three-liter pop bottle cap lined with the cork plug from the metal salt shaker. A hole had been poked in the middle of the cap with an ice pick so that a plastic tube from the kitchen's ice machine could be inserted. The long plastic tube stretched across the stove top to another contraption that was constructed from the metal salt and pepper shakers, two cooking pots, three hand utensils, and an empty coffee can. The coffee rested in a pile on the counter. The noise stopped.

"I said what are you doing?" Heather shouted again. But, without the noise, she was the only thing that was loud.

"You don't have to yell at me."

"What are you doing, Ryan?" Heather squinted her eyes as she tried to play at being nice. Any other attitude would be met with a rude response from her younger brother.

"I've made a, well, you could call it a...uh. A steam extractor. That's it. A steam extractor." R.O. smiled broadly.

"And what are you extracting with the steam, may I ask?" Heather said gruffly.

"Well, uh, I haven't gotten that far yet," he said as he leaned toward her just barely balancing himself on the stool.

Heather's eyes got wide but she didn't move. She knew better from past experiences. R.O. reached out with his left hand and touched her hair. Slowly he pulled his hand back and Heather's long blonde hair fell like a drape around her shoulders.

"I need a clamp. Your hairpin will work great. Thanks." R.O. turned back around and slid the pin over the joint between the teakettle and the plastic tubing. He turned the heat back up on the stove, and the kettle started to whistle again. R.O. pushed the pin on tighter and the whistling stopped.

"There. That did it." R.O. grinned again.

"Well, I am glad I could be of assistance." Heather was indignant.

Suddenly a loud boom echoed across the kitchen. The lid of one of the pots that was fastened with duct tape to the pipe blew off. It hit the stucco finish of the ceiling, ricocheted off and went flying like a Frisbee across the room. Chris, just coming in from outside, saw the flying metal object and ducked through the doorway. The lid sailed over his head and out the door for nearly twenty feet. It flew across the veranda before it crashed in a cloud of dust on the dry brown grass.

"What on earth is going on?" Chris shouted as he slowly got up and looked around the room.

"Einstein is at it again. This time he's invented his first weapon. The semiautomatic pot that belches lids like bullets," Heather remarked sarcastically as she pulled back her hair. She took an ever present yellow scrunchie out of the pocket of her robe and wrapped it around the knot of hair she had just made.

"Wow. That was so cool," R.O. said as he turned off the gas burner.

"Be glad mom is not here or you would be out the door with the lid," Chris said.

"Where is mom?" Heather asked. She opened the refrigerator door and retrieved a bottle of orange juice.

"She's at the market with Rachel. She was leaving when I was getting up. That was 8:00. Four hours ago," Chris said.

"Well some of us need our rest to maintain our health, figure, and good looks," Heather shot back. She gulped a big drink of the orange juice straight from the bottle.

"Heather, that's gross," R.O. shouted as she took another drink. Taking the bottle from her lips, she grinned.

"I'm sure I didn't get any backwash in it. Either of my brothers want a glass of this really sweet orange juice?"

"No thanks. I had my big drinks earlier," Chris said.

"Very funny!" Heather twisted the lid back onto the bottle.

"Now listen, both of you. Mom said that dad has a very important reception at the Kenya Wildlife Service headquarters this afternoon from two until four. She wants us dressed in nice clothes. No camouflage, R.O.

And Heather, no miniskirts."

Both gave Chris "the face." He ignored them and continued his instructions.

"A car from the ministry will collect us, as they say here, at 1:15. That's about an hour from now. Heather you can have our bathroom. R.O. and I will take mom and dad's," Chris said much like the drill sergeant he knew he had to be.

As the oldest, the responsibility for the three of them fell on him. If he didn't perform, they could all be sent back to Texas to stay with relatives while their parents continued on their year-long journey. His dad's book on endangered and threatened wildlife was just in its beginning stages. Chapter one had been about the sea turtles around the Cayman Islands. Chapter two is going to be written about elephants and big cats in East Africa and chapter three will take the family to Egypt. From there he knew that his dad had talked about traveling to Australia, India, and maybe even China or Japan. Chris realized that to miss this round-the-world trip would indeed be a tragedy for all three of them. He wasn't going to let the immaturity of either his brother or sister mess this up for him.

At exactly 1:15, a black Bentley arrived at the estate and the driver knocked on the door. By 1:20 they were on the highway to downtown Nairobi. Traffic was especially heavy as the Bentley cruised along with the flow. The majority of cars were old and in bad repair. Most belched blue smoke from the exhaust pipes and one even sprayed the Bentley with radiator fluid squirting from under the partially open hood. Rested and relaxed, the three kids talked about the safari trip, the wild dogs, the mother lion, and the Samburu warriors. By 1:50, the black handmade British automobile was coming to a stop in a parking zone marked for V.I.P.s in front of the Kenya Wildlife Service.

Chris, Heather, and R.O. walked down the sidewalk

toward the massive building. It was rather plain and, except for the sign, one would not know what it was or to whom it belonged. Mavis MacGregor bounded out the door and met them halfway down the steps as they were coming up.

"Right on time. I'm impressed. And let me see. Yes, properly dressed as I specified."

"Only for two hours," Heather said. She tried not to display too much attitude for this would only prompt her mother to focus on her that much more.

"Me too. Then it's back to shorts and T-shirts," R.O. echoed and stepped around his mother as she reached out and touched Chris on the shoulder.

"Get any more rest after I left, big guy?" Mavis hooked her arm through Chris's arm. Mavis MacGregor was indeed proud of her eldest son and the leadership role he had taken with his brother and sister. It made her life easier. And since the adventure in the Caymans with the lost Spanish gold, she had barely let a moment pass that she didn't touch him or hug him, sometimes much to his embarrassment. But Chris understood and let it pass.

"Yes. I went out to the hammock under the tree and dosed. When I woke up, I went back to the kitchen just in time to keep the house from blowing up," Chris said.

R.O. stopped and turned around.

"It was not going to blow up," R.O. said and gave Chris a dirty look.

"It was, Mother. I was there and I almost got my head blown off," Heather added and gave R.O. a drop-dead look.

"Mom. They're lying," R.O. yelled at both of them.

"Ryan. I told you not to use that word, and I meant it," Mavis said.

"OK. My two siblings are seriously misrepresenting the facts," R. O. shot back. He smirked at both of them.

Chris, Heather, and Mavis stopped and in unison

turned toward R.O. with raised eyebrows.

"Seriously misrepresenting the facts. Siblings? I'm impressed, my dear Mr. Ryan," Mavis said.

"That's what I said, and that's what they did." Ryan folded his arms across his chest.

"Then if that's the case, I will be glad to hear your side of it...later. But for now, we have to go inside and present ourselves as Dr. Jack MacGregor's wonderful, harmonious family from Texas. Truce everyone?" Mavis said. She looked each of them in the eye—her favorite thing to do when talking to her kids.

"OK with me," Heather said.

"Same here," Chris said.

"OK. Me too," Ryan said. He stopped and faced Mavis.

"Mom. What's harmonious mean?"

Chris and Heather both giggled as they tried to keep a straight face. They didn't want R.O. to get agitated again.

"I'll explain later, hon. Let's go. Dad's waiting and so are a lot of other important people." Mavis MacGregor shooed her brood through the massive front doors and into the lobby of the Kenya Wildlife Service.

Once inside the lobby, a young lady in a pretty navy dress ushered them through another set of doors that led to a large courtyard. Greeting them right away was a life-size bronze statue of a bull elephant. Its ears were forever pushed outward, its long trunk pointed toward the sky, and its massive tusks were aimed right toward their faces. A chill ran across Heather's arms as she remembered her dream on the train about the young Samburu girl, the soldiers, the raging bull elephant. The goose bumps ran up her neck.

"Wow, is that awesome or what?" R.O. said. He walked over and rubbed the end of one of the tusks. He could barely reach it.

The ceiling reached three stories high creating an

atrium. It also served as a giant skylight. Trees and foliage imitating a rain forest covered the room. In the very center was an open area where nearly a hundred people were going through a reception line and a buffet. Tables of four, five, and six were scattered everywhere among the trees and bushes to create a cozy but wild Africa effect.

"Mrs. MacGregor, we are so glad you could come. And these are your children?" a very tall man asked in his British colonial accent. He wore a gray suit with a black silk tie embroidered with a cheetah in motion. "Let me introduce myself. I am Benjamin Nyerere, chief liaison between the Kenya Wildlife Service and the native tribes of Kenya. I am Masai."

"Masai?" R.O. let slip out. He put his hand over his mouth.

"I don't look Masai?" The tall man spoke with a quizzical look on his face. He then burst into laughter.

The kids tried to join him but only Mavis caught on and truly felt the moment to be funny.

"I left my robe, earrings, and jewelry back at my hut with my goats and cattle," Nyerere continued. "No, seriously. I do wear my traditional dress when I work with the tribes. But you didn't come here to learn about me. Let's find Dr. MacGregor and introduce you to the people who are here today."

"And who is here today?" Mavis asked as she walked beside him toward the reception line. The kids followed.

"They are by far the most influential people in Kenya. Tourism represents our biggest industry. No other segment of our economy comes close. Farming is second, but a distant second. These people are from government, private safari clubs and businesses, aviation, railroad, food importing, telecommunications, and warehousing. In short, the top one hundred business and industry people in Kenya."

Mavis was impressed with the influential guests standing around her husband. She squinted her eyes.

"No teachers?" Mavis stared at Nyerere. He ignored her and turned away. "On your best, guys. No messing around today," she said to her three kids without looking at them. By the tone of her voice, Chris, Heather, and Ryan knew she meant business. And when their mom meant business, messing up was the last thing they wanted to do.

"Honey, kids," Jack MacGregor said as he walked up to them.

Mavis reached out right away to straighten his tie and turn the back of his dress coat collar down. It had curled up in one spot.

"You guys look great. You were still asleep when I left this morning. Daniel's here by the way." Jack knelt down to face Ryan. "You're getting taller. I have to look up to you when I kneel down."

"We had fun, Dad," Heather said before she wandered toward the buffet.

"And how 'bout you, R.O.? Have fun?" Ryan loved it when his dad called him R.O. It was something that had happened recently during their adventure on the Cayman Islands.

"We had a great time, Dad. Wish you could have been there. You would have loved seeing Chris shoot his rifle over Daniel's head at the wild dogs." R.O. smiled at his dad.

"What wild dogs? Chris, why were you shooting wild dogs?" Jack asked Chris.

"I wasn't shooting wild dogs, Dad." Chris was annoyed that R.O. had even brought it up.

"You guys didn't say anything about shooting wild dogs," Mavis said. She knew it would be a big deal with Jack. But she would take care of it as any loving wife and mother would, and it would not become a big deal.

"Can we discuss it later, Dad? Maybe with Daniel

present?" Chris pleaded softly.

"OK. But I want to know the whole story," Jack said firmly and stood up.

"Chris." Daniel walked over and the two embraced. Jack looked at them rather puzzled at the affection they were displaying. He raised his eyebrows and shrugged his shoulders.

"How did you get back so soon?" Chris asked.

"I caught a ride with a bush pilot. He landed at Tsavo Station to pick up mail just before dawn. Got here about ten this morning. Had just enough time to go home, shower, and change clothes. Didn't want to miss this. Your dad is an important man. Anyone with his reputation who writes about wildlife can influence a lot of people. The movers and shakers in Kenya don't want him to pass through here without a proper party."

"You exaggerate far too much, Daniel," Dr. MacGregor said. He took Mavis' hand and led the group toward the reception line.

Jack and Mavis were placed in line next to the Chairman of the Kenya Wildlife Service and a representative of the President of Kenya. The line was informal and flowed nicely as the Kenyans introduced themselves to Jack and Mavis. Daniel took Chris, Ryan, and Heather across the large expanse of the courtyard to a second buffet line.

"Look at that." R.O. pointed to a lamb carcass turning on a roasting rotisserie.

"It smells so good," Heather said.

She turned and stared toward the spot where the boys had stopped. Cold chills rushed all over her body. Her face turned white. Her knees felt weak. Suddenly she sat straight down on the floor. Chris rushed over to her and grabbed her arm. R.O. was right beside him.

"Heather. What's the matter. Do you feel sick?" Chris asked.

"Are you going to throw up?" R.O. asked. "I can

find a trash can for you."

Heather seemed in a trance as she looked in Daniel's direction. Standing next to him was a native girl with her hair in braids. She wore a pretty white cotton dress and had matching white socks and white shoes. But to Heather she was Samburu. Heather could only see the ivory earrings looped through her long earlobes. The red ochre painted across her shoulders and the rows and rows of colorful beads wrapped around her neck and woven through her black hair.

"Heather, are you all right? I'll go get mom." Chris turned to walk away.

"No, Chris. Don't. I'm OK." Heather looked around at the beautiful courtyard and the lush foliage. She then looked back toward Daniel. The Samburu girl was gone. Beside him stood a pretty Kikuyu teenager.

"Chris, Heather, Ryan. This is Rebecca, my daughter. I think she is the same age as you Heather. Fourteen? Are you all right? Let's get some food for you."

Chris was now steadying Heather on her feet.

"Yes. I'm Heather." She wobbled a bit as she walked over to Rebecca and put out her hand. The vision became human as their hands touched.

"Nice to meet you, Heather," Rebecca said.

"Daniel, you didn't tell us you had such a beautiful daughter," Heather said.

"Thank you. The two of you make quite a pair of beauties."

"Dad, please. That's embarrassing," Rebecca said.

"Yep, they're alike all right. I'm ready to eat," R.O. announced and headed for the roasting lamb and potatoes.

The three MacGregor kids and Rebecca found a table. During the next hour they exchanged information about their homes and how much they hated being at receptions and official parties.

By now, each teen had selected a full plate of food

and a large bowl of stew from the buffet. While Rebecca ate, Chris, Heather, and R.O. hesitantly tasted the odd looking stew.

"It smells wonderful." Heather looked at Chris and R.O.

"Yes, it does smell good...but, is that okra floating in it?" R.O. said.

"Yes." Chris took a big bite. "It's okra. And there are diced tomatoes, red peppers, celery, and chopped onions." Chris liked to cook and could visualize putting this stew together. Heather finally took a bite and smiled.

"I must be crazy, but I think I taste a little chili spice. And maybe cinnamon. This is good."

R.O. took his spoon, dipped it into the steaming bowl of stew and closed his eyes. Slowly he put the spoon in his mouth and started chewing. His eyes popped open.

"Man, this is good. Is that steak in it?"

Rebecca, who had been chowing down on the stew, looked up.

"No, it tastes like kudu to me."

"Kudu!" The three MacGregor teens said in unison.

"Yes, kudu. It's a wild antelope much like your North American deer."

"Well, whatever it is, it is delicious." Chris took another spoonful and ate it.

"You should have seen your dad run from those wild dogs. He was really moving," R.O. said as he ate another spoonful of stew.

"I'm not surprised. He's had lots of adventures out in the bush. I'm really proud of him," Rebecca said.

"Does he ever take you?" Heather asked.

"Oh, yes. Many times. I've been in every major park in East Africa. We've even sailed across Lake Victoria. And last year he took me to Rwanda to see the mountain gorillas at the Fossey Primate Center. They were just beautiful."

"Real gorillas?" R.O. asked with food stuffed in his mouth.

"Yes. Very real and very big."

"That's neat. I would love to see those creatures myself," Chris said. He took a drink of water from a crystal goblet.

"Heather, my dad is taking me with him to the Masai Mara Game Preserve tomorrow. He has to collect some data from the resident wildlife biologists about the giraffe and rhinoceros populations. Would you like to come along?"

"Yes. That would be fun," Heather said.

"We better check with mom and dad first, Heather," Chris said.

"I'm sure it will be OK, Rebecca," Heather said.

"Hey, Chris. Look at that big guy eat. He is really putting away the food." R.O. pointed to the opposite side of the courtyard.

"It's rude to point, R.O." Heather said.

"You're right little buddy. He is consuming it!" Chris added.

Across the room the big man put a strawberry the size of a walnut into his mouth and before he had swallowed, he stuffed in another.

"Mr. Hanes."

"Yes, sir."

"Would you be so kind as to retrieve for me another helping of that roasted lamb. It is so sweet and has such a delicate flavor to it. And Charles, another bowl of that delicious stew would be good, too. And ask the chef about the recipe, Charles?"

"Yes sir."

Soon the big man had another helping of lamb, stew, asparagus, and a bowl of fresh strawberries.

"The chef said he would personally write the recipe for you. It is called Marrakech Stew," Charles said.

"Thank you, Charles. You must remind me in about six months, right after we retire, you know. Remind me to be sure and buy a herd of sheep so we have an adequate supply of these precious little lambs. Fresh and juicy and oh so tasty. What a delight. You will do that won't you, Charles?"

"Yes, sir. I will make it a priority. All multi-million-aires should have roasted lamb whenever they want it. Any time of day."

"You will make a good companion, Charles. You must bring the Mrs. around and your children, too, so we can become one big happy family." The big man ate two more strawberries.

"I will make a point of it, sir," Charles replied. He poured a fresh cup of coffee for himself. "Um. Kenya's best. Straight from the hills of Ngomo." He took a sip and then another.

"Where's our next target, Charles?"

"Billy says that all of the major parks have game. But he says Amboseli and Masai Mara have the most remote herds of elephants and prides of lions. The further we are away from the photo safaris on this side of the Kenya border the better off we are. The hunting safaris just across the border in Tanzania only pose a problem between Tsavo and Kilimanjaro. It seems our predecessors have left us the more difficult herds to find."

"But, not to worry my dear Charles. That is why we are making young Billy, Mr. William Von Kryden from the former Rhodesia state, a new millionaire. Unknown to him, the ivory tusks we have already neatly stashed away will take care of him, buy us a large yacht to sail us across the Indian Ocean, and make my final payment on that mountain estate near Madras, India. With the new ivory tusks, lion skins and skulls, and rhino horns, we will live like kings—no, make that emperors among the poor masses of India. You will be able to send your children to the finest schools in Europe."

"I understand, Charles, the Swiss boarding schools are quite reputable. My very own brother sent his three daughters to a splendid academy in Bern. It had one of those strange P F Swiss names. You know, where the letter 'p' is silent. Pflin or maybe in was Pfinner, Pflex. No, no, I have it. It was the Pfund Academy for Girls. A very good prep school. All three went on to university from there."

The big man then cut a piece of lamb and stuffed it into his mouth. The natural juice leaked out of one corner and dripped down his face and onto the collar of his white cotton shirt. There it left a little brown stain.

"Yes. It will be a grand life." Mr. Hanes took a sip of his coffee. "But what if the international ivory embargo continues, sir?"

"Charles, we've watched the ivory trade fluctuate dramatically. You know that. The demand is once again growing in the Far East. The same chaps that kill dolphins and whales illegally will always be in the market for what we have to sell. We will easily dump this last load of ivory, and for a good profit. Then there are those tribes in Yemen that still want rhinoceros horns to fashion knife handles for their young men. And you know, Charles, my very good friend in Athens has peaked my interest in, shall we say, diverted foreign aid. It seems there are millions to be made in intercepting all that food and medicine those bleeding heart Americans send to the less fortunate souls of the earth. Bet we could market some of that in India, as well."

"You really are thinking ahead, sir." Mr. Hanes said.

"One can't always rest on one's laurels, can one, Charles?" He stuffed two more strawberries in his mouth.

# 7

# The Census

It was 6 A.M. when Daniel and Rebecca arrived at the government estate to "collect" Heather, as the British would say. The nearly four-hour drive to the Masai Mara Game Preserve would be rather mundane until they reached the safari tracks two hours from the capitol. The crowded roads around Nairobi were filled with buses taking people to work and home after long night shifts in factories.

There were dozens of safari vans headed to game parks on day trips. Their goal was to secure a good spot near a water hole or around a grove of trees. For it was at water holes and tree islands that the big cats would arrive during the day. They would drink or lie in the shade until their bellies told them it was time again to hunt and kill. Each species would exchange places with another until in the heat of the day a male lion, with his pride, would claim ownership and begin a long afternoon nap.

As Heather looked out the side window of the Range Rover, she could see three adult giraffes and two calves galloping across the plains, their heads held high above the umbrella trees. They reminded her of hand puppets dancing to the music of the puppeteer. Tall and majestic, their bodies and legs appeared in the opening between the trees, then it was back to viewing the bouncing and swaying necks and heads. To Heather, they represented the beauty and grace that she had dreamed about when her father told her she would be in Africa someday. It was an image far more beautiful than she had imagined and definitely better than the wild dogs or the charging lioness.

With the sun full in the morning sky, their bright gold coats with the black patterns shone brightly. Without being able to hear the noise of their hooves beating the ground or the wind blowing through the trees, Heather felt as though she was watching a silent movie. Only her imagination could provide the soundtrack.

Following the giraffes was a small herd of zebras with an occasional gemsbok leaping into the air and prancing away at a ninety-degree angle. Just as Heather was about to look away, confident of the peacefulness of the animals at play, she noticed a small object. It was something black and gold swiftly moving through the tall grass behind the menagerie of wild game.

The young male cheetah pulled hard with each long stroke of its body. Its hind legs nearly reached his head with every stride. He glided behind them like a tail of a kite that soared through the air following each movement of the zebras and giraffes. Obviously he was not trying to catch his dinner. Perhaps he just enjoyed the chase as he cruised along the grassy plain.

"Wow," Heather said.

Rebecca turned around and saw the giraffe, zebra, gemsbok, and the lone cheetah.

"Isn't that beautiful? I mean it's sad to see something that beautiful die. But the harmony of it all so amazes me."

"Yes, it's awesome," Heather replied.

Suddenly, as if it had received a silent command, the

cheetah burst ahead with a surge of energy and light-ning speed. An old lame zebra had become fatigued and was lagging behind the younger members of the herd. Realizing its opportunity, the cheetah's instinct told it that to pass up food was foolish indeed. Normally avoiding healthy young zebra that could with one kick kill a cheetah, the lithe cat sailed through the air. The old zebra fell after only one paw of the cheetah had touched its right back leg, its razor sharp claws digging into the black and white skin. The cheetah leapt forward and with it jaws applied a death grip to the zebra's throat.

The Range Rover moved along the road. Heather soon lost sight of the cheetah hanging on to the throat of its kill. Despite the increasing heat of the day, she shiv-ered a little. Goose bumps formed across the top of her arms. The giraffes ran off into the distance and disap-peared into the foliage of the Masai Mara.

Within a few minutes, Daniel edged the Range Rover off the highway and onto a rough road that had been a safari track. It led up into the hills and deep into the bush near the Mara River. After two hours of bouncing around and getting motion sickness, the girls were ecstatic when Daniel announced they were almost there. They topped a hill and below them in a beautiful valley, complete with a flowing river, was the ranger station. The ranger station consisted of a cluster of small houses, toolsheds, and a large equipment barn. It served as the home for three families.

The Rover came to a stop. The girls and Daniel eagerly jumped out and stretched vigorously. The trip had taken nearly four hours.

"I can't believe that we have to go through that again today," Heather said and looked at Rebecca.

"Me either. I mean, once I get here I love it and so will you. Just wait until you see all the animals. It will be worth it, Heather." Rebecca tried to encourage her.

In the distance, the popping sound of a helicopter

could be heard and all three looked into the sky just as a blue and white Bell Jet Ranger crested the top of the hill and began its descent. All of the kids, who weren't already racing toward the Range Rover, started running from the rangers' houses to the makeshift heliport next to the equipment barn.

At that moment, two rather beat-up Range Rovers approached through an opening in the trees next to the river and drove toward the helicopter. Converging on the strange bird from the sky were the kids, the rangers, Heather, Daniel, Rebecca, the families, and three dogs. A domesticated hornbill flew about two feet above the dogs and landed on the outstretched arm of one of the rangers.

Stunned, Heather stopped and gawked at the person who just stepped off the helicopter.

"I am so mad," Heather said as she turned to Rebecca.

"Don't be. It just means we get a fast ride home," she replied.

Dr. Jack MacGregor stepped from the passenger compartment of the helicopter as the rotor blades came to a complete stop and the motors went silent.

"Hey, babe," Jack hollered as he walked over to Heather and gave her a hug. "Long time no see. What? Uh, about four hours ago you guys left. You made good time. We took off about, let me think, was it forty or forty-five minutes ago? I can't remember."

"Dad, you snake." Heather gave him a soft punch to the stomach.

"What a way to greet your dad. You mean Daniel didn't tell you we were coming?"

"Daniel didn't know," Daniel said as he walked up to the reunion.

"That's right. You couldn't have. We only got the census report this morning. Probably after you left."

"The Wildlife Census?" Daniel asked.

"The one and only," Jack replied.

"I'm guessing that since you are here and the Deputy Director is here and let's see, the Director of Tourism is here, it must not be good news."

"Your deductions are accurate, my friend," Jack said with a serious look on his tanned face. His thinning brown hair was tousled by the wind that blew across river valley.

As Jack started to talk, the noise of two more helicopters could be heard. Then there was a third. Then a fourth appeared over the rise. All were now jockeying for a clear spot to set down. When the last one had landed, there were a total of sixteen more rangers added to the group and walking toward the large baobab next to the river.

"Is it bad news, Dad?" Heather asked.

"Yes, I'm afraid so. It looks like we're all headed down toward the trees next to the big metal building. You girls stay close by."

"Can we go with you?" Rebecca asked.

"Sure, honey," Daniel replied and took her hand.

Heather wrapped her right arm inside her dad's left arm and they walked along behind Daniel and Rebecca. When the group had reached the shade of the big baobab tree, the chattering of the monkeys got a little louder. One of the rangers took the safety whistle that was dangling from his shirt pocket and gave it a sharp toot. The monkeys scurried about jumping wildly from branch to branch. The chattering stopped. Being distracted by their instinctive defense behavior, their socialization came to an abrupt halt. The monkeys thought they could trust the humans who had never hurt them, but their instinct wouldn't let them totally relax. That's good for any species.

The Deputy Director and Chief of Ranger Services sat down on one of the dozen or so tree stumps, which had been placed around the baobab as natural seating in this beautiful setting next to the Mara River.

"I called this meeting for the western park region. Before dark tomorrow, we will have met with the entire ranger corps for our country. This is indeed an emergency meeting. What we discuss here must be kept a secret and only your field personnel should know. There are already some leaks that some of you may have encountered." Heather remembered the soldier talking about poaching at Tsavo two days ago. "The Director of Tourism, Mr. Armstrong, will not release to the press what I am about to tell you for one week."

Claude Metumbe, the chief ranger stood up and walked around behind the large tree stump he had been sitting on. A drop of sweat ran down his cheek and across a zigzag scar that he had acquired as a youth as a member of the Luo Tribe on the shores of Lake Victoria. Once a warring people, the Luo had been assimilated into a nation of tribes that is modern Kenya.

"We have some disturbing news. The game census, which was started last spring and continued through the summer, has revealed some interesting but sad numbers. First of all, we had expected a large increase in the elephant population since the arrest of the majority of poachers over the past ten years. The numbers of elephant carcasses we have found in the bush had gone down and safari companies' reports of elephant carcasses, meat-drying racks, and poachers camps had been reduced substantially.

"But our intelligence from Oman and other Arab countries revealed to us that there is still a tremendous amount of ivory, lion skins, and rhinoceros horns reaching middle eastern and far eastern markets. Initially, we thought this new animal contraband was coming from Zambia, Zimbabwe, Angola, and maybe even South Africa. As much as we would like to, we can't make the rest of Africa as wildlife friendly as Kenya. So we began the census confident we would find an increase in numbers among all of our wild game."

Metumbe began to pace around the group. He looked at each person and then back toward the river. "I am saddened to say we have less than a 10 percent increase in the elephant population. If poaching had truly been reduced to the level we expected and the habitat encroachment of our human population had been what we planned, the elephant population should have increased a minimum of 20 or 25 percent. We fully expected a 30 percent increase."

Heather heard the bad news at the same time as everyone else. She was losing interest in the numbers. But she tried to follow the chief as he spoke. She looked toward her dad and saw the concern on his face.

"Let's review the facts. In 1972, we had 45,000 elephants in Kenya. From 1972 to 1988, we lost nearly 40,000 elephants to illegal hunting and poaching. Our census at that time said we had 5,363 elephants. Then from 1988 to 1994 we had an increase of 27 percent in the elephant population to just over 7,300 elephants. But the current census finds that there are only 8,100 elephants in Kenya. Barely a 10 percent increase in population. If, now listen to me because this is important. If the elephant population had grown as it should have, Kenya would have nearly 10,000 elephants. But instead, based on expected growth, we have lost 1,692 elephants, almost 20 percent of our native herds."

There was silence. Even the monkeys weren't chattering. Down the bank only the movement of the river could be heard.

"And to make things worse, we've had a sudden drop in the lion population. Accounting for natural range migration between Tanzania and Kenya, the lion population has decreased 12 percent."

The ranger chief returned to his log seat and sat down. Without fully keeping up with the numbers, Heather could see the concerned look on the faces of everyone present, including her father.

"Questions?" he asked and looked around at the twenty plus rangers.

"What do we do?" asked one of the men from the Lake Victoria region.

"That is the big question," Metumbe replied. "Obviously we haven't been doing enough. But what more can we do? Look at your Range Rovers. They're rusted and many are broken down for weeks at a time. You carry guns that your grandfathers handed down to you. Isn't that right, Okere?"

"Yes. The old M-1 was my grandfather's rifle. My mamba gun."

Everyone smiled knowing the tale of Daniel Okere and his fear of snakes. But they also knew that with the rank of captain he carried a new .375 caliber double rifle. It had been a gift from a safari company.

"I am here to ask you what we should do. The safari companies loaned us these helicopters and pilots to use this week. They are being generous because the decline in big game affects their businesses. How can they sell African safaris if people see more wild animals at the local zoo?"

"Can I ask a question?" Jack MacGregor said.

"Go ahead. By the way, this is Dr. Jack MacGregor. He is a zoologist from Texas. He comes to us to write about elephants and lions for his book on endangered species." Everyone present already knew about Dr. MacGregor and his reputation.

"What has changed in the period between your increase in elephants and the current decline?"

"We have asked ourselves that question and we have come up with a few possible answers, none of which seem to fit the problem. But the census did discover something that was very puzzling. The elephant population decline is virtually the same in all regions," the chief said. He sat down again.

"Possibly the poachers are using high tech equipment to track herds. A quick slaughter and disposal of carcasses could also help them. Picking from each region so it wouldn't be noticed as quickly," Jack said.

"That was my feeling, too, Dr. MacGregor. But I hadn't thought of the quick carcass removal. If the poachers had the equipment and manpower, they could process one elephant on the spot in a matter of hours."

"And then fly out the meat with the ivory," Jack said.

"Even though it sounds feasible, the shear size of an elephant and the fact that several are killed at once prevents meat processing from becoming part of this puzzle," Metumbe said.

Everyone agreed. Jack sat down to think through all of the possibilities. While it was a new puzzle for him, it was an old and difficult one for the other people present. Metumbe turned to again address all the rangers.

"I still think that the high tech angle may be the correct one. And I am afraid I must include the fact that someone within the Kenya Wildlife Service may be involved. How else could elephant and lion herds be selected that would not draw undo attention? And how else could the reporting of carcasses be covered up? Someone within the service is involved! I am certain of it," Claude Metumbe said.

There was a hushed silence across the group. Then everyone in unison began talking to each other.

"Heather," Rebecca whispered from behind her. Heather turned around. "Let's go walk around until they get through."

As they strolled across the grounds, the hot sun reflected off their thick heads of hair. Rebecca's hair was braided and tied up while Heather had an ever present scrunchie holding her ponytail high on the back of her head. She normally wore yellow. But today she thought the red ones looked better with the drab khaki safari clothes she complained about wearing. "Mom, they're all the same color, no color!" she had said. Standing in front of her closet she had spouted off the options. "Red cotton top, yellow blouse with buttons, navy pullover, no color top, no color shorts, no color jacket."

"Well, princess," her mother had said, "you're going to be in the bush so I suggest you wear the 'no color' khaki articles, because they won't tear as easily nor will they attract wild dogs."

It was the wild dog comment that prodded her to choose from the "no color" selection. She had seen all the wild dogs she wanted to see for a lifetime.

But in the Masai Mara, one never knew what you were going to see next or what was going to see you.

# 8

# Masai Mara

Heather and Rebecca strolled down toward the river. The river was sluggish because of a lack of rainfall in the region. This was abnormal for the Mara River, which collected rainfall from the Kenya highlands most of the year. But the rains that normally fall from March through July had not come this year. Meteorologists had debated over why there had been a drought. Was it the weather patterns over the Sahara to the north? Or was it the El Nino that had haunted the Indian Ocean basin?

Even the mightiest rain clouds that appeared as angels bringing gifts of rain would drift off to the southwest toward the mountains of Rwanda and Burundi where only the mountain gorillas could enjoy the fresh water. There were only two weeks left for the long rains to come and then it would be October before the next rainy season.

"Why are all the sharp stakes sticking out of the ground?" Heather asked.

"They're bungee sticks. The sharp ends keep the crocodiles from crawling up the bank and surprising the families. See," Rebecca pointed, "they go for about two hundred yards in each direction."

"Can't the crocs crawl around them?"

"Sure, but by then the dogs would be barking and someone with a gun would show up and kill them."

"I thought crocodiles and alligators like to eat dogs," Heather said.

"They do. And they have lost a dog or two around here. But the big crocs down in the river don't seem to bother with them much. I think they hate the barking as much as we do."

"Alas, barking finally pays off," Heather said and smiled. "My dog never barks."

"What kind do you have?"

"She's half chow and half cocker spaniel. Just midnight black with the typical blue chow tongue. Her name is Mickey."

"She sounds cute. We have three dogs. Two dachshunds and a German shepherd. Dad wanted the shepherd around to keep nosy people out of the yard."

"Well, same here. We live on an acreage between Dallas and Ft. Worth. My brothers have two golden Labradors. They wouldn't hurt a fly, but strangers don't come around wherever you have big dogs." Heather turned when she heard someone following them. "Mickey and the two Labs have the run of the acreage."

"Don't you miss them?"

"Oh yes. But I know they're fine staying with my aunt in Newnan, Georgia."

"Newnan?"

"Yep. That's it." Heather smiled. "It's north of Atlanta."

"I know Georgia. I studied it in our world history class. North America, United States, Mexico, Canada... all that stuff," Rebecca said.

"You probably know more about my part of the world than I know about Africa."

"OK girls, let's go," Jack MacGregor walked up from behind them.

"Where to, Dad?"

Heather sensed a new adventure. She could always tell when her dad was off to an adventure. She could hear it in his voice, see it in his eyes. He was just like a little kid in a toy store.

"One of the safari pilots offered to fly us around the Masai Mara Game Reserve."

"This will be great, Heather," Rebecca said. "I've been there and you've never seen so many beautiful wild animals than you will today."

Soon all three were in the Aerospatiale helicopter and lifting off from the clearing, which on that day had become a busy helicopter hub. All of the other choppers had already left and Daniel had returned to Nairobi by air. He decided the game rangers needed his newer model Range Rover. He would try to convince the Kenya Wildlife Service it was the best thing to do. He also knew that he would be back to commuting in his own dilapidated Fiat with the hole in the floor. But it was worth the sacrifice. The newer Range Rover might help save a ranger's life, catch poachers, or take a needy person to the hospital. With the concern about the new census data, he felt it wouldn't be a problem with the administrators in Nairobi. It would be the least of their worries.

Heather and Rebecca crowded against each other nearly pressing their faces to the glass window on the side door. Jack sat next to them but closer to the other side. The chopper pilot had explained they needed to keep the passenger compartment balanced. The helicopter rocketed down through the valley following the river's every sharp bend or gentle curve. Giant hippos ducked under water to safety as the helicopter's rotors vibrated the surface of their river sanctuary. Crocs sunning on the banks of the river didn't move an inch, never acknowledging the strange bird overhead. The pilot carefully avoided a small lake that drained into the

river. The lake was full of flamingos. It looked like a
bright pink dot against the brown of the sun-scorched
grass. Three thousand flamingos would be difficult to
fly around and could easily down the helicopter with its
big turbo engines ready to suck in all those pink feathers.

Finally leaving the valley, the Aerospatiale flew
toward the flatland where the Serengeti joined the Masai
Mara. Both were crown jewel game parks in East Africa.
Herds of gazelles, zebra, and wildebeest could be seen
wandering from one water hole to the next. About three
dozen storks became airborne from a dead tree as the
helicopter passed overhead. Traveling over a hundred
miles an hour, the helicopter moved onward. The pilot
was unconcerned about the big beautiful birds.

"Dr. MacGregor," the pilot said over the intercom
connected to the headsets that everyone was wearing.

"Yes."

"There's a great lookout point ahead, a series of
kopjes, you know the large rock formations you find all
over East Africa. I can set her down there. You can break
out some of the goodies in the ice chest in front of you,
and we can watch what wanders by. What do you
think?" The pilot had a congenial smile on his face.

"Well, what do say girls? Do you want to set her
down for awhile and see what wanders by?"

"Yes," they said in unison. Big smiles were painted
across their faces.

In a few minutes the Aerospatiale was lowering its
landing gear and setting down about a hundred yards
from a large rock formation that stood forty feet above
the grassy plains. It was the highest point in the area.
Rebecca and Heather bounced out of the helicopter as
the pilot opened the door. Jack grabbed his satchel and
a cloth bag full of food he had retrieved from the large
chest. He had also thrown in three bottles of water for
their makeshift picnic in the middle of the Masai Mara.

He began to walk away from the helicopter but then returned to retrieve Daniel's .375 caliber double rifle. One of the rangers told him that Daniel had left it in the Range Rover. Jack agreed to take it back to Nairobi.

"Exactly where are we?" Jack asked the pilot.

"We're about ten miles south of Oloololo, at the north edge of the park," the pilot lied. He closed the passenger doors on the helicopter. "I've got some paperwork to do and then I plan on getting a nap. I had a late night in Nairobi. When you get ready to leave, just head back to the chopper and off we'll go."

"Thanks." Jack picked up his satchel, the bag of food and water and started to walk away. "By the way. I didn't catch your name."

"It's William Von Kryden, sir. My friends call me Billy." The pilot gave him a strange smile. Jack didn't notice.

"OK, Billy it is. We'll be right over here."

In a few minutes, Jack, Heather, and Rebecca were climbing the kopje. Centuries of weather wear made the sides smooth and difficult to find footholds, but even in the afternoon heat, the three adventurers made it to the top. It was flat with an area about fifteen by twenty feet. A warm breeze blew across the Masai Mara. However, they could feel the breeze cool them with sweat on their shirts and faces.

"Wow, isn't this beautiful. Look, over there." Heather pointed to a giraffe feeding on an acacia tree on the opposite side of the kopje from the helicopter. All three walked over to that side. Jack pulled his binoculars out of his satchel and handed them to Heather. She asked about the rifle.

"Why the gun, Dad?" She knew the answer before he said it. He began to answer her but Rebecca interrupted.

"Because, out here a human is prey. Most animals in this part of Africa, except for some of the birds, are carnivores, you know a meat eater. They would easily and eagerly love to find a two-legged mammal that had no sharp teeth or claws wandering around."

"I take back my question, Dad!" Heather said.

Over the next hour, the three of them observed a herd of zebras run by at full speed. They never could see what was chasing them. Four more giraffes rambled by. Then there were the male warthogs following the female warthogs around. It was that time of season.

After awhile they opened up the cans of chicken and sausages and the boxes of crackers that Jack had found on the helicopter. They were expensive but tasty snacks the safari companies keep around for their tourist clients that get a bit hungry. It was rare, however, that they would get hungry because the safari companies would prepare the most posh dinners one could imagine. Linen tablecloths, real silver flatware, crystal glasses, porcelain dishes, and roasted meats were common. Three splendid meals a day in the bush camps that dotted the game parks was generally the order of the day and not the exception.

As Heather, Rebecca, and Jack were climbing down from the kopje, a vibration could be felt through the soles of their boots on the solid rock. They all three stopped together.

"Wildebeest!" Rebecca said.

"Let's get going," Jack said and they all began to jog toward the helicopter. The vibration became a thunder in the distance. The helicopter pilot was already behind the controls, and the big rotors were turning. He had felt the same vibrations. Jack, Heather, and Rebecca could see the massive beasts stampeding toward them across the Masai Mara. Their jog changed into a run. They were only a hundred feet away when Billy pushed the collective and cyclic controls forward at the same time lifting the helicopter off the ground.

"No, wait," Heather shouted as they stood there and

watched the helicopter lift higher and higher.

"Sorry doc," Billy said aloud to himself. "But I can't take a chance those dumb animals might hurt the chopper. That might prevent my becoming a millionaire this month. And by the way, Mr. Big, no Mr. VERY Big," Billy laughed, "will be happy that someone with a big nose like yours is taken out of the picture. Happy trails campers!" Billy let out a hideous laugh and pushed a rock CD into the deck. The heavy metal music vibrated through his headset as he flew the Aerospatiale in an easterly direction at a high speed.

"The kopje," Rebecca shouted as she looked back at Jack and then toward the stampeding wildebeest.

"We would never make it. They would run us over about halfway there." Jack dropped his satchel and the food bag. He lifted the .375 double rifle to his shoulder.

"Stand behind me."

"Dad, what's happening?" Heather screamed over the noise of the stampeding wildebeest, which were now just fifty yards away and closing fast.

"Ten, eight, six, stay down, three, two, one." Jack squeezed the trigger of the rifle. It recoiled forcefully. The lead wildebeest was killed instantly but its momentum carried it like a spinning car on wet pavement toward the trio. With the friction of the earth pulling it down, the animal came to a sliding halt, its back legs suddenly knocking Jack to the ground. To his surprise a second wildebeest came crashing to a halt on top of the first one. The powerful .375 bullet had killed two animals with one shot.

Jack frantically reached out and grabbed Rebecca and Heather by the arms and jerked them up against the dead animals, pushing them hard into their warm and smelly bellies and groins. He then threw all his weight on top of them. He could hear them scream from the deafening noise of the herd and his sudden shove. The thundering of the hooves went on for nearly five minutes, but for the trapped trio it seemed like an eternity. Then finally the beating of the hooves ceased. Jack slowly pulled his body off of the two girls and looked over the side of the top wildebeest. Its hide and ribs were now mangled from the sharp hooves of the members of the herd that had jumped over the carcasses of their two leaders. Heather, Rebecca, and Jack were covered with the warm blood of the dead wildebeest.

"Stay down, be quiet," Jack said and pressed down on the girls again.

Suddenly three wild dogs jumped over the carcasses of the wildebeest and turned around. Jack knew their thoughts. Why continue the chase when there were two fresh animals all ready for eating? The dogs stopped, surprised by the three humans who were nestled quietly up against their food. The lead dog charged forward and snapped at Jack as he jumped over the top of the wildebeest to distract them away from the girls. He felt a sudden pain in his ankle and foot. He grimaced. But he could only think of the girls. Jack looked around on the ground for the double rifle. "Where was it?" He was frantic to find it.

The other two dogs charged and one grabbed Jack's already injured foot and bit hard. Jack kicked back and Heather screamed. A deafening boom filled the Serengeti sky. The dog was knocked six feet backwards in the air and fell with a thud to the ground. Because of the recoil, Rebecca was jammed into the bloody side of the wildebeest.

Jack reached over and took the rifle from Rebecca's hands and tried to stand up. He was met nearly face to face with the last of the wild dogs. The dog snapped wildly at him. From twelve inches away, Jack slammed the butt of the rifle into the head of the wild dog and knocked him backwards. He quickly reached into his pocket and found a handful of extra shells the rangers had given him. All he needed was one.

The dog charged again. Jack swung with the butt of the rifle but missed.

The dog jumped on top of the dead wildebeest and barked wildly for his companion, which had been mounting charges toward Jack and then retreating. Jack found the release and cracked open the rifle that loaded like a double-barrel shotgun. He jammed in one bullet and closed it, pinching off a chunk of his hand. As the blood dripped from his hand, he leveled the barrel with the face of the dog and pulled the trigger.

The results were the same. Heather and Rebecca slowly stood up next to him and wiped tears of fear from their cheeks. Neither girl complained nor whined. Never looking back, the other wild dogs continued chasing the wildebeest herd.

"I was laying on the gun, Dr. MacGregor. It must have flown out of your hands when the wildebeest knocked you down. I think I have a permanent barrel mark on my leg."

"You're a brave girl, Rebecca."

Jack opened the gun, ejecting the spent cartridge. He loaded two more rounds.

"No problem. I've been hunting with my dad before in Tanzania. We usually just shoot antelope to put in the freezer. That was for sure my first wild dog." Rebecca wiped the tears from her eyes again.

Heather came over to her dad. She ripped off the right sleeve of her safari jacket and helped her dad wrap it around his hand. She was no stranger to field-dressing wounds. The bleeding had already stopped.

Jack looked around in the sky for the big helicopter. Instinctively he knew that it wasn't coming back. Later he would try to put the pieces together. But for now, he had to get these two girls back to the kopje and out of harm's way.

"I think my foot is broken or severely sprained. The hooves hit it square on," Jack said as Rebecca and

Heather supported him under each shoulder. Heather also carried his satchel, which had fallen under him. What was left of the food bag hadn't been so lucky. It took them thirty minutes to walk a hundred yards to the rock formation that stood forty feet high above the Serengeti.

"How are we going to get you up there, Dad?" Heather asked as she let go. Jack leaned against the smooth rock wall.

"Slowly," Jack said.

And slowly it was. It took nearly forty-five minutes, with breaks every five minutes or so, for Jack to reach the top. All three of them fell to the hard rock and stretched spread eagle looking into the blue sky. The sun was now at 4 o'clock.

"Heather. Hand me my satchel, please." Jack forced himself to sit up. His foot and hand were both throbbing.

Reaching into the satchel, which he carried everywhere, he pulled out a hard case covered with leather. He usually stored breakable items in it. This time was no different. He opened it carefully and lifted out an electronic device about the size of a pocket watch.

"What is it, Dad? It looks like one of Ryan's toys."

"It could be one of his, but this one has been tested. It is a G.P.S. locator. I simply punch in my code and it begins to send a signal to a satellite passing overhead. Then someone at the control center lines up the coordinates and comes to get us."

"Sounds, simple. So when do they arrive?" Rebecca asked with obvious excitement in her voice.

"I don't know."

"What do you mean you don't know, Dad?"

"This is a test device that I was planning to use on an elephant. I was going to attach it. Then I would use my Iridium phone to call the control center to track the elephant. It was going to be a good experiment."

"Where's the control center, Dr. MacGregor?"

"Well, Rebecca, it's…"

"Nairobi?" Heather interjected.

"No…"

"Mombasa!" Rebecca smiled as if she had guessed the right answer.

"No…"

"No?" Heather said with disbelief in her voice.

"If it's not Nairobi or Mombasa, then it's got to be Cairo. Cairo is only two thousand miles away and the biggest city that would have such tracking capabilities," Rebecca said confidently.

"Not Cairo either."

Both girls looked bewildered.

"No more twenty questions, Dad. Where is it?" Heather stood up looking toward the acacia tree where the giraffe had been eating earlier.

"Houston."

"Houston!" both girls exclaimed in unison.

"Dad, what's this all about? We need to know." Heather squatted down next to her father.

"Heather. All I have in my hand is a little experiment that I was going to use tomorrow on an elephant. Nobody at NASA will even have the satellite turned on for another twenty-four hours. I'm afraid we're stuck here on this rock pedestal for another day. Unless, of course, a safari company comes by and rescues us. I can't walk out of here, and I sure wouldn't let the two of you try it."

"It's only ten miles. You said the pilot told you we were near Oloololo. I've been there before. There are two rangers stationed there," Rebecca said.

"I'm sorry girls, but the pilot lied. I knew something was funny when he said we had turned north from the Mara River. I was watching the compass on my watchband and it indicated southeast. His fancy flying was meant to disorient us and prevent us from finding our way out. I think he had orders to kill us but just didn't have the stomach for it. When the wildebeest stampede happened by, he must have thought he had been living right or something. A perfect way to leave us to die."

The girls looked at each other and then back to Jack. They walked over and knelt down and hugged him.

"My guess is that we are deep into Tanzania. Somewhere in the Serengeti and not the Masai Mara. Where exactly? I couldn't even guess. How about you Rebecca? Any guesses?"

"No, Dr. MacGregor. I've only been down the main road between Bologonja and Lobo. And that was two years ago." Rebecca patted Heather on the back.

"Well, ladies, I believe we are stuck for at least another day. We better count our provisions and water and settle in for the night. I suggest the two of you hustle down the kopje and bring back as much of the dried wood you can pick up around that grove of acacia. Rebecca, you carry the rifle. Heather hasn't shot that caliber before."

"Dr. MacGregor, that was my first time to shoot the double rifle, too," Rebecca replied sheepishly. "The recoil practically ripped my arm off."

"I know that, hon. But we had no choice. You used it under pressure. You knew what you had to do and you did it. You saved my life. You hang on to it while Heather gathers the wood."

Both girls nodded in agreement and climbed carefully down the back of the kopje. They discovered a new path they had missed before that allowed them to literally walk all the way to the bottom. They also mentioned to each other that lions could walk all the way to the top on the path, as well. It was something they would hold in their thoughts for much later, when it was time to go to sleep.

The small fire burned long into the night, preventing the chill from creeping into them. It dropped to only sixty-one degrees. The trio huddled close together and soon the girls drifted off to sleep. Dr. Jack MacGregor, having checked the rifle again, laid his head back on his satchel and closed his eyes. He was hoping that the people at NASA would remember to turn on the satellite as it flew over to test his little experiment. He told them that he would call them because of the ten hour time difference.

As he looked up at the big sky of the Serengeti, a meteor bounced off earth's thick atmosphere creating a shooting star effect. Without interference from city lights and at the high altitude of the plains, the effect was spectacular. On any other night, a display like this would have brought a smile to his face. But tonight, he lay injured on a rock mound in a most desolate area of East Africa. He could handle that. But with him were two young ladies whose whole lives lay ahead of them. The thoughts about the girls and his responsibility to them were too grand to let him sleep easily.

The hour hand on his luminous dial reached 2 A.M. Loaded with fatigue, his foot and ankle aching, Jack MacGregor finally nodded off to sleep.

# 9

# Mavis

The phone rang. Mavis MacGregor laid the mystery novel on the soft yellow comforter. Sliding her reading glasses down her nose so she could see the telephone on the bedside table, she picked up the handset.

"Hello, Dr. MacGregor here," she spoke in her polite British accent, which was tainted a bit from eighteen years in West Texas.

"Dr. MacGregor, this is Daniel Okere. Have you heard from Jack this evening?" He sounded alarmed. Mavis sat straight up in the bed.

"No. Is something wrong?" She turned around and put her feet on the floor, sliding her long slender feet into a pair of sheepskin house slippers. African days and nights were hot in the summer in the lower altitudes. But in higher altitudes, the nightly temperatures could drop to sixty-five degrees or lower.

"No one at the Wildlife Service has heard from Dr. MacGregor since he left the meeting at the Masai Mara ranger station. That was about noon. We checked with all the safari companies, and they said their pilots returned with no passengers. The pilot we thought they were with said he left the ranger camp without any passengers. But since he was flying the last helicopter to leave, we can't verify that story. We sent someone back to the camp and the Masai Mara rangers said that everyone had left. They couldn't remember which helicopter Dr. MacGregor and the two girls had been on.

"What do you mean they couldn't remember? They either saw them or they didn't!" Mavis said with a mixture of astonishment and building anxiety.

"Dr. MacGregor, I am as alarmed about this as you. Rebecca is my only child."

"I'm sorry." Mavis stood up and walked across the room, the cordless telephone in her right hand. "Where do we go from here?"

"We know we don't have a helicopter crash to deal with, and we can thank God for that. We also know that the two girls are with Dr. MacGregor, most likely in the bush camped out for the night. Did Dr. MacGregor have any communication equipment with him?"

"I don't think he had a radio or cell phone with him. He had ordered one of those global telephones, the Iridium, but it wasn't due for arrival until, wait, that's tomorrow." Mavis ran her free hand through her long auburn hair.

"Well, Dr. MacGregor, I can't see that we can do anything tonight. I've got a helicopter ready to collect me at first light. You're welcome to come along."

"I was hoping you had a plan."

"I will be there at fifteen minutes after daybreak."

"Thank you," Mavis replied and pushed the off button on the telephone. She walked across the room and placed the phone back in the cradle. She hurried down the hall to check on the boys. Both were sound asleep in the oversized bunk beds. Chris was on the bottom. The other two bunk beds were full of their gear from the camera safari. She decided that she needed Chris to go with her. Since there was no one to leave Ryan with, he would come along, too.

Returning to her bed, she had barely closed her eyes when there was a knocking at her door. The seven hours till dawn had passed in the wink of an eye. She couldn't believe she had slept so soundly with such a worry on her mind. Her intuition told her that all was well. The morning cook poked her head in the door.

"Mr. Okere called and said he would be here in twenty minutes."

"Thank you, Rachel," Mavis said and bounded out of bed. In another couple of minutes she was walking down the long hallway toward the boys' room.

"Chris, Ryan," she announced in her motherly voice. "Time to wake up. We're going on a helicopter ride."

"Helicopter," Ryan, still half asleep, repeated.

"Do I have to go?" Chris mumbled without ever lifting his head from the pillow. Most kids would jump at the chance, but these two young adventurers weren't most kids.

"Yes. Heather and dad are missing."

Both boys sat up straight and looked at their mother. The look on her face revealed that this was no trick to get them out of bed.

"Where? When?" Chris asked as he stepped on to the cool tile floor.

"We don't know yet. But Daniel is here with a helicopter to fly us out to the Masai Mara Game Park where they were last seen. Everyone thinks that maybe they went on a hike, got lost, and spent the night camping. I'm buying that for now." Mavis looked determined. "So get dressed. Bush gear, survival packs, the whole works." She turned to walk out the door. "And Chris…"

"Yes, Mom," he replied as he pulled off his pajama top.

"Bring your 7mm rifle and several spare clips of ammunition."

"Got it, Mom." Chris looked at his mom with her

steely-eyed expression. He knew it when she meant
business and this was one of those occasions.

Mavis MacGregor, Ph.D, paleontologist, wife, and
mother of three teenagers returned to her bedroom. She
opened the free-standing armoire and pulled a large
backpack onto the floor. Unzipping the oversized steel
zipper, she checked it for first aid supplies, freeze-dried
food, water purification tablets, compass, five hundred
feet of nylon rope, spare socks and underwear, sun
block, and a knife, which she took out and clipped to the
belt of her safari shorts. On went the shorts, a white T-
shirt, thick socks, and over-the-ankle leather and fabric
bush boots. She unsnapped the clasp on the expensive
gold watch that Jack had given her last Christmas. She
held it for a moment, then kissed it and laid it on the
dresser. Unzipping a small side pocket of the pack, she
lifted out a rugged outdoors watch that her father had
given her when she graduated from Oxford. It was a
Rolex Explorer. She then pulled out a summer weight
safari jacket from the armoire and slipped it on. Out of
one pocket she retrieved a khaki hat that was rolled up.
She unrolled it and after she fixed one of Heather's
yellow scrunchies to her long auburn hair, she pulled
the hat on.

Chris and Ryan appeared at the door and looked at
their mom. They knew she could swim, run, bike, hike,
and climb with the rest of them. But to see her fresh for
the challenge, dressed like she had just stepped out of a
safari camp magazine, was a bit overwhelming. Tall,
trim, and curvy, both boys appreciated her femininity.

"Mom, you look great. Too bad dad can't see you,"
Ryan said.

"Ditto that, Mom," Chris added.

"He will see me. So let's get moving. Daniel's waiting."

As they walked through the kitchen and out the
back door, the pilot flipped the switches and the engines

came to life. The rotors were barely moving when they had thrown their gear into the passenger compartment. Daniel proceeded to tie down every pack. Loose cargo and people could cause a dangerous weight shift on a helicopter. The Bell Jet Ranger hovered for just a few seconds as the engine increased its speed. Then, like a big wasp jumping into the air in search of its prey, the helicopter leapt upward and moved toward the southeast, the direction of Kenya's most prized game preserve.

The Masai Mara was a protected park that joined Tanzania's famed Serengeti. While a "no hunting law" was strictly enforced in Kenya, Tanzania allowed big game safaris. For years, the tourists would arrive in Kenya, only to cross the border to Tanzania, kill their game, and then return to Kenya. Eventually, Tanzania retaliated by closing its borders for many years and raising hunting fees and taxes on tourists who came into their country from Kenya. But this defeated the tourism industry, and Tanzania once again opened its borders.

The recent appearance of hundreds of elephants was a sign that food and habitat were being cut off from the south and the east. Both the Serengeti and the Masai Mara never had dealt with the potential destruction that could be caused by thousands of elephants. But most everyone in East Africa knew that poaching was not the answer. Almost everyone, anyway.

R.O. and Chris talked to each other and pointed at different herds of animals or the lone beast wandering across the plain. Mavis talked to Daniel about the meeting the previous day.

"I can't believe the census count was down that much. Was it just the elephants?" Mavis asked.

"No, the lion and leopard population were also impacted. We're not sure about the cheetah. They've had an unexpected drop in life expectancy from fourteen years to nine years. The hoofed animals are doing well. With reduced predation from the big cats, they only have the hyenas and wild dogs to fear, neither of which take massive amounts of game. The hyenas like to steal from the wild dogs and the wild dogs steal from the lions and hyenas. Lots of animals eat off of one dead zebra or gazelle. And a pack of hyenas likes nothing better than to ambush a wild dog or jackal."

"It is definitely survival of the fittest," Mavis said. She was still thinking about Jack and the two girls but trying to carry on a conversation.

"Fit meaning lean, mean, smart, cunning, all of those things. When pitted against the natural carnivores of East Africa, man doesn't fare very well. That is until we start manipulating the habitat."

The pilot interrupted their conversation.

"Captain Okere. We're nearing the ranger camp. How long will you be there?"

"About an hour. Just set her down and take a break. I'll let you know our plans after we get more information."

"That's a roger, sir," said the pilot. He was one of only six helicopter and fixed wing pilots in the ranger service. R.O. had noticed the three single strands of braids that hung from the back of the pilot's neck and were neatly tucked inside the khaki uniform shirt. Ryan had also noticed the gruesome scar that ran around the base of the pilot's head and the enlarged left earlobe where a circle of ivory once hung. But R.O. had learned one thing in Africa. Never ask about tribal stuff unless you knew who you were talking to.

The Bell Jet Ranger came in for a smooth landing next to the toolshed. Waiting for their visitors, two rangers stood away from the flying dust and dry grass.

"Captain, good to see you again. Twice in two days. That is never good news in this business." The older ranger shook Daniel's hand.

"This is Dr. Mavis MacGregor, her sons Christopher

and Ryan." Daniel introduced everyone.

"Let's go into the house and have a bite to eat and talk about some strategy," the older ranger said.

Mavis was getting a little exasperated, but she had learned in her travels around the world that usually it was the Americans, Germans, and Japanese who tended to be in a hurry. The rest of the world operated on a much slower pace. It made more sense, but in situations like this, the stress was overwhelming. As the rangers' wives laid out a table full of fruit, fried plantains, and jerky of some kind, the boys dug in since they had missed breakfast. Mavis realized she was hungry, too, and experimented with the fried plantains. She listened to Daniel and the rangers map out their search plans.

"How many more helicopters are coming?" the ranger asked.

"None." Daniel forked a long plantain. To Ryan it looked like a giant banana.

"No others? With only one helicopter it will be like searching for an ostrich egg on top of Mt. Kenya," the ranger said in an exasperated tone.

"Are we looking for ostrich eggs, Mom?" Ryan asked as he chewed hard on dried gazelle jerky.

"No, Ryan. It's just an expression. It means that without more help we are going to have a tough time finding your dad, Heather, and Rebecca anytime soon."

"Isn't dad some sort of big shot or something? Shouldn't they call out the army or the National Guard to help look for them?" Ryan asked.

"Honey, they don't have a National Guard like ours. And dad is an important man, but right now he's just another zoologist wandering around the Masai Mara studying wildlife. For these people, it's no big deal for a scientist to stay in the field for days, weeks, or even years. After awhile they think we're all nuts."

"R.O.," Daniel said, "I'm sure that your father, Heather, and my Rebecca are fine. They may have gone for a hike and gotten lost. Another ranger may have come into camp and taken them off to see more animals somewhere else. They could have hitched a ride with a safari company. There are dozens of possibilities. Out here, Ryan, everyone must watch out for themselves. This is a big place, with good people, bad people, and lots of animals that want you as their next meal. I'm not worried, I just want to know. All parents like to know where their children are." Daniel rubbed Ryan's hair and then patted him on the back.

"Thanks Daniel. We all needed that. Especially the part about being someone's next dinner!" Mavis said and reached for a piece of jerky. She glanced out the window as the kids kicked a soccer ball around the grassy compound. She sensed that Jack was OK but, like Daniel said, she wanted to know. She also knew that if Jack had intended to stay overnight, he would have called her or had somebody contact her. She had a fleeting thought. Maybe the messenger had forgotten to call her. But who was the messenger?

"I suggest we fly southwest toward the Tanzanian border and then work our way back toward Nairobi. We can set down along the way and question the safari companies we encounter. That should give us some idea if they are still in the Masai Mara district," the older ranger said. He took a drink of water from a new bottle.

"Why wouldn't they still be in the Masai Mara Game Park?" Chris asked.

"If they did fly out with a safari helicopter, they could have been dropped off just about anywhere. The fact we haven't heard from them may indicate they are further out into the bush than we first thought," Daniel said.

"But I thought the pilot said he left without them," Mavis said.

"That's what he said." Daniel avoided making eye contact.

"Are you holding something back from me, Daniel?" Mavis moved around so she could look into his eyes.

"We checked the pilot's license. Seems he is fresh in from Zambia. His records indicate he was a safari pilot down there, but when we tried to verify it, no one had heard of him. Usually that means he is from a rebel or anti-government force of some kind and was brought in to help with illegal activity. We've seen it before. The bad guys are always recruited because they have the stomach for evil and usually have no fear of arrest or sometimes even death."

"Thanks for picking me up and then dashing me against the rocks." Mavis took off her hat and looked at the kids who were now playing "chase the stick" with two of the dogs.

"I'm sorry, Dr. MacGregor. I don't want to unnecessarily alarm you. I still think that Rebecca is safe. That means they are all safe. But there is that slight possibility that they have encountered evil forces." Daniel put down the bottle of water and gazed at the playing children. More reason to get going and cover some ground before dark."

"I agree. Boys, let's go," Mavis said to Chris and Ryan, who had just polished off a piece of fruit.

Soon the three MacGregors, Daniel, the older ranger, and the pilot were cruising 250 feet over the grasslands of the Masai Mara. Daniel knew that if Jack and the girls were out there, they could hear the turbines of the Bell Jet Ranger from a mile away and get a fire going pretty fast. He had taught Rebecca how to build a fire. She always carried a specially made butane lighter in her bag wherever she went. Yes, she could always build a fire to signal rescuers. A fire to warm herself from the cold night. And a fire to frighten away the big cats.

# 10

# Tanzania

---

Mavis, Ryan, and Daniel sat next to the windows of the helicopter. They were all staring at the vast expanse called the Masai Mara. The Mara River rolled along in a lazy fashion carrying a meager amount of water. However, the rains on the Kenyan highlands that rose upward to 10,000 feet sustained the Mara during the dry season. The season of the long rains was only a few days away, and soon the river's banks would be swollen. Regardless of the season, the Mara always managed to capture every drop from the region that it possibly could as it flowed toward the great lake called Victoria.

The Bell Jet Ranger hummed along stopping occasionally at a safari camp to seek information.

"No, Captain Okere," the bearded safari boss said. He took off his green floppy canvas hat and ran his tanned fingers through his oily hair. "We haven't seen any choppers in this area for about a week. You're the first. Nice helicopter for government property."

"Have you been in contact with any of the other safari companies?" Mavis asked as she took a scarf from her pocket and tied it around her neck, catching the sweat dripping from the back of her head.

"Well, yeah. We passed one yesterday. A group of Germans headed across to Tanzania. They were hunting trophy antelope. Gazelle, impala, and kudu. There weren't any Americans or kids with them."

Thirty minutes later, after a cool drink from the portable refrigeration unit of the safari company, the group boarded the helicopter and was back in the air. It was nearly two hours later before they landed again. This time it was near the Tanzanian border alongside a hunting track. Hunting tracks were old animal tracks that the hunters used to follow the animals. Over time they became roads.

Frustrated and not knowing where to turn, they decided to fly into Tanzania. Daniel knew that it was risky for him to cross over the border. Even though game rangers cooperated regarding the migration of animals from the Masai Mara to the Serengeti and back, there were still some politics involved.

The Bell Jet Ranger was in the air only twenty minutes when three army helicopters zoomed in at a high speed. The Kenya Wildlife Service pilot was startled and pulled the collective back, reducing the lift and forcing the helicopter to dive. At the same time he pushed the cyclic forward to maintain forward motion. He then quickly pushed both pedals, spinning the helicopter around and gliding between two acacia trees. A small branch was chopped off and sent flying.

Before he could increase altitude and gain airspeed, the military helicopter had circled the helicopter and was hovering nose to nose with the Bell Jet Ranger. Two military pilots, in camouflage uniforms, looked through the glass bubble of the cockpit. The military helicopters had rocket launchers and machine guns mounted on each side.

"I'm going to set her down, Captain," the pilot said.

"I agree. They mean business," Daniel said.

"Who are they?" Mavis asked. Chris and R.O. sat

still and didn't say a word.

"They bear the markings of the Tanzanian Air Force. But I have never seen these new helicopters before and never with this type of aggressive behavior."

The Kenya Wildlife Service helicopter came to a rest in a short grassy clearing. A bat-eared fox darted into a hole between two bushes. As the three military helicopters landed, the dust from the hot, dry grass blew up like a Texas dust devil.

"Stay inside the helicopter," Daniel said as he got out.

However, he didn't know Mavis very well. She was right behind him tossing her hat toward R.O. as she hit the ground in a jog behind Daniel.

Two of the pilots approached. Between them was a short man in an officer's uniform of the Tanzanian Air Force. Daniel noticed the stars on the epaulet on his shoulder.

"General," Daniel said, "please explain why we were forced to land."

"It's a long story. But for now let me say I wanted to check your papers. Will that satisfy you? It is routine after all," the general said.

"Routine! Is it routine for a general of the Air Force to force down a Kenya Wildlife Service helicopter, endangering the lives of two children?" Mavis said as she stepped in front of Daniel.

"Dr. MacGregor, wait," Daniel said but Mavis continued anyway. It was time to vent her pent-up frustrations.

"Is it routine, General, for an officer of your rank to fly around in an attack helicopter checking papers that a sergeant could check?"

He knew her story, but she didn't know he knew. He would excuse her insolence this time.

"I assure you it is. Whenever criminal activity is suspected, the rank of the officer present is immaterial.

Your helicopter obviously does not have permission to enter Tanzania."

Mavis relaxed her posture and squinted toward the south where two ostriches strolled across the plains. She turned back toward the general. He was still standing in the same place staring at her.

"General, I am Mavis MacGregor and these are my two sons. Along with Captain Okere, we are searching for my husband, my daughter, Heather, and Captain Okere's daughter, Rebecca." Mavis looked toward Chris. He smiled at her, giving her a touch of confidence.

"I know why you are here, Dr. MacGregor," the general replied.

His words didn't sink in quickly. They were so unexpected. Mavis looked first to the general then back to Chris and R.O.

"What did you say?"

"We have been monitoring unidentified radio traffic for about thirty days across the northern tier of Tanzania. We have even employed one of your American AWAKS planes to fly down from Saudi Arabia for a few days to help us. We first thought the traffic to belong to unregistered safari companies. Then about a week ago we heard the name Dr. Jack MacGregor. Our investigation revealed your husband's identity, impressive credentials, and his whereabouts in Nairobi. We also learned of his concern for the wildlife census. All East African nations are participating in the census. Our lifeblood depends on tourists and hunters to visit our nation."

Mavis was dumbfounded. Speechless, she stood in the hot sun. The general continued.

"Then two days ago, my analysts in Dar es Salaam broke the poachers' radio code. It was very sophisticated and quite similar to the code used by the insurgents during the Rhodesian wars to the south. This particular illegal safari company is involved in a poaching and smuggling ring of unbelievable proportions. We have reason to believe that this may involve criminal elements of drugs, slavery, and terrorism. But before I go on, let's walk over here to the shade of this tree and remove ourselves from the sun." The general moved toward the grove of acacias, also known as thorn trees, the favorite food of giraffes.

"Yes, why yes. That would be wise." Mavis was still amazed at what she had just heard about drugs, slavery, and terrorism.

In a few minutes the boys joined them as they were seated on the grass out of the direct sun. The Kenya Wildlife Service pilot had retrieved some bottled water from the helicopter and passed it around.

"Go ahead, General," Mavis said as she twisted the white cap off the bottle of water.

"Two days ago we identified the source of the radio transmissions. We're getting close, but we have yet to catch up with them. By the time we get to the coordinates all we find are dead animal carcasses. But they're not your normal poacher remains." He took a sip of water.

"What are they?" R.O. asked.

"It appears the poachers have set up a field butcher shop. They strip all the hides and tusks. Of the lions, they cut off the heads even after taking the hides. Then they drag the largest body parts with heavy equipment into the bush for the vultures and big cats to fight over. Obviously, they're are using a big helicopter. It has to be either a Sikorsky or Aerospatiale."

"Why do they go to so much trouble? Aren't they after just the ivory?" Chris asked.

"Not anymore. The skin off the elephant ear makes a nice leather that is used for shoes and purses. Same for the short tails. Then there are the feet. Lion skulls are being sold to colleges and universities around the world for science labs."

"That's what Jack said yesterday," Daniel said.

"Obviously the locals have to cooperate or they won't get the added meat in their diet and the extra meat to sell. Everyone from the poacher to the village chief profits."

"But why didn't you inform my husband of the investigation. He had no idea he was at risk." Mavis shot back at the general.

"We did. I personally called the Kenya Wildlife Service in Nairobi and talked to Mr. Nyerere. He assured me that Dr. MacGregor would be informed immediately. I also called my counterpart at the Kenya Defense Ministry. They agreed to launch an immediate investigation."

"But why would they want to hurt dad?" R.O. asked Mavis, who was now pacing back and forth. The general stood up and dusted the grass from his green trousers. Taking off his hat he wiped his head with a handkerchief.

"I can answer that, I think." He walked over to the massive trunk of the acacia tree and leaned against it. A vervet monkey screeched overhead. R.O. looked up.

"Son, your father is a world famous zoologist. All of East Africa knew that Dr. Jack MacGregor was coming our way with a United Nations' mandate to look at the problems with the elephant herds. What we didn't know and your father couldn't have known is that the elephant population was being selectively reduced. We expected a huge increase since the last census."

The general paused and took a sip of water. He continued as Mavis paced back and forth.

"Apparently, the poachers didn't expect the census to reveal their presence. They also weren't expecting your husband to arrive the week the census results became public. I suppose, in their evil minds, if they killed your husband they could divert attention long enough to wrap up their operation and leave Africa.

Maybe to go after walrus ivory in Alaska, Canada, or Norway. And of course, drug trafficking and terrorism is big business. Who knows how those deviants think?" The general turned to face Daniel, but Mavis spoke first.

"Daniel, why didn't Mr. Nyerere tell you about this?"

"I don't...wait. I didn't see it coming. It was Benjamin Nyerere who suggested that Jack fly out to attend the rangers meeting at the Masai Mara ranger station. Only he and the chairman knew the results of the census. It was his staff that computed the data." He turned toward the boys. "I'm sorry. Your father walked into a trap and in my own ignorance I let Rebecca and Heather go with him." Daniel looked sullen and anxious. He knew he couldn't have prevented the unknown from happening but he felt responsible just the same.

Mavis turned toward the open grasslands just as a gemsbok bounced from behind a tree about a hundred yards away. Obviously it had been disturbed from its midday hiding place by a possible predator nearby.

"OK. So we know we have real live poachers. They probably have connections deep in the Kenya Wildlife Service. They have the ability to extract large animals from the parks without hardly a notice. They've been there, how long?"

"We estimate about twenty-four to thirty months," the general said.

"That's more than enough time to accumulate a large amount of wealth through ivory, rhino horns, and animal skins," Mavis replied. "But what about my husband and the girls?" She said already knowing the answer.

The general also knew the answer. There was nothing that could be done today. Chris stood up and walked over to his mother. Mavis' facial expression revealed no weaknesses. She was still determined as ever.

"Let's just keep looking, Mom. Then before dark we

go back to Nairobi. We convince the government there's a traitor in their midst. From there we try to find dad, Heather, and Rebecca," he said looking into her blue eyes. Chris and his mother were about the same height.

"I don't think that would be wise. I know Benjamin Nyerere," Daniel said. "He's served Kenya well with tribal relations and he has powerful friends. He's been known to be ruthless. We can't confront him directly or our families will disappear. Forever."

Mavis turned back to the general.

"How did you know we were out here?"

"I know your every move, Mrs. MacGregor."

Daniel raised his eyebrows.

"I see. We're wasting time here. I agree with Christopher." Mavis turned to walk away and stopped.

"I don't think that's wise, Dr. MacGregor," the general said.

"I know. But it is the only hope we have. Good day, General. And thank you for your information. I apologize if I seemed rude." Mavis reached out to shake his hand.

"I understand completely. I would have felt the same way. Just know you are never very far away from me."

In a few minutes all the helicopters were airborne and flying in separate directions.

One hundred miles to the northwest, the big Aerospatiale radioed to the three trucks that were tracking a herd of elephants.

"Safari 2, this is Safari 1," Billy spoke into the radio.

"Go ahead Safari 1," Mr. Hansen replied.

"You've got a small herd about two miles west of your 20. Over."

"Roger that. Heading west as we speak."

In about thirty minutes the three trucks surprised the elephant herd as they had stopped to try to find a drink at a nearby water hole. The three females and two calves were playing in the mud to give their thick skins a coat of mud to protect them from the sun.

The noise of the trucks drove them out of the water hole and onto dry land. As the three trucks stopped, several men emerged from the rear of the trucks and started firing automatic weapons. Soon all five elephants lay dead. Even the babies. Within another thirty minutes, their ivory, ears, and feet had all been chopped off. The ivory would be sold to the Asian market for trinkets and jewelry. The soft thin skin of the ears would be treated and manufactured into boots, shoes, and handbags. The feet would be fashioned into stools and ottomans to furnish the homes of the rich and insensitive. In less than an hour the poachers were thousands of dollars richer, leaving Africa that much poorer. It wasn't just the ivory tusks that were being hacked away. It was the soul and spirit of a wild continent that was in the last throes of death.

The Kenya Wildlife Service helicopter landed in the dark on the heliport, which was located on the visitors' estate. Mavis, Chris, and R.O. trudged across the garden and into the house where Rachel, the housekeeper, had prepared a hot meal. It was waiting on the stove in the kitchen. With low spirits, their appetites were also suffering. But Mavis knew that they had to eat. She coerced them all through a brief meal of hard rolls, lamb stew, and a bowl of fresh fruit. When finished, everyone fell into bed after deciding to rinse off the African dust in the morning.

As the sun peaked over the Indian Ocean and began to warm equatorial Africa, Mavis awoke. She had spent the night tossing and turning never slipping into a deep sleep. Through the big window that overlooked the lush grounds of the estate, rays poked Mavis in the eyes and she decided it was time to get up.

Mavis slipped into her sheepskin house shoes and wandered down to the kitchen. She noticed a piece of paper sitting on the coffee pot. It was a note.

> "Mom. I've got an idea. I left before day-
> break and took a cab to the Wildlife Research
> Center on the north side of Nairobi.
>     You and R.O. go ahead and do what you
> think you need to do. Trust me on this. Have I
> ever let you down?
>                                          Love, Chris"

# 11

# The Kopje

---

Perched high above the plains of Africa, Jack, Heather, and Rebecca had slept despite their obvious worries. They were totally oblivious to a safari company that came within two miles of their ancient rock formation. All Jack would have had to do is reload the .375 caliber double barrel rifle and fire off two rounds. The safari company clients would have come to check it out. They would have been fearful of another group of hunters in the area. Bullets from high-powered hunting rifles can travel for miles with the right trajectory, proving dangerous for unsuspecting hunters or field scientists. But it was not to be.

The morning found Jack, Heather, and Rebecca all huddled close together as if they were in a cocoon awaiting to be separated at birth. The small fire was just enough to knock off the chill and give them a sense of safety. The normally warm summer nights had turned cool the last few days. The weather patterns were shifting, finally making way for the much anticipated and long delayed rainy season.

Jack awoke first. As he tried to stand, he painfully remembered the bad ankle and the sprained or broken foot. He didn't know which it was. But it was still painful. Visions of the stampeding wildebeest and the wild dog trying to chew his foot crossed his mind. It was not a pleasant thought.

Hobbling around, he finally was able to stand up using the double rifle as a crutch. His foot was extremely swollen and felt as though he had a layer of concrete all around it. The pain told him he didn't. He checked to be sure the firing chambers were empty. Something caught his eye overhead. Three vultures circled the kopje, making a premature claim to their two-legged victims. Obviously they wanted to be ready for the moment of death in order to swoop down and begin the feast. The African vultures were big and deadly and, as a flock, they could defend themselves and their claim from the wild dogs, jackals, and foxes. They were no match, however, for the big cats or the hyenas.

"Daddy," Heather said as she opened her eyes.

"What babe," Jack replied and hobbled over to her.

Heather was now sitting straight up with Rebecca beginning to wake up.

"Dad, what's on the menu today?"

"Well, who knows. Got any ideas?"

"Thanks a lot. It's at this moment, as the adult, you are supposed to reassure Rebecca and me that everything is going to be okay." She started to get up.

"We just have a day or two of challenges ahead of us. But after that we'll be okay. Good morning, Miss Rebecca." Jack looked down at her.

"Good morning, Dr. MacGregor," she replied and stood up. "It's freezing out here."

"Just a bit chilly. But I heard that the cold nights give way to very hot days in Africa. Is that right?" Jack tried to engage the girls in a conversation that would distract them. He already knew the answer to his question.

"That's right," Rebecca said. "Since we are on the equator, it's difficult to ever notice a change of seasons.

The closer you get to Kilimanjaro or Mt. Kenya, the more the weather changes and the nights get even colder." Rebecca walked over to the edge of the kopje. She looked down at the tall dry grasslands forty feet below. "But this is July. July always marks the beginning of the rainy season. Once the rain comes, then the warm air follows and nights like last night won't be around for a couple of months." She walked back to Heather and gave her a hand up.

"Thanks," Heather said and dusted off her shorts.

"Well, let's just hope it doesn't start raining today. We need good weather for an air search. In the meantime, I need for you two guys to gather more wood. I've got to keep our fire going all day and night as a signal."

"That's a roger, Dad." Heather walked over and gave Jack a hug. He noticed that Rebecca was standing alone.

"Come on, it's time for a group hug," he said.

Rebecca quickly joined them and they felt better already. The two girls followed the path back down the south end of the kopje and returned to the large baobab tree. As they approached the tree, the vervet monkeys screeched and gave off a barking sound. With their long skinny tails tipped with a black tuft of hair, their black faces, white-haired chest, and brynnel colored hair, they were pretty and entertaining.

"I've had all the monkeys I want for awhile," Heather said. She told the story to Rebecca about the wild dogs, lions, R.O., and the baobab tree.

"My dad did what?" Rebecca stopped picking up wood and looked at Heather.

"He dove straight to the ground and let Chris shoot over his head to stop the charging of the wild dogs."

"Oh, my gosh, he never said anything about it," Rebecca said.

"My dad never brags either. We always find out later about some risk he took or an animal that almost got him. Then Mom turns on him like a duck on a June bug, chews him up and spits him out."

"She does?" Rebecca said trying to literally visualize what Heather had said not quite figuring out how ducks eat June bugs.

"Oh yeah. She gets really mad, then they kiss and makeup. Chris, R.O., and I leave the room because it gets real embarrassing sometimes." Heather smiled. "If you know what I mean?"

"Oh, I know."

The two girls wandered around the baobab stacking small piles of wood that they could easily retrieve on future trips without having to search very long. Heather noticed a large branch protruding from a hole under a thorn bush. She reached out and pulled on the branch and heard a loud grunt. She froze, her hand still on the branch. She didn't move, but she heard the grunt again. Slowly letting go, she stepped back a foot but it was too late. Before she could turn and run, a full-grown 180-pound female warthog charged from the hidden den under the thorn bush. At the last second, she veered to the right slamming her stout body into Heather's legs and knocking her to the ground.

"Rebecca," Heather yelled as she hit the ground with a hard thud. Before she could get up, six twenty-pound piglets came popping out of the den, each one trampling on her as if she were part of Mother Africa.

"Oh, stop, no, stop!" Heather yelled as she tried to protect herself from the onslaught of pigs.

Rebecca arrived just in time to take a whack at the last piglet with one of the branches she collected.

"Are you all right?" Rebecca asked. She knelt down next to Heather.

Heather sat in a daze, out of breath, covered with dirt and mud from the den and smelling a little foul. Her soft blonde hair was a twisted mangled mess. Grass and twigs hung from her locks of hair and her bangs. She calmly reached up and touched her painful nose. Dark red blood dripped from her nose where a piglet had kicked her during the mini-stampede.

"I hate pigs," Heather said. She tried not to cry as she looked at Rebecca.

"Hold still, you have a little cut over your right eye," Rebecca said. She took her scarf off from her neck and dabbed the little drop of blood that was trying to escape the wound.

In a few minutes, both girls were carrying an armful of twigs and branches up the trail to the top of the kopje. As they neared the top, they could smell something cooking.

"Am I dreaming, or do I smell roasting meat?" Heather said.

"It must be a parallel dream, because I smell it too," Rebecca replied.

As they took the last big step up the rock trail, they came into view of the fire and Dr. Jack MacGregor holding a long stick over it. Dangling from a stick was a huge agama lizard. It had been gutted, skinned, and beheaded. The reptile's muscles were now a dark brown and released an almost pleasant aroma. But both girls knew that since they hadn't eaten in nearly twenty-four hours, anything would smell good.

"Dad, that is one 'mongo' lizard. It smells great. I can't even believe I'm saying this. Like, I would eat that right now!" Heather said as she dropped her wood on the ground next to the fire.

"I agree, Dr. MacGregor." Rebecca dropped her wood on top of Heather's and walked over to the fire.

"What happened to you? And what's 'mongo' mean?" Jack asked calmly, trying not to cause any more anxiety than necessary. Making a big deal over spilt milk was not his style.

"You might say, I now have a very good reason to hate pigs, even more than I did before," Heather replied and sat down. "Oh, and 'mongo' is one of Ryan's words. He says it's short for humongous. You know, really big."

"Warthogs," Rebecca replied.

"Warthogs? That explains it. Mongo warthogs too?" Jack smiled, trying to carry on two conversations at once.

Jack was proud that Heather had responded so adult-like. He knew many adults that wouldn't have taken it so coolly. He could tell she was growing up and he never regretted for a minute bringing Heather, Chris, and R.O. with him on this adventure, until now.

"Okay. Roasted lizard is ready to eat," Jack proclaimed and laid the cooked reptile down on a smooth rock surface. Carefully, he pulled the legs off of the lizard and passed them to Rebecca and Heather.

"How did you catch him, Dad?" Heather asked as she took a bite of the leg.

"Let's say that he thought I was just part of the kopje and when he stopped directly on my arm, it was an easy catch. Then I…"

"Stop, don't go there. I don't want to know anymore," Rebecca said. She grimaced at the thought of Jack killing the lizard and prepping it to eat. She then closed her eyes and bit into the leg she was holding. The sinewy and tough leg muscles were hard to chew and almost tasted gritty. No doubt the dirt of Africa had attached itself to the skin either when Jack cleaned it or when the stick was pierced through it. Nonetheless, all three ate the gift they had received and were glad to have it.

The kopje proved to be a magnificent tower from where they could watch the life of Africa's wild and strange creatures. It was as if they were on nature's greatest stage.

From a distance, Heather watched a cheetah chase its prey. She was ecstatic when another appeared from the bush just a hundred yards away. The exotic gold and black animal, defying gravity and the unseen laws of motion, sped hungrily behind a gazelle. With a furrowed brow of determination, it reached out through the air and snagged the right hind quarter, bringing the gazelle down in a whirlwind of dust. A quarter mile away a herd of nearly two hundred zebras stood motionless watching the high drama of death on the run. A female elephant pulled her trunk from the small watering hole to the south. She nudged her eight-hundred-pound baby toward the shelter of the bush, leaving the great elephant path behind them.

"Wow. That is awesome, Dad," Heather said as she watched her father hobble over to her.

"That's why I became a zoologist, Heather. I wanted to understand more about what you just witnessed. I wanted to make sure that nothing interfered with the natural order of life…and death."

"I've heard you talk about it before, Dad. But not until I saw this did I ever realize what you meant. I mean, like the smelly pigs that knocked me down. I was in their space, not mine."

"It's all right to be there, Heather. We are, after all, higher up the food chain. We just can't interfere."

A clap of thunder suddenly echoed through the air. Jack, Rebecca, and Heather quickly turned to the north and noticed a large thunderhead forming across the horizon.

"The rains are coming. I knew they would. Everyone has waited so long," Rebecca said.

Jack frowned. His concerns had just increased a hundred fold. If the rainy season began today, their chances for survival dropped dramatically. They couldn't walk out because there were simply too many large predators and, of course, his bad ankle and foot. If the sky filled with clouds and lightening, the aircraft wouldn't search for them. For the first time, his heart sank. He thought about Mavis. He remembered how she hadn't been willing to give up on Chris at Cayman. He now realized that her tenacity and "never say die" attitude was their only hope.

"We've got to find shelter," Jack said as he looked across the tall grass toward the fast moving thunderstorm.

"Dad. If we leave the kopje, we'll be down in the middle of nowhere with all the big cats, the hyenas, you name it," Heather said with a frantic look on her face.

"I know. But if we stay here, we'll be a prime target for a lightening strike."

"What about the baobab tree?" Rebecca asked.

"That would be even worse. Never gather around trees during a lightening storm."

Suddenly a clap of thunder could be heard miles away across the Serengeti. The herd of zebras that had been watching the cheetah eating the gazelle began to move toward the south in a slow run.

"Ahhhhhhhhh," Heather screamed as something dropped on top of her from the sky. She fell to the ground tangled up in a rope.

"What's going on?" Jack shouted as he looked up.

"Oh, my gosh!" Rebecca followed.

Suspended in midair about a hundred feet over the kopje was a gorgeous white balloon with a rainbow pattern stitched into the material. The hot air balloon held perfectly motionless.

"Dad, Heather, grab the rope!" Chris shouted from the gondola of the balloon.

"Chris," Jack said in a whispered voice. He couldn't believe his eyes. Then he yelled "Chris!"

Heather untangled herself from the rope and started jumping up and down.

"Grab the rope. Start pulling them down!" Jack shouted to the girls.

Heather, Rebecca, and Jack, with only one good

foot, grabbed the rope and pulled with all their might. Slowly the balloon inched its way closer to the top of the kopje.

"Let some of the hot air out," Jack shouted as the balloon reached the fifty foot mark over the ancient rock formation. Jack could see two young people in their twenties standing next to Chris.

"They can't. There's a storm coming and they said we've got to save the hot air so we can get out of here fast. Hurry, pull harder," Chris shouted.

Heather was practically hanging from the heavy knotted rope until the gondola was now only ten feet over the top of the kopje.

"Get on board, quickly," the young man shouted. He was obviously the pilot of this rescue balloon.

"Up, go up, Heather, Rebecca," Jack ordered.

"No, Dad. You first. We can steady the rope. You can't hold it for us with your bad foot," Heather argued.

"Quit fussing and get on board," shouted the young man again.

"Come on, Dad. Go first. They can hold the rope." Chris could see his dad had a bad foot from the way he was hobbling around hanging on the rope.

"You're right. Hang on to it and then both of you get up the rope quickly. Understand?" Jack gave them a both do or die look.

"Roger, Dad. Go!" Heather shouted as Jack began to pull himself hand over hand up to the gondola. The cut on his hand from the rifle began to burn as he squeezed the rope. With great upper body strength, he was up and in the gondola in just about two minutes.

"Come on. Who's next?" Chris yelled as he pulled his dad inside the expansive gondola. It was big enough to hold ten people.

Rebecca was next. She started up the rope when suddenly a blast of wind from the north gusted violently across the top of the kopje causing the balloon to start drifting toward the south. Heather wrapped the rope around her waist as the balloon began to pick up speed. Rebecca was halfway up to the gondola when the balloon reached the forty-foot rock cliff of the kopje. Heather was skidding along the smooth rock surface, her bush boots acting as skis. The balloon began to rise. Heather worked at letting out as much rope as she could when finally the rope had reached its maximum length. She was now perched at the edge of the kopje looking down the forty foot cliff.

"Heather, Heather!" Jack shouted as his heart sank.

"Heather. Jump and hang on. We'll pull you up!" Chris yelled.

Another blast of wind hit the balloon and pushed it even farther. Finally she had nowhere else to skid. With one last bit of strength, she took two big steps and jumped. Her hands tightened with all her strength around the last knot on the rope as she swung free from the kopje and was now hanging from the hundred-foot rope as the balloon drifted toward the south across the Serengeti.

"Hurry, let's pull them up," shouted Jack to Chris and the young couple who had attempted this daring rescue.

"Heather," Rebecca shouted from ten feet below the gondola. "Hang on!"

But the monsoon rainy season was upon them without mercy. The large thunderstorm rumbled quickly across the Serengeti bringing with it its fury and full force of nature. The winds gusted to thirty miles per hour. The young couple fought to hold the balloon steady and not gain altitude too quickly with the two young girls dangling precariously on the rope.

"We can't hold this altitude very long. We've got to get up and away from the crosswinds. If we don't, the thunderstorm will pound us flat in a hurry. At this speed, we can't outrun it," shouted the blond-haired young man with a Norwegian accent.

Jack and Chris, with the help of the young woman, frantically tried to pull the rope in. But the very athletic, muscular girls had a combined weight of 240 pounds and the vertical lift was just too great.

"We've got to land," Jack shouted to the pilot.

"I'll try to get us close, but if we set down, there's a chance we won't get back up.

"You've got to try," Jack shouted as he looked down again. "Hang on Rebecca. Hang on Heather."

"Hang on Heather," Chris yelled again.

But nature wasn't willing to cooperate. The gusts picked up and in a couple of minutes the balloon was moving up and down with the motion of the incoming storm.

The jerking motion was taking a toll on Heather's hands. She tried to relax her grip on one hand, then the other. But now she couldn't feel anything as the rough rope began to bite into her flesh. Her shoulders began to ache. Tears appeared in her eyes. She glanced the direction they were drifting and noticed she was headed straight for a tall acacia tree. The tree was also known as giraffe food with thorns. The balloon was still falling a few feet every minute. They were now two hundred yards away and closing.

She looked up to call her father's name, but the pain kept her from saying anything. She could see his tortured face, but she couldn't hear the words his lips were saying. She had no strength left and decided she couldn't hang on any longer. Then she felt a warm hand around her wrist. It was Rebecca.

"Heather, I've got you. Hang on," Rebecca shouted. During the excitement and the pain, Heather hadn't realized what was happening. Rebecca had lowered herself down the rope nearly ninety feet.

Suddenly the balloon started losing altitude quickly and it dropped a hundred feet in just a few seconds. The acacia tree was upon them when Heather felt her feet and then her seat touch the ground. She instinctively let go of the rope and tumbled through the tall grass. Rebecca let go at almost the same instant and hit the ground running, never losing her balance. The rope drifted through the acacia tree, miraculously not getting caught or tangled on anything.

"Heather!" Jack shouted as the balloon, now free of two hundred forty pounds of ballast, jumped higher in the sky and soared to an altitude of nearly five hundred feet. In less than a minute, Heather and Rebecca appeared as two small animals sitting on the face of Africa.

"Heather," Jack whispered to himself, a lump forming in his throat. "Oh, Heather, what have I done?" Tears filled his eyes.

Chris looked quickly around the gondola. He spied two large green duffel bags. Grabbing them, he slung them over the side and watched them plunge five hundred feet toward earth. The first one snagged the outstretched branch of a tree and bounced lazily to the ground. The second one dropped like a missile and ripped apart at the seams when it hit the ground, its contents bursting out in all directions.

"What are you..." the young balloon pilot started to say. He knew the answer and gave the balloon a much needed burst of flames to heat the air. Soon the balloon was a thousand feet up and catching a wind that would keep it ahead of the approaching storm.

Chris then jerked open the lid of a plastic cargo box. He knew what he was going after. He had seen them load the two parachutes before the balloon had taken off from the wildlife center in Nairobi. Quickly he grabbed one and threw it over his shoulders.

"Son. What are you doing?" Jack shouted over the noise of the approaching storm.

"I'm going down there with them. They won't stand a chance of survival by themselves. You know that,

Dad. I'm healthy, you're not." Chris snapped the front clasps of the parachute and started to climb over the side of the gondola.

The balloon had now risen to twelve hundred feet and was gaining speed. Jack knew Chris was right. He quickly leaned forward and they hugged each other tightly.

"Gotta go, Dad. Later!" Chris said and swung both legs over the side.

Without hesitation, he leaned outward and dropped from the gondola.

"One, two, pull," Chris said to himself as he pulled the parachute release handle called the rip cord. A small parachute about two feet in diameter popped out first. Then the wind caught it and the small chute pulled the bigger chute out. Chris had fallen three hundred feet before the big parasail was fully expanded in the air. As he felt his weight begin to pull on the chute, he breathed a sigh of relief. Reaching up over his head he found the control handles to the parasail. He was now at five hundred feet and descending smoothly.

Quickly he looked back toward the kopje and assessed his situation. He was nearly a mile away. Pulling on one side and then the other, he closed the distance by a quarter mile before the ground leapt up to meet him. Putting his ankles together and flexing his knees, he prepared for a hard landing. But he surprised even himself when the sail softly deposited him on the run in the tall dry grass. The wind gusted and whipped the sail as he unsnapped the harness and dropped it to the ground.

Looking back into the sky, the balloon was now a small round dot in the clouds. He started walking quickly toward Heather and Rebecca. In awe, they had watched as Chris had parachuted out of the balloon.

Already to their feet and standing with mouths agape as the balloon grew smaller in the distance,

Heather and Rebecca ran toward the fallen duffel bags.
They reached the intact one first and with each girl
holding an end strap, they carried it over to the one that
had exploded. They could now see Chris about a quarter mile away walking toward them. They felt better.
    "Let's get this picked up before he gets here." Heather
said.

    Scattered on the ground was an assortment of freeze-
dried food packets, a water purification kit, and an
Austrian made Karl Kahlese 12X night scope still tightly
sealed in its metal case. Ten feet from the torn duffel lay
a backpack. Rebecca unzipped the pack and discovered
a "bag tent" just big enough for two people in sleeping
bags. It was folded and compressed to fit in an eight-
inch by ten-inch vinyl case that snapped neatly over one
end. Also included in the pack was a multipurpose
survival knife and utility belt.

    "Wow, Heather. Your dad was thinking fast," she
said as she put on the belt around her waist.

    Filled with emotion, Heather looked at her aching
hands, and then toward the balloon that was now just a
dot in the sky far away.

    "Yes. I know he must feel awful right now. I bet he
suspected that the balloonists had all their survival gear
in these two bags. He knew he had to get them to us."
Heather sorted through the mess and found a small first
aid kit. Removing a small tube of ointment, she rubbed
it on her rope-burned hands. A sudden gust of wind
blew their way. She felt better knowing Chris would be
with them soon.

    "We need to get back to the kopje, don't you think?"
Rebecca said half confident, half questioning.

    "I think that would be a good move. We better get
going before the rain hits or we won't be able to use the
rock path on the south side," Heather added as she
started picking up the rest of the supplies. "Chris can
catch up to us there."

In a few minutes they were lugging the two duffels toward the kopje, a half a mile away. The wind kicked up and a few sprinkles of rain began to fall when they finally reached the ancient stone structure in the middle of the Serengeti.

Chris caught up with them as they reached the kopje. Not many words were spoken. After a couple of big hugs they resumed their task. They knew what they had to do. Hauling only one bag to the top at a time and allowing for the beginning drizzle of rain, they were on the summit in about twenty minutes.

"Look, the double rifle and shoulder bag," Rebecca said. She walked over to the edge of the vertical cliff.

"Bring them over here with the rest of the supplies. We've got to get the tent together and the bags stuffed down inside them quickly," Chris said as he opened the vinyl case.

In a matter of minutes all three were securely tucked inside the "bag tent" with the duffels jammed at their feet.

The rain began to pour. Even though it was the middle of the day, the sky grew dark as the rainy season began. A family of warthogs darted around the baobab tree and tried three dens before they found an empty one. A young male leopard bounded out of the bush and up into the tree to ride out the storm. The vervet monkeys screeched and climbed hurriedly to the top of the tree, using each other as stepping stones and ladders. Some of the limbs bent nearly to the breaking point from the new weight. The monkeys knew better than to tempt the leopard, an agile tree climber. They quickly became silent so as not to draw attention to themselves.

A clap of thunder echoed across the plains as nature ruled once again.

# 12

# Trek

The storm rumbled in quickly and hammered the
Serengeti for six hours. The dark gray sky was now
becoming black with the arrival of night. Unrelenting
rain, lightening, and thunder prompted Chris, Heather,
and Rebecca to cover their heads in fear. Lucky for them,
the balloonist's tent was waterproof. Weighted down
with the duffel bags, Daniel's .375 double rifle, and their
bodies, they held steady on the top of the kopje against
the onslaught of winds, sometimes gusting to thirty
miles an hour. In time they became accustomed to the
pouring rain and howling winds and began to talk to
each other over the noise of the storm. Well into the sixth
hour of the storm, one would have thought that the
coming of the summer rains was no big deal. They had
been taught by their fathers that if fear rules your life,
then your ability to think and act clearly disappears.
This was no time for cloudy thinking.

"Chris, I still can't believe mom let you do this."
Heather looked at her brother in the face from only a
foot away.

"She didn't know. I spotted the balloon from the air
when the helicopter came in last night. The pilot was

testing the flame and you could see the rainbow on the side from miles away. Daniel told me it was leased to the Kenya Wildlife Service by a couple of Norwegians and was set to fly out early this morning. It was a long shot. I hoped it would be flying west or southwest into the Serengeti and it was. I called a cab after everyone went to bed, got up early and here I am. Just be glad dad kept the fire going. We could see it from nearly ten miles away at a thousand feet altitude."

"Where did you learn to sky dive?" Rebecca asked.

Heather chuckled. Chris smiled at Heather then Rebecca.

"I never have. When we were on Grand Cayman Island last month, I went parasailing behind a boat two or three times. They use the same kind of hand controls. I hoped that if I got the chute to open, I would figure it out."

Rebecca's eyes got really big. She put her hand over her mouth. They all began to laugh. After awhile Chris fell asleep, but the girls talked for a few minutes longer. The storm raged on, but with the flashlight on, it seemed they were in another world, protected from the danger outside.

Heather talked about her home back in Texas and the friends she left behind in school. She would miss the swim season but she wouldn't miss the 3,000 meters a day of stroke practice nor the constant feeling of being wet.

Rebecca talked about the school she attended in Nairobi. She told about her mother who worked as a textile consultant for the International Trade Center so that she and her brother and sister could attend the school that specialized in math, science, and languages.

Even though they had eaten the agama lizard, it was not lasting all day. They avoided talk about food. Growing weary of talk, the girls soon fell asleep within the blackness of the tent. The rain stopped.

Chris was sound asleep with thoughts of Natalie dancing through his head. First he was in Texas with her. Then he realized they were walking across the campus of Oklahoma State in Stillwater. Then just before he woke up, they were in the Caribbean fighting off the shark, all over again.

As the sun crept over the Indian Ocean to the east, the clouds hung low and blanketed the Serengeti like whipped cream on a chocolate fudge brownie. The golden rays of the sun were blocked from reaching the surface of the earth.

Rebecca awoke first and stretched inside the tent as much as she could with the duffel bags stuffed around their feet. She nudged Heather. A faint glow of light penetrated the nylon tent. Chris was snoring softly.

"Heather, you alive?"

"Yes. I was having this great dream. I was on a big jet flying back to Texas and a cute steward on the plane had just handed me a cold Dr. Pepper. On the movie screen was Leonardo de Caprio. It was the sixth time I had watched *Titanic*. I had just taken a bite of a blueberry bagel, and then…you woke me up. Thanks!"

"Sorry, but we better wake up and analyze our situation." Rebecca sounded like an adult.

"I agree," Heather replied. She unzipped the tent flap to the outside world.

Her eyes widened and she held her breath. Rebecca sensed something wrong and poked her head out of the tent.

Surrounding them in a perfect circle were fourteen baboons ranging from adults to babies. Both girls were perfectly still. Chris opened his eyes to the same scene as twenty-eight eyes looked back at him.

The baboons gawked at them and then back at each other. Baby baboons ran around the top of the kopje playing and jumping on each other. Twice they nearly rolled off the cliff only to scurry back to safety.

"What do we do now?" Heather said softly and slowly.

"I don't know," Rebecca replied.

"Hold still and be very quiet," Chris whispered.

Suddenly, as if he had sized up his enemy as being weak, a large male baboon reared up and charged the tent, barking loudly and showing his long canines. Just as he reached the flap where the girls had now ducked back inside, he jumped over the front of the opening and onto the tent running down their backs to the end.

"Ouch!" shouted Heather.

Rebecca fumbled around and found the .375 double barrel rifle and shoved it out the flap.

"Wait, don't do that!" Chris said and he reached for the rifle.

Just as the large male started his second trip across their backs, Rebecca pulled the trigger. A boom exploded from the end and echoed across the top of the ancient rock formation. The bullet whizzed five feet over the heads of the baboons, but the noise was enough to cause them to scatter down the sides of the kopje to the plains below. When the troop had gone about a hundred feet from the base of the rock formation, they regrouped and looked back up to the top.

"Rebecca, I said not to do that," Chris said angrily. He took the rifle out of her hands.

Rebecca crawled out of the tent. Heather was next out. Walking slowly over to the cliff, they could now see the entire troop of baboons that had tried to take over this kopje.

"This is our kopje. Stay away!" shouted Heather.

"Yea, stay away." Rebecca repeated.

"Oh, man." Chris knew this would be a challenge. But until now he didn't realize just how much of one it would be as he looked at the two girls yelling at the baboons.

The two girls turned toward each other and gave a

high five. But reality sunk in after taking a couple of steps. They turned and hugged each other, both fighting back the tears. They knew in their hearts that if they were to ever see their families again, it would be up to their own will, faith, and the survival skills that their fathers had taught them. Chris walked over and put his arms around them. In a moment they were OK.

Keeping their eyes on the trail and peering over the cliff for the baboons, whose large canines could be deadly in a second, they pulled the large duffels out of the tent. Folding up the blue nylon tent, Rebecca stuffed it back into its compact case.

"All right, let's take inventory." Chris began to open the duffel bags.

"And we need to have a plan. My dad always told me that if I got lost in the bush, I should make a plan and stick to it. That way search parties would have a better chance of following my logic rather than trying to guess what I am going to do, wandering around and such," Rebecca said.

Chris sat by as the girls pulled each item out and laid them in two rows next to them.

Small first aid kit
22 freeze dried food packets
water purification tablets
one empty canteen
a Karl Kahlese 12X night scope
five pair of women's panties
five pair of men's briefs
flashlight and four spare D batteries
all purpose utility knife and scabbard
80 feet of nylon rope
three Bic butane lighters
a compass
six large animal radio collars
two rain ponchos
a hair brush

two tubes of lipstick

two tubes of sunscreen

The girls sat wide eyed and giggled with each new discovery. High fives were popping with each new item pulled from the bag.

"Wow, look at this. A stopwatch and pocket binoculars," Heather said and slapped another high five with Rebecca. She handed them to Chris who sat to the side and enjoyed the show they were putting on. You would think they were back in Texas in Heather's bedroom.

"Here's something interesting," Rebecca said. She pulled a nineteen-inch-long mahogany box with metal hinges from the duffel. "So cool."

"What is it?" Heather leaned closer.

"It's a dart gun. But not just any old dart gun. It's a Tomme 960. Handmade in Belgium. Guaranteed to shoot one hundred yards with less than a two-foot drop. The metal tube stock folds out like this," Rebecca said and lifted the gun from the case. Chris got up and moved over next to Rebecca. He watched intently.

As if well trained, she quickly popped the stock in position. They heard a click. "Then you screw on the barrel here." Rebecca took the short ten-inch barrel and screwed it in place. "Then you put the bolt action piece here." She reached into the case and set the bolt mechanism in place and pushed. Another click was heard. "Now all we do is load the dart and *voila*, we're in business."

"That is way cool. How did you learn to do that?" Chris was wide eyed.

"My dad's taken me with him several times to tag big game for the Wildlife Service. We use an old dart gun that is rusted and misfires half the time. But this gun is of premium quality. It's brand new. Looks like it's never been fired." She reached down into the case and retrieved a dart and held it up to look at it. "This is great, Chris. This is the kind of dart scientists use on big cats.

It can be loaded with a drug called M-99. It's a combination of sodium bicarbonate and acetic acid. It's so powerful that it can literally drop a lion before it can run ten feet."

"What's this?" Heather said and held up another case exactly like the first one.

They opened it and found over two dozen darts and several vials of M-99. Next to the M-99 vials were six syringes filled with the antidote for the drug. They were overwhelmed with their treasure. Suddenly they remembered how hungry they were.

"Anybody hungry?" Chris asked.

Heather walked over to the duffel bag and pulled out a handful of freeze-dried food packets. "You can place your order here, please." She lifted two packets of freeze-dried food in the air. "Beef stroganoff or chicken tetrazinni?"

"That's disgusting. But it beats eating another agama lizard," Rebecca said.

"Who ate an agama?" Chris asked. He put the Tomme 960 back into the case.

"We did. Your dad, Heather, and me. Trust me. Anything is better than that lizard."

"Ditto that," Heather replied and tore open the beef stroganoff bag.

The ancient and weathered rock formation had provided several pools of water across the top of the kopje from the heavy rain. Rebecca took the empty canteen and in a matter of minutes had filled it up and dropped two water purification tablets inside. Shaking the canteen, she started the stopwatch and in four minutes she was pouring the slightly milky colored water into the beef stroganoff packet.

"Well it's not chicken cordon bleu, but it will fill us up," she said. They all ate from the packet with a set of utensils they had discovered in the duffel bag. Rebecca used the fork while Heather ate with the spoon. After

Heather took a few bites she would hand the spoon to
Chris. Then he would take his turn. The small packet
didn't last long and soon they were experiencing the
fine dining of freeze-dried chicken tetrazinni. They finished both packets without saying a word. The food was
cold, tasteless, and generally disgusting. But no one
wanted to be the first to admit it.

Completing the inventory, they found one backpack and, of course, there was Jack's satchel.

Dividing everything up, they had decided that staying on the kopje might be more of a risk than trying to
hike their way across the Serengeti.

"Won't dad send a helicopter back to find us, Chris?"

"I don't know Heather. It was just pure luck that the
balloon was traveling the course that it was. I don't even
think that Evan, the pilot, and Kristen, his sister, knew
how far into the Serengeti we had come. We had spotted
several fires from the air, but yours was the only one
that the wind was carrying us toward. I mean it was
mainly all luck. I don't think we can afford to wait."

"What do we do with these?" Heather asked as she
held up the six large animal radio collars.

"Hand me one of them," Rebecca said and took one
of the bright orange nylon collars from Heather. She
wrapped it around her waist, looping it twice, and then
slid the end through the buckle next to the small electronic device.

"Makes a great belt!" Rebecca smiled. "Just leave the
rest of them here. We don't have any use for them.
Unless you want to collar a lion or leopard along the
way?" She smiled, already knowing the answer.

Heather picked one up and fashioned a belt for
herself and they both gave each other a high five. Chris
rolled his eyes with the continuous high fives. They
were getting old to him, but he knew it lifted their spirits
so he didn't say a word.

With the protection of the Tomme 960 dart gun, he

was hoping they could walk far enough to find a safari company. The satchel fully loaded and the backpack bulging at its limits, Heather picked up the double rifle and handed it to Chris.

"Rebecca," Heather said.

"Yes?" Rebecca pulled the zipper across the top of the backpack.

"I was wondering how you got a shot off at the baboons when my dad unloaded the rifle to use it as a crutch?"

"What about the crutch?" Chris asked. "I've been meaning to ask. I saw dad limping but in the excitement I didn't have time to ask him about it."

"He broke his ankle when the wildebeest tumbled into him during the stampede. Then Rebecca picked up the rifle and shot the wild dog."

"Wildebeest stampede. Shooting a wild dog! You must have been really busy." Chris seemed impressed.

"I was thinking about that myself. Your dad must have loaded it the night before. Probably more worried about us on this rock in the middle of nowhere than he was letting on," Rebecca said.

Chris opened the rifle, breaking it in half like a double barrel shotgun. He found another live round still in the left chamber.

"We have only one bullet left. The others went over the cliff during the storm and I really don't want to spend time looking around the baboons for extra bullets. It's not too heavy, but with the satchel, the backpack, and the dart gun, I say we leave it here," Chris said. After thinking through the options, that was the only one that made sense. "Otherwise it may prove to be just extra baggage."

"I agree. One bullet wouldn't help us. At least I don't think it would anyway," Heather said.

"I'm going to point it toward—which direction did you say we should go?" Chris asked.

"Southeast, toward the old safari tracks," Rebecca said.

The compass was hanging around Heather's neck. She held the compass for a few seconds and located the southeast bearing they needed. Chris laid the rifle on the rock surface of the kopje. He let go of it carefully, all the while thinking of his dad. He then picked up some loose stones and fashioned an arrow from the tip of the gun barrel pointing southeast.

"There. If someone comes along, they will know which way we went and come looking for us." Chris stood up and looked toward the southeast.

Chris, Heather, and Rebecca stood motionless and silent for what seemed a long time. In truth, only a couple of minutes had passed. It was time to leave. It was their big moment to blend into nature and become part of the community of animals that roamed this wild land. It was time to be strong. They looked at each other and knew each others' thoughts. Pushing their fears deep inside, they allowed only caution and will to rule their minds.

"It's time," Chris said.

"Yes, it's time," Rebecca said.

"OK, let's do it." Heather picked up her dad's satchel.

As they followed the pathway down the kopje, a young male baboon ran across the trail and barked at them. Rebecca kicked a rock in his direction and never flinched. After nearly two hours of following the compass's direction of southeast, they came to a massive grove of umbrella trees, the trademark tree of East Africa. They're called a tree island when they are standing alone in the middle of the grassland. In awe of the view, the teens could see dozens of species of wild animals roaming, grazing, or playing among the trees in the grassland.

As Rebecca pointed out the different animals, she began teaching Heather how to count in Swahili.

"Now there are *nne* giraffe."

"That would be four," Heather said.

"Good. And look up there at the birds. I count *sita.*"

Heather looked up in the sky at the flock of cranes.

"That would be six."

"Great. Now repeat after me one through ten. *Muja, mbili, tatu, nne, tans, sita, saba, nane, tisa, kumi.*"

As Heather counted back to Rebecca, Chris noticed the trees ahead were filled with monkeys.

Not only were the trees filled with the cute black-faced vervet monkey but with the more exotic colobus monkey. The colobus has a beautiful black and white alternating ring pattern up its body and tail. It, too, darted and pranced across the forest oasis in the broad expanse of the Serengeti grassland. Grazing between the trees were a herd of mixed antelope. Impala, bush bucks, duikers, kudus, and tsessebes all roamed about as if they had no cares in the world. But Heather and Rebecca knew otherwise.

"Look over there." Chris pointed to the far fringe of the tree island.

"I see them. A pride of lions." Rebecca took the binoculars out of her backpack. "I count *tatu* females, *mbili* young males, and *mbili* cubs. No dominant males."

"What do we do?" Heather asked nervously.

"I say we walk around the other side of the tree island." Chris tried to stay relaxed.

"Ditto that." Rebecca looped the binocular strap around her neck. Setting down the backpack, she pulled out the Tomme 960 dart gun and loaded a dart into the firing chamber. She gave it to Chris.

"I loaded a dart with enough M-99 to knock down an elephant. Just in case one of the lions picks up our scent, I'll have two others ready to load if we need to."

"We *are* facing the wind, so we should be all right," Heather said.

She had been on several deer and elk hunting trips

in West Texas, New Mexico, and Colorado with her brothers and her dad. She understood well about letting an animal catch a human scent. As the three teen adventurers carefully chose their path to the south of the umbrella trees, the lions didn't move from their midday napping spot. Their faces were stained with blood from an early morning kill. Lions with full tummies and the increasing heat of the day made it easy for Chris, Heather, and Rebecca to trek around the menagerie of wildlife, exotic plants, and trees.

But they had made a near fatal mistake and didn't realize it. The soft breeze had shifted and was now blowing in their faces. Two of the younger males from the lion pride had been left out of the morning feast and still needed fresh meat. They had been born together and raised together. Now the two males often hunted as a team. As one circled around the three unsuspecting teens, the other approached quickly from the rear. Rebecca heard something behind her and spun around. Horror streaked across her face. The young male, about 250 pounds of predator, was running full speed. When she saw him he was forty feet away.

"Lion," she screamed with all of her power.

Chris pivoted quickly and brought the dart gun up like his rifle. Heather jumped to the side out of the line of fire. Rebecca fell backwards toward Chris. Chris felt his heart pounding. His thoughts raced through his brain like a bolt of lightening screaming at him that he had one shot. The alternative was too horrible to think about. He waited and counted.

"One, two." The lion's burst of speed brought him to within twenty feet of Rebecca.

Chris pulled the trigger. He was shocked that there was no kick like his hunting rifle. His mind's eye could see the dart traveling like a stinger missile from under the wing of a supersonic jet fighter. The lion made one last giant stride before he put every ounce of strength he had into a final jump. The dart struck him squarely in the chest. The scene played out as a slow motion picture for Chris, Heather, and Rebecca.

Chris and Heather watched as the lion showed his massive teeth and writhed in midair trying to bite at the sting in his chest. Rebecca could see that he was going to land directly on top her so she started rolling to her left. As the young male came flying through the air, his body went limp like a rag doll and he rolled with feet, legs, and tail moving in all directions. And then it ended. Just as if it were the last note of a symphony. The cymbals crashed and then there was silence.

Rebecca opened her eyes to find a tail laying across her shoulder. It twitched once and then was still. Chris ran over to her.

"Rebecca. Are you all right?" He knelt down beside her.

"Oh, man. That was too close. I'm fine. How about Heather?"

"Not a scratch," Heather responded as she crawled up on all fours and looked around. She saw the other lion charging from the other direction. He was about a hundred feet away. "Lion, Chris. There's another one." She jumped to her feet.

"Quick Rebecca. Another dart!"

Rebecca was stunned for a second and then realized that clutched in the palm of her right hand were the other two darts. She slapped them into Chris's hand. She rolled to one side and got up to her knees. The young male lion, not yet an expert in hunting techniques but nonetheless deadly, kept on charging. Chris knew he would be on them in less than ten seconds. His subconscious was thinking about the rest of the pride.

Chris stood up and was counting in his head. He remained calm. "One, two," he had opened the breech and slipped in the dart, "three, four." He leveled the dart gun up to his shoulder. "Five." He pulled the trigger. But he had second guessed that the young male would jump like his brother. He didn't. The dart hit the lion's shoulder and barely stuck. The lion jerked to his left and charged onward. But for a reason no one could later explain, he ran directly to the downed lion and growled toward the three teens. He jumped around his fallen brother and waved his paws in the air. Lunging forward twice, Chris swung the dart gun toward the lion but it didn't connect. Then the M-99 drug began to hit. In less than a minute the second lion was sprawled across the body of the first one. Both were unconscious.

"Quick," Rebecca said as she opened her backpack. "There are a lot of drugs in those lions. We need to administer some of the antidote so the drugs don't kill them."

For the next few minutes, Rebecca, Heather, and Chris worked with the two downed lions. It took all three of them to pull the second lion off the first lion so he wouldn't suffocate.

"That should do it. How long did you say they would stay knocked out?" Chris asked Rebecca.

"About ten minutes."

"Good. That should give us enough time to get down the track. Heather, hand me the first aid kit." Heather took out the small kit and Chris rummaged through it. "Good, I was hoping it had some." He took out a bottle of eyedrops that was labeled "most like natural tears." Gently he dropped the liquid in the eyes of the lions. Then he squeezed their eyes shut and placed a gauze pad over the closed lids.

"That should keep the sun out and their eyes moist until they wake up."

"Where did you learn to do that?" Rebecca asked.

"I've seen my dad do it many times. I was with him on an expedition to tag black bears in northern New Mexico. Same thing with them. Gotta keep their eyes from drying out and being damaged while they're unconscious. It's easier to use a special ointment, but this will work for the short term. Let's go."

In a couple of minutes they were about three hundred yards away and paying better attention to the wind. After nearly an hour of walking through the grasslands and watching for big cats, they all agreed it was time to stop and eat something. Maintaining their strength was important.

"OK. Your choices are beef stew or chicken noodle soup, room temperature of course," Rebecca said and forced a smile.

As the girls bantered back and forth about the food, Chris thought about their situation. He started thinking ahead a few hours when they would need to camp for the night. He reloaded the Tomme 960. It had proven to be a powerful friend with a very big kick indeed.

"I'll take the prime rib with broccoli," Heather said and chuckled.

"Yea, right. And I want the roasted lamb and strawberry jello," Rebecca shot back.

"Beef stew sounds better cold than chicken noodle," Heather said.

After a cold serving of freeze-dried beef stew, a long drink of water, and a short twenty-minute nap, the young adventurers were back on their feet and trekking across the grassy plains.

As the sun began to dip in the afternoon sky, the clouds began to form to the north. Soon the first drops of rain found Chris, Heather, and Rebecca tucked away securely in their tent nestled between two umbrella trees that had tried to grow together. Their boots and socks were stripped off and shoved to the end of the tent. No one commented about the obvious foot odor. But then no one had had a bath in two days either.

The soft grass under the tree helped cushion the hard ground, but fatigue had done its job. Chris thought about his mom, dad, and R.O. But his mind quickly jumped to Natalie. Before the third thunderclap of the nightly storms of the Serengeti, all three went fast asleep.

The threesome had discovered that the spare under-wear, all rolled together, made great pillows. But this night, they slept soundly enough that the pillows could have been chunks of the kopje they had left behind.

As the rain began to pour, a cry of a hyena in the distance could be heard. It was just another instrument in the symphony of sounds that have been part of this ecosystem for centuries in the past and hopefully for centuries to come.

A growl of a lion answered the hyena. Having faith in each other and their will to survive, Chris, Heather, and Rebecca slept soundly. Fatigue had something to do with it, too!

# 13

# Ngorongoro

Mavis MacGregor had suffered through two near sleepless nights, falling asleep only when sheer exhaustion engulfed her whole body. R.O. walked across the large room and sat down on the floor next to the couch where Mavis was napping. It was eight o'clock in the morning, and she had been asleep only a couple of hours.

"Mom," he reached up and touched her soft auburn hair. "Mom, there's someone from the Kenya Wildlife Service on the telephone."

"OK, honey. I'm awake," she said as she sat up on the couch and took the phone.

"Hello," she said sleepily.

"Dr. MacGregor?" the voice said.

"Yes, I'm Dr. Mavis MacGregor."

"Please hold the line while I connect you to a cell telephone. It will sound kind of garbled, but if you listen well, you can hear the other party."

"I understand," she said and brushed the hair away from her face.

"Honey, this is Jack." He spoke loudly into the telephone.

Mavis jumped to her feet, her heart racing. She was barely able to speak.

"Jack, Jack, where are you? Where's Heather?" She shouted into the telephone.

"I'm at a paleontology base camp near Olduvai Gorge. It's in the old Norongoro Crater. That's southeast of the Serengeti. Chris found us."

"Oh, honey, we have been worried sick. Let me talk to Heather," Mavis said expressing her motherly concerns. There was a pause.

"Jack, I said let me talk to Heather."

"I can't."

"Oh, Jack, no, don't tell me this," Mavis said as tears welled up in her eyes.

"She's not dead Mavis. That's all I can say. She and Rebecca are alive and waiting for us to pick them up in the Serengeti. I know the spot. We can find them today."

Mavis was holding her hand to her mouth and fighting back the urge to collapse on the couch. "Where's Chris?" She held her breath for the answer.

"He's with them. That's why I'm not worried. It's a long story that can wait a couple more hours. Call Daniel. Get his big helicopter and come get me. Do you understand?"

"Yes, honey, I understand."

"You can be here in ninety minutes with the big Bell Jet Ranger. Then we can go get Heather, Chris, and Rebecca. They'll be all right," Jack said confidently trying to mask his own fears.

"We're on our way. I love you," Mavis said and pushed the off button on the telephone.

"Where's Heather?" R.O. asked the second he heard the telephone beep off. "Is she dead?"

"No, she's not dead," Mavis said nearly biting his head off with the statement. It actually made her feel better to hear her impatient tone. "No, Ryan...Heather is OK. Chris found them, but I don't know how. He's with them in the Serengeti. Dad knows where. Now get your gear while I call Daniel."

The wheels of government grind slowly, especially in Africa. Nearly three hours passed before Daniel was able to convince someone to let him have a helicopter to go pick up Dr. MacGregor. It was as if someone was deliberately stonewalling the effort. Someone who didn't want Dr. MacGregor rescued so quickly. By noon, however, the helicopter, complete with R.O., Mavis, and Daniel were approaching the Tanzanian border.

"Keep your eyes peeled for the military escorts," the pilot said over the intercom inside the cabin. They all remembered meeting the general two days earlier. In thirty minutes they would be at Ngorongoro.

Jack had handed the cell phone back to a pretty brunette, who had about three layers of dirt over her tanned arms and legs. She wore khaki shorts and a powder blue tank top. A red bandana held her hair up and away from her face.

"Thanks, Dr. Crewson," Jack said.

"You're welcome Dr. MacGregor. I wish we could do more. Sounds like you've been through quite an ordeal."

"Let's say it's been exciting."

"Well, we don't get much excitement here at Olduvai Gorge. A fossilized digit or tooth once a month really gets us all worked up," the attractive paleontologist said as she led Jack out of the tent toward the balloon. He was now using real crutches that the paleontologists kept with their first aid equipment that was stocked like a mini-hospital. Being properly prepared for medical emergencies was the rule in Africa when hospitals were so far away.

"Under different circumstances, my wife Mavis would be ecstatic to visit with you. She finished her "paleo" degree from Oxford. But until our daughter and son are safely within our reach, there is no other world out there to consider," said Jack from a fatherly perspective.

As with mammals of the wild, humans were no different in this respect. Caring for their young was a priority. As Jack and Dr. Crewson neared the balloon, the last of the air was finally pushed out and Jack's two rescuers came over to talk to him. During the all day flight across East Africa and the three hour return trip, Jack had learned that these two Norwegians had no business flying a balloon anywhere.

"Wow, what a trip back," the tall young blond Norwegian said as he finished coiling up a rope. "If we hadn't gone up another thousand feet by accident, I bet we would be over Madagascar by now instead of catching the air stream back over Tanzania. A bit chilly wasn't it?" Evan Grieg smiled at Jack.

"It was more than chilly. I never want to go back to Norway and be cold again," his sister Kristen Grieg said.

"I appreciate your rescuing me from the kopje, but trying to freeze me to death was not what I expected," Jack said. For the first time he looked around the camp and noticed the primitive conditions in which these dedicated scientists lived.

"What were you doing ballooning over the Serengeti in the first place," Dr. Crewson asked.

Kristen, the more talkative of the pair, spoke up.

"We've been in Uganda for a month as volunteers helping spot lions and other big cats from the air for several zoologists from Germany. We would radio back to camp and then the zoologists would drive toward the pride. Occasionally, we would land and help them put on the radio collars. We stopped in Nairobi, hoping to catch another wind south into the Serengeti when your son showed up. We couldn't resist his appeal. And he is cute," the strawberry blond said and smiled.

"Wait, stop. Radio collars. Who carried them, you or

the zoologists?" Jack said quickly. His heart began to race.

"We both did. Just in case we got there first, Kristen is an expert marksman. First place on the Norwegian Olympic team. She would dart the animal, I would collar it, and then back up in the air we would go. At least that was the plan. Occasionally we would get hung up in an umbrella tree or the wind wouldn't cooperate," Evan said.

"Where are the collars?" Jack asked.

"They were in the duffel bags you dropped overboard to the kids," Kristen said.

"Were they activated?" Jack asked hoping to hear the right answer.

"We had activated one just a few minutes before we spotted the three of you on the kopje. Kristen, what did you do with the collar we activated?" Evan asked his sister.

"I put it back in the duffel bag."

"Then the kids still have it," Jack said with hope in his voice. "That should help us pinpoint their location." Jack took a deep breath and released a sigh. His spirits were picking up. He forced himself not to think of the alternative.

Dr. Crewson tried to play the congenial host, but she knew that Jack's mind was elsewhere. The Norwegians, well they were a different story altogether. Obviously from a wealthy family, they had decided that "volunteering" to help scientists in Africa would make a great summer project. Little did they know that amateurs sometimes became more of a hindrance than help and occasionally ended up as someone's lunch! Studying wild game in the heart of Africa was not a Saturday trip to the local zoo.

As the Bell Jet Ranger neared the Ngorongoro Crater, an ancient volcano, the pilot flew low to the ground and followed the ancient Olduvai Gorge. Within a few minutes, he spotted the paleontologist's camp and spoke into the intercom.

"We're here. Everyone stay inside until the rotors come to a complete stop. That means you, too, Dr. MacGregor."

Mavis got the message. Her stomach had calmed down during the flight, but now she was full of butter-flies again. She could see Jack standing at the edge of the clearing next to the deflated balloon. Tears welled up in her eyes.

While the rotor was still moving, she bounded out of the helicopter ducking her head and ran directly to Jack. She nearly knocked him down as she lunged into him.

"Hold on, I'm OK," Jack said as he hugged her. Then they kissed, not once but three times.

Evan, Kristen, and Dr. Crewson smiled as they watched the reunion. But they also knew that the real challenge lay ahead. R.O. gave his dad a hug, and they were all led over to a tent where they sat down in canvas chairs. The pilot spoke first.

"Do you have any recollection of the direction you were going when you left the kopje?"

"We were headed southeast, but when I gained altitude the winds pushed us due east," Evan said.

"So you made a hook due east toward the Indian Ocean?" Mavis asked.

"Yes, that's about it."

"What was your air speed?" the helicopter pilot asked again.

"I think we hit about forty-five knots once we reached altitude and headed east."

Everyone was feeling the same and thinking the same. It would be like finding a needle in a haystack.

"I mean, I do remember passing over Lake Natron on the way east. But when we hit the airstream at higher altitude and reversed our course, we then flew south by southwest."

"That helps," the pilot said confidently. He looked at his notebook that held a stack of maps. If we start at Lake Natron we can fly straight toward Lobo and Tabora at a northwesterly direction. We should be able to pick up any radio collar signals along the way if we stay low enough. There's a fueling station on the Mara River twenty-six miles northwest of Tabora. Then we can zigzag our way back filling in the spaces we missed."

Everyone felt better that the pilot was confident of the search. But the reality of possibly finding three teenagers among hundreds of thousands of wild animals in an area the size of the state of Vermont was overwhelming.

R.O. had wandered from the tent during the discussion. He followed a long path toward a dig. The dig location had been in Olduvai Gorge since the famous Louis Leakey had begun his studies some fifty years earlier. R.O. noticed a table that was full of sand and screens. He walked over to it. No one was there so he strolled around the area between spots that had strings and ropes marking sections that had been carefully dug around. Tools of the paleontology trade, small brushes and dental picks, lay stacked neatly here and there. R.O. checked his watch. He figured they had all gone to lunch.

A small red and green lizard peeked over the top of the ledge in front of him and darted across the sand.

"Wow," R.O. said to himself and took off after the lizard.

Down the gorge and up the side to a flat grassy area, R.O. pursued the lightening fast lizard until it finally darted down a hole. The hole was way too large for a lizard and R.O.'s curiosity got the better of him. He crawled on his stomach down to the entrance. Taking a small flashlight out of the right cargo pocket of his shorts, he shined the light down into the hole. It appeared to be a den of some kind.

Suddenly the light reflected on six round shiny objects. They were three sets of eyes. He moved the light around and realized they belonged to three bat-eared fox kits.

"This is so cool," he said to himself. He reached in and picked up one of the kits.

Little did he know that just twenty feet away hidden in a row of tall grass were two hungry jackals. With ears pulled back and their predator senses focused on the den, they considered R.O. a messenger who would now deliver them their much desired morsels of food. Usually hunting in pairs and mainly at night, this pair had been watching the fox den for some time. They were just waiting for the opportunity to steal the kits for a quick and easy meal. Jackals, considered to be real dogs by zoologists, usually opted for the easy meal and avoided conflict as much as possible. But having staked a claim on this den, they were not going to be cheated out of their prize.

R.O. stood up and petted the soft little fox as it licked his hand.

"Hey, little fella. What's your name?" R.O. had the compulsion to name everything.

"Wait till Mom sees you. She will *love* you."

Carrying his new friend, R.O. walked back down the incline into the gorge toward the camp. The two jackals adjusted their position and stalked closely behind ready to charge at any second. When R.O. had reached the dig tables, he turned around. Had he had heard something? As he petted the baby fox, he decided it was nothing. He started up the pathway toward the tents where all the adults were still talking about the search plan for Chris, Heather, and Rebecca. Then he heard gravel and rock falling. He turned around in time to see the two jackals, each with teeth showing, literally flying down the rock incline toward him.

"Oh, no," R.O. said. He took off in a run, tucking the

baby fox under his arm like a football. He reached the tent in a few seconds with the big jackals hot behind him.

"Dad, Mom," he yelled as he blasted inside sliding on the soft dirt floor and landing on his back in a cloud of dust. Before any of the adults could react, the two jackals bounded into the tent and crashed into the table. They were barking loudly, snarling, and becoming confused about what in the world they had just entered.

"Ryan," Mavis yelled. Jack ducked as a jackal jumped across his lap, his teeth snapping, one of its paws digging into his sore ankle.

It was all over in a few seconds. Tables and chairs were spilled everywhere. Adults had fled the tent like rats leaving a sinking ship. R.O. had become permanently fixed in the dirt, the baby fox tucked safely under his arms. Mavis walked over to him and glared down at him.

"OK, mister. Get up," she said sternly, pushing thoughts of Heather and Chris from the front of her mind for a moment. "Explain yourself."

Ryan, hoping that it would work, held the baby fox out toward his mother. It did, but just for a second.

"How cute!" Mavis said and took the fuzzy little fox in her hands.

Jack, Daniel, and the rest of the adults wandered over and stood around the two of them. Mavis smiled and looked at Ryan mocking a pleasant look.

"And I suppose, Ryan O'Keef MacGregor," she said slowly, still smiling. But Ryan knew what was coming when he heard his name spoken like that. "I suppose, that this furry, cute, little friend of yours just jumped up into your hands and told you to take him for a walk. Right?"

"Well, Mom..." R.O. started.

"Don't well Mom me, young man. Where did you get him?"

"Well, I, uh, I'm sorry. I was following a lizard and it went down in this hole. So when I looked in the hole I spotted three little bat-eared foxes. I figured..."

"You figured what?" Mavis interrupted in a strong tone.

"I thought he was cute and you might like to have one!" Ryan exclaimed. He had formulated a reason he thought perhaps his mother might like to hear—one that would lessen the level of punishment he knew he was about to receive.

"How thoughtful of you, Ryan. But as you well know, I have a lot on my mind at this moment. And you have managed to terrorize these nice people who are trying to help us find Chris, Heather, and Rebecca. Now I suggest that you take this wild creature and find the hole that you stole him from. Put him back before his mother shows up. Now! "

"I'll go with them. I'm sure the jackals didn't go very far." Daniel picked up another rifle he had brought along and followed Ryan out of the tent.

In a few minutes, they were standing in front of the small hole in the ground. As R.O. leaned down to release the kit, the mother bat-eared fox leapt from the den and practically snatched the baby fox from his hands with her teeth as he placed it on the ground. Secure in her mouth, she scurried back down into the den where she investigated every hair and fold of skin and licked the baby from nose to tail.

"Wow, did you see that?" R.O. said and stepped back quickly.

"That should teach you not to mess with baby whatevers anymore," Daniel said.

"You're right about that. Unless they're lost or need help or something."

"Now come on. We've got to go find these kids and end this mess," Daniel said with determination in his voice.

In a few minutes, everyone was loaded into the helicopter. Jack, in the copilot seat, had the radio-positioning device in his hand to try to home in on the animal collars. Mavis leaned back in the passenger seat and looked out across the gorge as the helicopter circled the camp. They flew north toward Lake Natron, where they would begin their search. She didn't like the *deja vue* she was experiencing from the Caymans. But at least Chris, Heather, and Rebecca weren't in danger from any humans.

"Mom, sorry about the kit," Ryan said as he leaned across from the other seat.

"It's all right, honey. We've just got to stay focused."

Soon the helicopter was banking to the west over Lake Natron. A dozen or so fishermen waved to them from their small boats.

The pilot spoke over the intercom.

"OK. Start looking and don't talk unless you see something."

# 14

# Gentle Giants

The breaking of branches awakened Chris, Heather, and Rebecca from a hard night's sleep. The trek across the Serengeti was taking its toll, and they weren't getting enough to eat to keep up their strength. They had agreed to eat more the next day.

"What was that?" Heather said. She had just awakened.

"I don't know," Rebecca replied rubbing her eyes.

"Chris, it's your turn to look out first. I did it yesterday," Heather suggested. She gave him a delicate push.

"I know," Chris replied reluctantly as he slowly unzipped the small opening in the end of the bag-like tent.

"You aren't going to believe this," he said.

"Trust me. I'll believe anything now," Heather said. She crawled forward next to Rebecca.

What they were all viewing was the hind end of one giant elephant. The elephant was busy tearing branches down to get at the soft supple leaves that had come with the rains. When she moved a few feet to the right, the girls gasped. For beyond her and all around the trees were fifteen elephants. There were six females with

small calves and three young females not yet in repro-
ductive age. Each mature elephant was busy foraging
trying to eat the four hundred pounds of roughage a
day that their massive bodies required.

"This is awesome," Heather whispered to Rebecca
as they watched from the front row seat of nature's
theater. Safely wedged between two big umbrella trees,
the teens were secure as long as they didn't attract
attention. In their brief role as African adventurers, they
had learned that keeping a low profile contributes to
longevity.

The herd of elephants roamed around the cluster of
trees gently breaking branches and chomping down on
the fresh new leaves that seemed to be bursting out
everywhere. When one smaller female seemed to tug
for over five minutes to fall a small tree, another larger
female casually strode over. Together they pushed it
down. Then the larger female left to return to her baby,
while the younger elephant began to forage on the fallen
tree. The kids were amazed at witnessing such coopera-
tion over and over again among the herd.

The smallest of the baby elephants continually ran
from one mother to the next, quite often tripping over
his own little trunk and rolling to the ground. The
closest adult would always turn and inspect him and
touch him with its trunk before the baby hurried on to
the next one. Finally locating his mother, he eagerly
began to suckle his morning milk.

"They look so happy," Rebecca said.

"I even think I can see them smiling," Heather replied.

"They are smiling," Chris agreed.

"My dad says," Rebecca said, "that the increase in
the human population to the south has forced the herd
north into the Serengeti. As the trees and grass die, they
walk onward into Kenya. He says that elephants are the
smartest animal he knows. They can count, they have

compassion for other animals of different species, and they talk to each other at long distances by something called infrasound."

"Oh yeah, I've heard of that. My dad," Heather added proudly, "gave a lecture on that one time. We all had to go because the zoological society wanted to meet the whole family. It was the first lecture I had heard him give that didn't put me to sleep. He said that the elephants make a vibrating noise through their trunks. The noise travels through the bones in their foreheads. He said we can't hear it. But they can hear it miles away. It's kind of like that noise that bats make that we can't hear either."

Chris was having fun just listening to the two girls challenge each other with the amount of knowledge they had in their heads and how great their fathers were.

"That is really cool. Wish we could talk like that so our parents couldn't hear us," Rebecca said. They all laughed.

They were startled by a cracking of a limb that fell just a few feet from their tent. A baby elephant ran over to the limb. It stopped when it realized there were strange looking animals lying on the ground between the trees. Instinctively, he tried to belch out a cry, but he only squeaked and ran back to his mother. The large female walked toward the umbrella tree. Heather and Rebecca sunk back down inside the tent and lowered the flap.

"Oh, boy. Put your boots on—fast." Chris said. He curled around and jerked on his socks and safari boots. But it was too late. They had been "made."

Sliding as far as they could back inside the tent, they were surprised to see the end of a trunk snaking its way through the flap toward them. When it reached Heather's face, she stifled the urge to scream. Rebecca quickly reached deep in her backpack and pulled out a packet of freeze-dried food. She tore off the top and shoved the food out toward the inquisitive trunk. It stopped. Then in one quick motion, the trunk sucked the entire contents out of the bag. Suddenly it disappeared from the tent and they heard the female elephant trumpet.

There was no other noise for nearly five minutes. Slowly Heather, Chris, and Rebecca crawled to where they could peek out. They could see the large mother elephant about twenty yards away sucking water up her trunk and blowing it back out. She was draining a small pond that had formed from the night's heavy rains.

"What was in the packet?" Chris asked quietly.

Rebecca pulled the empty packet up to the front of the tent where they all could see it.

"This would have made me thirsty, too. It's the freeze-dried version of taco surprise."

They all chuckled softly. For the next two hours they were entertained with the daily routine of earth's gentle giants. Several elephant calves milled around, played and interacted. There were large mature females, obviously longtime friends spending their lives together raising their young. Touching. Always touching.

"Have you noticed how they touch each other all the time?" Heather said.

"Yes, I did. I think it's neat. You can tell they really love each other. It's not just a wild animal thing. You know, a 'behavior pattern' of some kind."

"Yea, behavior patterns. My dad goes crazy over birds and their behavior. He gets all 'weirded' out when he sees a bird doing something like bouncing its head up and down or sticking it tail feathers straight up. If we are in public, he can really be embarrassing," Heather said.

"My dad's the same way," Rebecca replied.

"Give them a break, guys. They both love animals," Chris said.

By the heat of the day, the girls had dozed off. Chris kept watch but eventually fell asleep as well. When they awoke, the elephants were gone. The presence of large elephant patties and broken branches everywhere were the obvious signs that a herd of elephants had spent a half a day in this spot. In a few minutes the teens were all packed up and walking again toward the southeast. The heat made them forget to eat, but by two in the afternoon, they agreed that food was needed.

"There are some kopjes ahead," Chris said. "We can head there to eat."

He turned toward Heather as they were walking under a massive umbrella tree just as something dropped on her face from above. Heather instinctively wiped away what she thought was a drop of water. Chris and Rebecca looked at her in astonishment.

"What?" she said and looked at the back of her hand. It was red. "Oh my gosh."

Her face was smeared with blood. They all three looked up at the same time. Neatly positioned fifteen feet off the ground was a 200-pound impala that was hanging from a limb by its horns.

"A leopard kill," Rebecca said.

Chris swung around quickly looking in all directions for the cunning cat. It was not to be found.

"That is awesome," Heather commented still cleaning the impala blood from her face. She was fast becoming a seasoned explorer. "A 150-pound leopard dragging a 200-pound impala up that far. I'm impressed!"

"I've got an idea," Chris said. He put the backpack and the dart gun on the ground.

In a few minutes he had climbed high up in the tree and was standing on a limb next to the impala. Retrieving his field knife from his pocket, he began cutting a large muscle from the hind quarter of the impala. The sharp knife did its job and in just a few minutes, Chris was holding a four-pound chunk of muscle. His hands were covered with blood.

"Dinner!" Chris jubilantly held up the large impala steak with a big smile.

"Heather, catch." Chris dropped the meat down to her and she caught it. In a few minutes, he was back on the ground.

"Now, let's get out of here before the owner of this dead impala comes back." He picked up the backpack and took the meat from Heather.

"Good idea," Rebecca agreed.

About thirty minutes later they had reached the row of kopjes and found one that was easy to climb. They had gathered some wood on the way from the tree island where they had found the impala. Chris quickly started a fire using Rebecca's butane lighter.

The meat, now cut into four smaller pieces was draped across the burning limbs and began to broil.

"Oh, this smells so good," Heather cooed. She added a few small sticks to the fire.

"Ditto that. Man am I hungry," Rebecca said.

When the meat was about medium cooked, Chris used his knife to retrieve it from the flames and pass the pieces around. While the outside was good and black from the charcoal affect, the inside was pink and juicy. The three kids didn't talk much and ate every stringy fiber of the lean impala steak. They passed around the canteen and soon all three were laying on their backs in the afternoon sun. It was warm but it wasn't unbearable today. They were stuffed.

"Lose the freeze-dried stuff, Chris. I'm having steak from now on," Heather said. The dried blood on her face looked like a mosaic of face paint.

"Time to go." Chris got up first, then the girls followed. They all felt better.

As they were leaving the ancient rock formation, three giraffe wandered toward them and poked their heads up to look at them eye to eye.

"R.O. would be just going crazy right now if he were here," Heather said. She laughed.

Not finding anything of interest in the three humans, one of the giraffes opened his mouth and out shot his long tongue. It came out nearly three feet before wrapping itself around a small bush. The giraffe pulled the bush from where it had rooted itself in the cracks of a rock and popped it into his mouth. After about two minutes of chewing, he took one big swallow and the bush was gone. He turned and walked away.

"No one will believe that one," Rebecca said.

"No one will believe anything that we tell them after this trip," Heather said. They crawled back down the kopje.

"They'll believe us all right. It would be tough to make up something like this," Chris said.

As they were climbing down, several hyraxes jumped from one rock to the next before disappearing into a small cave.

"What was that?" Heather asked.

"Hyraxes, I think. I've never seen them in the wild before," Chris offered.

"Those *are* hyraxes. They're kind of like rabbits. They have a face that's a cross between a beaver and a bunny. My dad says they are the closest living relative to an elephant," Rebecca said.

"An elephant?" Heather said.

"Yea, no kidding." Rebecca sensed doubt in Heather's voice. "It has to do with DNA or something."

"Wow! An elephant and a rabbit is really strange." Heather made the last few steps down to the plains.

Three hours and two miles later they came upon a small lake. Just as they arrived, an African fish eagle snared a fish and soared high into the air before disappearing to the west. A small herd of bushbucks were drinking on the far side.

"That's a good sign," Chris said.

"Yea, no lions around if they're drinking. But that doesn't mean a leopard isn't stalking them or us," Rebecca said.

They decided to take the animal path around the north rim of the lake. Heather checked the compass and showed it to Chris. Rebecca refilled the canteen and dropped in two more water purification tablets. She shook it for a few minutes. They all took a long drink and refilled it to the top. Heather added another tablet, just for safety's sake, and returned the canteen to the satchel.

As the day grew long, the clouds began to reappear. Since they had spent half the day in the tent watching the elephants, Chris, Heather, and Rebecca weren't excited about crawling back into it anytime soon. They came upon a lone umbrella tree and decided to build a camp, start a fire, and eat more hot food. Before the sprinkles began, they had gathered small sticks of wood and some dried elephant dung. They put on the rain ponchos they had found in the duffel bags and set up the tent just in case the water became too much to bear.

At the equator, the twilight of the day only lasts a few minutes before it is totally dark. By nightfall the rains had come, but the dung burned on and provided heat for their bodies and their food. With a stick, Rebecca held the metal canteen carefully over the fire so the strap wouldn't burn. When the bottom had been thoroughly blackened, Heather, using her socks as oven mitts, poured the hot water into the aluminum packets of freeze-dried food. They had lined up four packets and propped them up with small rocks they had gathered.

"OK, madam and sir," Heather role played. "What can I serve you first. Would you like beans and weenies, chunky chicken noodles, beef stew, or taco surprise?"

"I've got to tell you something, Heather. Whoever picked out this food really needs some help."

Chris remembered meeting the zany brother and

sister team from Norway.

"I agree but let's eat." Rebecca picked up the chunky chicken noodles first.

The kids stuffed themselves with the hot food even though it didn't match the impala steak. But they knew they had felt better after the impala and were determined not to become weakened again. When they had dipped and forked all they could, they picked up the aluminum packets and drank the last drop, even from the taco surprise. With their ponchos in place, Heather put her socks back on, making her feet black from the soot from the bottom of the canteen. Neatness was still important to them so they cleaned up around the campfire, packed everything away and crawled into the tent. With the rolled up underwear under their heads, they soon fell asleep. Chris always struggled to stay awake the longest. He felt a responsibility for all of them. But tonight he fell asleep first.

Within thirty minutes a lone female hyena strolled into the camp and sniffed around the tent and fire. Fortunately for Chris, Heather, and Rebecca, three days on the Serengeti had defeated the delicate floral scent of their colognes and soap. As far as odors were concerned, they had become one with Africa. Sheltered by the massive umbrella tree and feeling the warmth of the hot coals amid the drizzling rain, the hyena curled up and shared the heat for nearly three hours. Then she was up and foraging the night for the remains of a lion kill she could devour and head back to her den. With the strongest jaw muscles of any animal its size, even a leg bone with its rich marrow was a prize to be found. Once at the den she would suckle her young and regurgitate some of the food for the older pups.

Life on the Serengeti was not subject to a clock or any measure of time. It was ruled only by the forces that make some animals predators and other animals prey.

# 15

# Killing Fields

The Bell Jet Ranger had traveled hundreds of miles in the two days of searching. It was on the morning of the third day that a signal was finally picked up.

"I've got something, Jack," Daniel said as he looked at the dial on the radio tracking device.

"Give me a direction," Jack responded quickly from the copilot's seat on the helicopter.

R.O. and Mavis, each with a pair of binoculars, sat still. Anxiety was building within them.

"Go west and let me check the signal." Daniel adjusted the dial trying to find the strongest reading. "OK now turn north a few degrees. Yes, that's it, hold it steady. We're not more than a mile away."

Everyone was pressed hard against the glass windows of the helicopter. Their emotions were raw from days of near misses and fleeting signals that belonged to nothing more than an old radio collar hung on a bush still emitting a weak signal.

"We should be…"

"There's the kopje," Jack shouted cutting off Daniel in mid-sentence. He recognized its unique boat shape with one end reaching over forty feet above the Serengeti.

The helicopter made a tight circle and set down as close as possible. Everyone's hopes were dashed with no obvious sign of the kids. But Mavis was first out of the helicopter, again ducking underneath the still spinning rotors. The pilot had exhausted his patience giving her warnings the day before.

"The path to the top is over here," Jack said. He hobbled on his taped foot, which was now much better. His injury had been diagnosed as a bad sprain.

R.O. helped him up the steep and narrow pathway. Upon reaching the top, they found Mavis sitting on the rock surface next to the rifle and holding a lion's radio collar in her hands. She was gazing across the beautiful grasslands that was the home of the wildest animals on earth. Everyone walked up to her in silence.

"They left the live one here," she said quietly. "They didn't know." She was fighting back tears. "They took the collars that hadn't been activated. They didn't even have a clue that one of them was working."

"Sorry Mom," R.O. said and touched the back of her hair with his right hand. He then walked around the top of the kopje.

Jack limped around on one crutch looking down the sheer cliff and then back toward Mavis. He leaned over and examined some animal spore. It was dry. He picked it up and crumbled it in his hand looking for seeds, grass, or small animal bones. By the contents and texture, he would have a good guess as to what kind of animal had left it.

"Baboons." He dropped the crumbled feces on the rocks and dusted off his hand. "If a troop of baboons had invaded the kopje, they might have had to move on. Baboons can be very dangerous." He looked over to where the rifle lay on the rock surface. "I don't think I left Daniel's gun in that exact spot. It was over there next to the round boulder. I'm afraid they may have used it."

He limped over to it and started to reach down to

pick up the double barrel rifle.

"Dad, stop," R.O. shouted.

Everyone looked toward R.O., who was standing on the boulder behind the gun. He was looking across the Serengeti to the southeast.

"They left us a sign. See the rocks on the side of the barrel. They make half of an arrow. The other side must have been blown away or kicked around by the baboons." R.O. jumped down and ran over to the gun. He quickly took the small rocks and lined them up on the left side to match the existing right side. "See, it points that way."

Mavis jumped to her feet and ran back to the boulder and stood on it and looked to the southeast.

"Ryan, I love you, I will never punish you again. Let's get moving. Heather, Chris, and Rebecca, we are coming to get you." Mavis jumped down and kissed Ryan hard on the mouth and headed for the trail.

"Mom, you didn't have to do that. And by the way, everyone here is a witness to the punishment thing you just said."

"We are lucky they were baboons. Less likely to pick up something like a rifle. A chimpanzee would have picked it up, carried it around, maybe even pulled the trigger," Jack said in a professorial tone.

"Is the baboon dumber than a chimp, Dad?" R.O. asked as they were leaving.

"No, not dumber. They just don't have the cognitive thinking ability that chimps, gorillas, and humans have."

"Jack, we can talk about it in the helicopter. Let's go," Mavis said in a stern voice.

"I can only walk so fast, hon," Jack replied.

Daniel picked up the rifle. He and R.O. helped Jack down the kopje and to the helicopter. The Bell Jet Ranger's rotor blades turned hard and fast. It was soon up in the air following the directions that Heather and Rebecca had left. They all figured that the girls would be no further away than twenty miles, at the most. That meant they could catch up with them in less than fifteen minutes. The turbo engine of the helicopter screamed along. All eyes on board strained to watch for any sign of a two-legged mammal walking across the plains. Ten minutes passed, then fifteen minutes, then twenty, then twenty-five. Soon forty minutes of flying in the south-easterly direction had passed and no sign of the teens could be found.

There was total silence on board as the Jet Ranger turned around to retrace its flight back to the kopje. The mood was darkened even more when Jack told everyone that one shot had been fired from the rifle and the other was left untouched. They couldn't believe that Chris would willingly leave a loaded gun behind. But they didn't know about the Tomme 960 either!

Seventeen miles to the southwest, Chris, Heather, and Rebecca forged ahead through the tall dry grass. The new sprigs from the rain were pushing up everywhere and so was the insect population.

"I haven't seen as many bugs as this since we were at Great Slave Lake visiting dad's cousin Geoffrey." Chris swatted three insects that landed on his face.

"He's the Canadian Mountie, isn't he Chris? Remember, I stayed home for a regional swim meet. Man…my arm is tired from swatting these nasty things," Heather said.

"That's him. Dad says he's doing some top secret police work in London with Scotland Yard. Ouch." Chris swung at a few dozen more of the biting flies and gnats.

"This has got to stop," Rebecca said firmly. "Let's try this."

Rebecca paused next to a low spot in the plains that had collected water from the night before.

"Dad told me that elephants roll in the mud to protect themselves from the sun and the insects."

Heather reached up and touched her swollen lips, which had been burned by the sun. Even though she was a blond, she tanned well. Only her lips, eyelids, and the top of her ears were suffering. Rebecca's dark native skin ordinarily protected her from the solar exposure. But even she was suffering because of too much sun, something she normally avoided. There was no sunburn on Chris who loved the outdoors and stayed there as much as he could. But, like Heather, the top of his ears were blistered. They all wished they had their canvas safari hats.

Rebecca knelt down and formed a mud ball and rubbed it on her arms. The insects chose somewhere else to land. Soon every bare spot on her body was covered in a layer of mud. Heather joined in and before long they were laughing and making faces. Things girls always enjoy. Chris finally smiled at the two of them and decided to jump into the fun as well.

"Finally, no more bugs," Heather said joyfully, her blond hair framing her dark muddy face.

"I mean you really look strange." Rebecca laughed.

"Time to take a bearing while you get more water." Chris put one last layer on his forehead and handed Heather the compass. Heather had taken the last three readings after Chris had refreshed her skills with a short lesson.

She held the compass at stomach level and looked down at the face. After standing and looking at it a few seconds, a frown slowly formed on her face.

"Rebecca, look at this."

Rebecca set the canteen down and walked over to Heather. Taking the compass in her hand she tried to make a reading. Chris turned around, quickly sensing something wrong.

"I don't believe it. It says we are going southwest."

As Rebecca dropped her arms to waist level, the needle swung to the north, then northeast. She glanced at her belt. The lion's radio collar was just a few inches from the compass.

"Oh my gosh, Heather. The radio collars have a small magnet in them. Most older radios do."

Chris reached out and took the compass from her hands without asking. He checked the reading.

"Rebecca's right. We've been traveling southwest." He turned quickly and held the compass against Heather's lion collar belt. The needle swung wildly around before it settled on one direction. He shook his head.

"Oh no. I took the reading while holding the compass at my waist, next to…" She stopped and burst into tears.

Rebecca pulled her close to her as Heather sobbed. The whole time they had been walking in a different direction than the arrow they had made from the rifle. Chris put his arms around both girls.

"It's OK, sis. If there were a search party anywhere near here, we would have heard them. It's OK."

A hundred yards away near a small watering hole was a herd of fifteen elephants. The kids decided to sit down and think it over for a minute and watch the beautiful beasts. It gave them confidence and strength. They didn't feel so alone with the mother elephants taking care of their babies.

Chris wanted to inventory their food and ponder the possibility of walking out of the Serengeti during the rainy season. The thought depressed him for a minute. Then he started reviewing the survival skills he learned in scouting and began a checklist in his head. Plenty of water. Capture some food. There were two freeze-dried bags left, but they couldn't stomach them anymore. Check each person's feet for blisters and bug bites. Wash out socks and keep feet dry. The list was continuing when his thoughts were interrupted.

They heard a strange noise. A thumping sound. Both girls looked at Chris and rose slowly to their feet. They knew it was the sound of a helicopter.

"I hope that's what I think it is." Chris stood up next to Heather and Rebecca.

"They've found us," Rebecca exclaimed and dropped the backpack next to the canteen.

"I don't know what to say," Heather said. She looked around until she could see the dot in the sky that grew larger by the second.

When the helicopter got closer, they started waving and jumping up and down. Their legs ached but they didn't care. All they could think about was going home. As the helicopter got closer, it suddenly veered to the north and hovered over the herd of elephants.

"Safari 1, this is Safari 2, come over," Billy said into the radio of the Aerospatiale, hovering over the herd of elephants.

"We read you Safari 1," Mr. Hansen said into the radio.

"We have a group of friendlies about two miles west of your 20. I count twelve carrying big sticks, over."

"That's a roger, Safari 1," Mr. Hansen said. He turned to the driver of the truck. "Billy's struck gold with this herd. Says there are twelve big tuskers. Mr. Big says," and he laughed at the nickname Billy had given his boss. "Mr. Big says he only needed ten more ivory tusks and two lions to make his goal. Looks like this will be our last little hunting operation."

"Suits me. These guys you hired to do the killing make me nervous. They could kill you and me just for their jollies, if you know what I mean."

"I do. Today is their last day, too. On the planet, that is! They just don't know it yet."

They both laughed.

The Bell Jet Ranger landed back at the kopje for the fourth time and everyone got out to regroup their thoughts and stretch. Today their hopes had been dashed too much.

"Dr. MacGregor," the pilot said. Both Jack and Mavis turned around. "I'm getting some radio traffic a few miles from here. Sounds like a safari company and a game spotter talking to each other. They're talking about friendlies carrying twelve sticks. I don't make it out. Maybe we can call them and ask for their help?" the pilot asked. So fatigued from the flying, he collapsed in his seat and began to gulp down a bottle of water.

"Did you say twelve sticks by friendlies?" Daniel asked.

"Yes, that's correct," the pilot answered.

"That's poacher's code for elephants and their ivory. We cracked that code just last month."

"Poachers. We've got to go there." Jack moved as quickly as he could.

"What about Heather and Rebecca?" Mavis pleaded.

"I've got a hunch. No time to discuss it. Let's fly."

The weary pilot buckled his belt and flipped all the right switches. Soon the helicopter was in the air and moving swiftly southwest. In ten minutes they hovered over an old umbrella tree as a campfire smoldered. The dried elephant dung was still burning.

"They've been here. I knew it!" Mavis shouted over the noise of the rotors.

In a second they were back on the trail flying over another group of kopjes that whizzed by below them.

Waving their arms at the Aerospatiale, Chris, Heather, and Rebecca ran toward the group of elephants.

"Hey, we're down here, we're down here."

The roar of trucks could be heard coming from the east. Before they knew it, gunfire blasting across the serene grasslands echoed and shattered the calm. Instinctively they dove into the tall grass. Mr. Hansen's men drove among the gentle giants killing them at close range with their automatic rifles.

"Stay down. Don't look up!" Chris yelled at them. Heather and Rebecca looked up anyway and were horrified. Realizing what was happening, they began to cry. They thought they would be next. But in a few minutes, the killing was over and all the animals lay dead. Mothers and babies were slumped together.

But the tragedy was not completely over as the men quickly took chain saws and cut out the tusks. Another helicopter flew in with a large metal storage container that was ten feet long, six feet wide, and seven feet tall. The killers took the bloody tusks and, with the help of four men, pushed them over the top into the container. The killing, taking the tusks, and loading the container took less than fifteen minutes. They were efficient.

The men climbed back into the trucks while Mr. Hansen talked to Billy, who had landed nearby.

Chris was on his elbows watching the whole drama play out. He was thinking about their struggle and made a quick decision. He hoped it was the right one.

"Heather, Rebecca. Listen to me. No one is next to the container. They've got to take the ivory back to civilization. If we stay here another day, we may die. It's just that simple. The container may be our only hope."

"I'm reading your mind," Heather answered.

"Me too. I'm for it." Rebecca shook her head in agreement.

In a split second they were running with all of their strength. In about twenty seconds they were leaning up against the large container. One at a time they used the metal ladder rungs on the side to climb in. Just as Chris had ducked inside last, the second helicopter lowered a steel cable. Billy and Mr. Hansen came over and attached the cable to the harness on the container. The helicopter crew reeled in the cable until the container was twenty feet below the helicopter. Then it lifted gently off the ground and quickly gained altitude. Moving to the southeast, it was on its way.

The Wildlife Service's Bell Jet Ranger came bolting in from the northeast.

"Look, Jack, there," Daniel said. He pointed to the two helicopters and three trucks leaving the clearing.

"Oh my gosh," R.O. said as he spotted the bodies of the dead elephants scattered all around. "Mom, look at that. They're poachers."

The Wildlife Service's pilot zoomed in close to the Aerospatiale as it lifted off the ground.

"Mr. Hansen, we've got company." Billy radioed the elephant killer. "Would you mind giving them a proper greeting?"

"My pleasure. OK, everybody out."

The trucks stopped and suddenly eight automatic rifles were trained on the incoming Bell Jet Ranger.

"Hang on everybody," the pilot yelled. He pushed hard on the collective while increasing air speed.

As he banked hard to the right, seven bullets found their mark and either punctured the skin of the aircraft or lodged in the motor. Its hydraulic functions ceased. Two bullets had entered the cabin. One lodged in Daniel's backpack, but the other had creased Mavis' left ear. Blood dripped down the side of her face. She could feel it running down her neck. Jack couldn't see it from the copilot's seat, but R.O. immediately reached over and put his hand on his mother's ear. She was already holding it tight.

"Mom!"

"I'm all right. I don't feel pain anywhere else. It was just a nick."

"We're going down," was the last thing the pilot said as he worked frantically to turn off all the electrical systems to help prevent a fire when they hit the ground.

The rotary blades began to come to a halt and gently turn in reverse. They were beginning to autorotate, slowing the aircraft down. Then the earth jumped up quickly. The skids broke off and all the glass shattered as the Bell helicopter dug into the small watering hole next to the dead elephants. The shallow pond was deep enough to cushion the blow as the muddy bottom worked like an air mattress. Water rushed inside and stopped at the top of the seat cushions.

Jack looked around quickly. Everyone was alive but shaken. Daniel pulled a glass shard out of his arm. Looking beyond the killing field, Jack could see the poachers were gone and so were the two helicopters.

"Let's take it easy getting out," Jack said calmly.

Jack saw the blood on Mavis' face and neck. He turned a shade of white.

"I'm all right, Jack. Get Ryan out first," Mavis said. She reached over to help Daniel with the glass. They were all totally wet. Jet fuel from the helicopter floated on the surface of the water around them.

In a few minutes, Jack, Mavis, Daniel, Ryan, and the pilot were standing next to the dead elephants. They were horrified at the sight. Glancing back at the downed aircraft put a whole new meaning on the phrase "game wars." Their emotions were so full and strong, no one said anything. R.O. wandered off around the watering hole. Daniel and the pilot waded back to the helicopter and retrieved the packs, satchels, and the two rifles with spare ammunition from the first aid box. First aid in Africa could mean many things.

They all gathered in a makeshift circle to evaluate their situation. Ryan was on the other side of the pond nosing around, as usual. Mavis kept a keen eye on him.

"Jack. I've been meaning to tell you this. I got a package for you before I left." Daniel began to rummage through his pack.

"Two days ago? That's all right. What was it?"

"I don't know. I just put it in my backpack here, and I remembered it when I was digging through to see what got wet or broken."

Jack took the package, about the size of a shoe, and unwrapped the wet brown paper from the outside. Luckily, the next layer was shrink-wrapped plastic. Using his field knife to cut through this, he found another layer of brown paper and then another layer of plastic. Totally frustrated he finally reached a hard plastic case that had a small push button snap on the front. Pushing the button, it popped open. He smiled from ear to ear.

"Mavis, you won't believe what Daniel just handed me. My new Iridium."

She turned around and became wide eyed at the sight of the handheld telephone that was capable of calling anywhere in the world at anytime. Based on a network of satellites, the Iridium telephone could reach any active telephone network in any city or field office.

Mavis snatched the telephone out of his hand and started dialing a series of numbers. After the 26th number, she heard a ringing tone.

"Hello," said the soft female voice with a British accent.

"Hello, Mum," Mavis said.

"Is that you, Mavis?"

"Oh yes, Mum."

"When did you get back to London? I thought you were in Africa."

"I still am, Mum. I'm talking on Jack's new telephone. We can call anywhere with it. I just wanted to hear your voice. Got to go, Mum."

"Call me tomorrow?" her mother asked.

"I will, Mum. Good-bye."

"Good-bye dear," her mother said and hung up.

Mavis handed the telephone to Jack and gave him a stern look.

"Now get us out of here," she said and walked away.

R.O. was yelling and running toward them. They all turned around as he coasted up to them out of breath. He had Jack's satchel in his hand.

"They were here. This is your satchel, Dad."

In a couple of minutes, they were standing around the spot where Chris and the girls had dropped the packs and witnessed the killing.

"They're with the poachers. That's for certain," Daniel said.

"I agree," Jack said.

"But what do we do now?" R.O. asked the adults, hoping for an answer.

"I know who we can call," Mavis said. She took the Iridium telephone from Jack.

They rested in a dry grassy spot away from the dead elephants and hoped no lions would arrive too soon. An hour later, five military helicopters arrived from the south and landed.

As the Tanzanian general walked toward the beleaguered searchers, Mavis leaned over to Jack and spoke.

"Here comes the calvary. It's time to kick butt!"

A roar of a lion could be heard nearby.

"And it's time to go," Jack added.

# 16

# Kilimanjaro

---

Heather and Rebecca pushed up against the inside wall of the container. Chris tried to move a couple of ivory tusks but had no luck. They were wedged in tightly and each tusk weighed as much as he did. He finally gave up and sidled in against the girls and looked up toward the helicopter. There was no lid or top. But the container had been painted black, so Chris and the girls blended in with their mud pan coating.

"Heather," Rebecca shouted over the noise of the wind and the helicopter, "your hair is too bright."

"She's right, Heather. You stand out too much up against the black. You could sit out there on the ivory and blend in, but I wouldn't recommend it." Chris attempted a little humor. Finally Heather smiled.

"I know what I have to do."

She reached out to one of the elephant tusks that she was leaning against and rubbed her hand over the bloody flesh at the end. She then wiped the blood on her hair. After the first stroke it became easier. She had already become accustomed to the worst odors on earth. This was nothing new. After a few strokes, her hair was reddish black from the blood that had begun to dry in the wind. Their clothes, already full of dirt and mud, were now coated with fresh blood. If they didn't move, no one from the helicopter above would be able to see them.

They sat with their backs against the wall, their feet propped up on the stack of ivory tusks. Their days on the Serengeti had prepared them for this moment. They held hands and leaned on each other. The wind buffeted around their faces. It was warm at first and felt good. But the longer the helicopter was in the air, the cooler the air became. Soon they were clutching each other and shivering.

"I don't know how much longer I can take this cold wind," shouted Rebecca over the noise.

"Me either," Heather said.

"We must be at a very high altitude," Chris said. His teeth began to chatter. "We've got to hold on. Helicopters can't fly at high altitudes very long. We've got to come down soon."

Each girl nodded. They were too cold to cry. The mud on their skin had contracted and began to crack. They looked like they were made of clay.

But just when they felt their teeth were going to shatter, they sensed the helicopter descending. The wind whipping around their faces began to slow down.

They sat perfectly still until suddenly the container hit the earth and jarred them apart, bouncing two large tusks over toward them. Pushing with their legs with all of their strength, they kept the tusks from rolling on top of them. They saw the cable being lowered from above and then there was someone standing on the side of the container just above them. Chris, Heather, and Rebecca didn't move. They laid flat against the tusks and the metal sides.

The man unfastened the harness and jumped back onto the ground. The helicopter quickly gained altitude and disappeared from their view. The chopping noise was gone in a couple of minutes. There was silence outside until they heard a vehicle of some kind fire up, shift into gear and drive away.

Slowly they stood up. They knew not to speak. Eye contact was enough for Chris to tell them to stay put while he checked out their situation. Chris reached the top of the container. He inched up slowly until he could peer over the top. He waved the girls up behind him as he crawled over the side and out of their sight. The two young girls, who had already seen a lot, weren't prepared for what they now viewed. Around them were dozens upon dozens of storage containers. They could tell from the dried blood on the sides that they contained either elephant ivory or dead animal parts. There was no sign of life, especially human.

"Rebecca, look behind us," Heather said. Chris was on the ground walking around the container.

The two girls emerged from the container and sat on the cold metal side. In awe they viewed the snowcapped summit of Mt. Kilimanjaro. They were only 5,000 feet down from it, at the 14,000-foot mark. Climbing down from the container, they walked around the frigid abandoned camp. They agreed they had counted forty-seven black containers. Peeking inside some of them, they found most contained elephant ivory. Many of the others contained the frozen carcasses of lions, leopards, and cheetahs. They walked toward the upper edge of the storage grounds where they spied a toolshed about half the size of one of the containers. When they finally reached it, they noticed it had a large padlock on it.

"If it's locked, then it must have something valuable inside. Right?" Rebecca said. Chris picked up a large rock.

"Makes sense to me," Heather said rubbing her arms trying to get warm.

Chris wasn't much for small talk. He simply started hammering the lock. It didn't give. Searching around

the area he found a small metal rod and a two-foot
chain. He brought both back to the locked door. Chris
tried to use the metal rod as a pry bar. Finally the screws
in the frame began to give way while the lock never
budged. After thirty minutes, he was warming up with
a sweat that felt good in the mountain air. The hinges
gave way and the door swung open, hanging only from
the padlock.

"Finally," they all three said in unison.

Once inside the small building, they found a box of
hand tools and a large brown nylon duffel bag. Opening
the bag, they couldn't believe their eyes. Insulated coveralls. Five pair. Without saying a word, they pulled
them out and crawled inside them. Heather reached
into the tool box and retrieved a pair of tin snips. She
started cutting the legs and arms on Rebecca's coveralls.
Then Rebecca did the same for her. Standing and looking at each other, they slowly began to smile. They
started to give their jubilant high five but when their
hands touched they stopped and squeezed tight. Chris
was rummaging around looking for anything they could
use.

"Let's go home," Rebecca said. They left the toolshed. Each girl had stuffed a couple of screwdrivers in
their pockets. Chris found a small ball pin hammer and
did the same.

"Good idea. Let's head for the road. But we've got to
listen all the time. Those guys are definitely going to
come back to this place. Either by chopper or truck."
Chris led the way out of the shed.

As they reached the road that descended the 14,000
feet down the mountain, they stopped and looked across
the broad expanse of East Africa. They could see the
patchwork of farms blending into the mosaic colors of
the wild bush. To the east they could see a ribbon of blue
on the horizon, the Indian Ocean.

"This is so awesome," Heather said.

"I know. No one will believe this either," Rebecca replied.

"Rebecca," Chris said as they walked along in their insulated coveralls, "do you still have that butane lighter of yours?" They were finally enjoying the brisk light air of the mountain.

"I had forgotten all about it." Rebecca unzipped her coveralls and reached inside to her cargo shorts and padded around. A smile came on her face. In a few seconds she was pulling a fist out of the coveralls. She opened her hand and in it was the unusually fat lighter. Scavenging around they found a stick that looked like it belonged to a crate. They surmised it had probably fallen off a truck. Flipping the top back off of the lighter, Chris quickly rotated the wheel with his thumb and the flame appeared. Heather held the stick steady. In a few seconds a large yellow flame appeared on the end of the stick.

Heather leaned down carefully and put the stick on the ground. They all crouched around the small flame and began to warm their hands. Their faces began to soften as a sense of well being came over them.

"I never thought a little stick on fire would mean so much." Heather looked into Rebecca's eyes.

"Me either. Now I know why my dad always told me to carry the lighter with me whenever we went into the bush. I remember I forgot it one time and he grounded me for two weeks."

"Two weeks!" Heather replied.

"That's right. And man did I always have it with me after that. Just think. We used it to light our fire yesterday. I am so glad I didn't put it in the backpack."

"That's for sure."

Chris had learned to listen to the girls. He finally got to where he enjoyed it.

Soon the flame had died and the stick had been reduced to charcoal. The girls kicked dirt on it with their boots so no one would notice it coming up the road.

"Well, it looks like it will be a long walk down. With no food, we'll just make it by tomorrow. There are several villages at the base." Chris walked ahead of them a few feet.

Rebecca reached out and took Heather's hand as they began their trek down Mt. Kilimanjaro. Little did they know that on the opposite side of the mountain a storm was forming and snow was beginning to fall. Before the day's light would be gone, they would again be fighting for their lives.

"General, is there any way your radar can track the poachers?" Jack asked.

"We have limited capabilities. So we must focus those toward the west, Burundi and Rwanda, from where most of the wars have spread. We are concerned about poachers but at this moment we have to think about our national security."

"What about radio-tracking devices. Do you have any equipment we can use," Daniel asked. Jack had an inquisitive look on his face after hearing Daniel's question.

"What are you thinking about, Daniel? The lion collars can't be remotely activated. Even if they still have them, they are useless to us."

"I'm not thinking about collars. It's a long shot. I gave Rebecca a special made lighter last year. She has orders to carry it with her at all times in the bush. I don't know why I didn't think of it earlier. I could kick myself."

"What's the lighter have to do with all of this?" Jack asked impatiently.

"I had our electronics department implant an experimental microchip in the base. They built a special case for it and everything. It is thermal powered. All you have to do is strike the lighter once a day and the heat transfers and powers the fuel cell that directs the energy to the radio transmitter. I don't know exactly how it works, but we tried it out on two rangers before they made a duplicate for me. Then I gave it to Rebecca."

"What kind of monitoring equipment do we need?"

"A basic Mark IV receiver would work. The transmitter works on a special frequency that I knew only the Rangers would be using. We've got several back in Nairobi."

Jack turned toward the general. Mavis was hanging on to every word and never let go of Jack's arm, partly to help him stand up and partly for hope.

"General. You heard what he just said. Can you help us?"

"We have several we use in the military. I can have one here in a few hours, maybe as early as in the morning." It was getting late in the day.

"That won't do. We need help now. In two hours, those kids could be gone forever." Mavis bit her lip to fight back the tears. She reflexively reached up and stroked her bandaged ear. It was throbbing.

Jack limped away from the crowd.

"Think! Think!" he said to himself.

He suddenly turned to R.O.

"R.O, what day is it?"

"It's Thursday, July 17."

"When did the Atlantis lift off?"

"On Sunday, Dad. Why?"

Jack grabbed the Iridium telephone that was hanging around his neck on a strap and starting dialing. In a few minutes a voice could be heard. It was a female with a strong Texas twang.

"Hello."

"Julie, this is Jack MacGregor."

"Hi Jack, I thought you were in Africa."

"I am..."

"Now don't tell me how it is we are able to be talking to each other like this," Julie said. "I never ask Ronnie how he gets in touch with me. I just accept that astronauts and scientists can do just about anything."

"That's flattering Julie, but I need your help. Is Ron still in orbit?"

"Oh, yes. This is one of those long missions. A CIA satellite and all that spook stuff. They usually take a few extra days. I think they play with the satellite for awhile before they kick it out of the cargo bay." It was no big deal to this veteran NASA wife.

"I need a big favor, Julie. Chris and Heather are in trouble. They're missing."

"Oh, no. Are Mavis and Ryan OK?"

"Yes. I need for you to get a message to Ron. When's the next family call from the Atlantis?"

"Well you're in luck, Jack. I'm expecting his call any minute. In fact, I thought your ring was from Mission Control."

"Julie. Heather's life is in danger. I need to talk to Ron. This is my number on this Iridium telephone." Jack read off the seventeen number code with letters, pound and star signs all mixed in.

"I don't know Jack. I'll try. But you know the government when it comes to personal stuff. I mean, politicians get away with just about everything. But for the rest of us, it doesn't matter whether you mop floors or drive space shuttles, you're just another hired hand."

"I'm hoping and praying this will work, Julie."

"Give Mavis my love. Good-bye."

Everyone had been gathered around listening to the one-sided conversation. Mavis wiped a tear from her eye. R.O. sat quietly holding the double barrel rifle that Daniel had retrieved from the downed helicopter.

"Are you talking about the space shuttle Atlantis?" the general asked politely.

"Yes. A classmate of mine from college is the commander of this flight. It's his fourth time in space on shuttles. I don't know if they can help, but they control a lot of satellite equipment."

The Iridium telephone started beeping. It had only been five minutes. All were stunned and fully expected that bad news would be coming from Houston.

"Jack MacGregor," he spoke into the telephone.

"Jack, ole buddy, what's happened to that cute little girl of yours?" Colonel Ron Springer, USAF, Commander of the United States Space Shuttle Atlantis said. The Atlantis was cruising at an altitude of 145 miles at a speed of 17,500 miles an hour.

"Ron. I can't believe it. Julie got through."

"Believe it cause here I am. Now what can I do to help?"

"Ron, Chris and Heather are lost in Tanzania. With them is another fourteen year old who is carrying a radio transmitter that can be picked up by a tracking device similar to the ones found in the Nimbus series satellites. You know, the early ones used to track big animals. Our problem is that we can't get the smaller version, the Mark IV receiver, to our location for about twelve hours...."

"So you want me to turn on the big eye in the sky and take a peek, right?"

"That's right."

"Well you know, officially I can't do. But if I remember correctly, during the Rwanda-Burundi War, the CIA watched the gorillas at the Fossey Primate Center on top of a mountain just west of your location. They kept track of them in case the rebels moved toward the mountain. If necessary, they could send in a military force to protect them. They used a nice little geosynchronous satellite over that part of Africa. Problem is, Langley changed its orbit so now it looks straight down at the Middle East. But that's all I can tell you."

"That's right about the gorillas. I'm surprised you remembered," Jack said.

"Surprised? Ole buddy, that was my idea! You forget I was a zoology major before I got caught up in all of this space tech stuff. Tell you what. You sit tight and I'll make a few calls. Be back soon."

Jack heard a click and then dead air.

"What's he doing?" Mavis asked.

"He said he would call us back."

It was getting late in the afternoon when Chris, Heather, and Rebecca decided to stop and rest. They convinced each other it was safe to build a fire. They hadn't seen anyone all day. Even in the dampness and cold, the meager collection of sticks caught fire. The girls were too tired to talk. Their tummies growled from hunger and their feet were freezing. The excitement and stress of the day finally caught up with them and they fell asleep, wrapped up in each others' arms. Chris, curled up on the opposite side of the campfire. He decided it was time to take a nature break. He walked down the side of the mountain a few yards.

The frigid air fell on the trio from the summit above. The powerful hand of nature on Mt. Kilimanjaro was gripping their delicate bodies. Even in their sleep, the girls' senses were still very much alert. Their minds had never let go of the events of the past few days. Total exhaustion and unconsciousness were looming at the door but they weren't there yet. They felt someone's presence and simultaneously opened their eyes to find a man standing over them with an Chinese made AK-47 automatic assault rifle in his hands.

"Good evening ladies. Aren't you a long way from home?" Mr. Hansen said in his strong South African accent. In a few minutes they were tied together by two other men and literally thrown into the back of the truck. Chris was crouched behind a large boulder. He had no weapon and if he rushed in they would all probably be killed. He watched the truck drive up the road toward the container camp.

"Who are they?" the driver asked Mr. Hansen.

"I haven't the foggiest. But two girls alone on Mt. Kilimanjaro is not a good sign. We can't afford to leave them behind. And we can't afford to get rid of them just yet. We'll transport them back up to the storage camp. The choppers start hauling right away. By morning, all the containers will be on board a Malaysian cargo ship headed to India. And you and I will be millionaires." Hansen laughed and picked up a cell phone.

"Yes," the voice at the other end said.

"We got the last load here, sir," Mr. Hansen said to Mr. Big. "The choppers dropped me at the base of the mountain so I could ride up with the men."

"Excellent. Our villa on the coast awaits us, Mr. Hansen. You have done a wonderful job. And how many sticks did we bring in this time?"

"Twenty-four, sir."

"Twenty-four! How exciting. We only needed eight more. Mr. Hansen, the other sixteen are yours to do with whatever you wish."

"But, sir, that's nearly $200,000 worth of ivory. I couldn't."

"You can and you will. See you on board in the morning."

The truck arrived at the storage compound and two men carried the girls to the toolshed. They noticed the ripped hinges but neither seemed curious or cautious. Neither had been to the camp in over a month. They figured someone had lost the key to the lock and simply ripped the hinges off.

"A few days in the shed and they won't have any stories to tell. We'll be long gone by then." Mr. Hansen shoved the door closed.

Heather and Rebecca lay on the floor not believing their change of fortune. Luckily for them they still had on their insulated coveralls.

The Iridium telephone began beeping. The noise broke the somber silence of the group. Only R.O. had managed to keep himself entertained by flipping insects at a frog he had spotted. The frog's tongue would pop out and grab them up and pull them in like an efficient fishing line system.

"Jack here."

"Hey, Jack. Good news. We need to test this electronic toy we're hauling, and I've got the OK to open her eyes for one hour. We are over the coast of Brazil. With a slight course adjustment, we will be looking right down on you in exactly twenty-one minutes and fourteen seconds. You realize that we will be reading every radio telemetry device across East Africa. Can you help us pinpoint the area?"

"Yes, we are talking four degrees south latitude and thirty-six degrees east longitude. A twenty-mile radius would work," Jack replied.

"Got it. It's already programmed into the computers. Stay by the phone. We'll call you back in twenty minutes. Hey, and tell Mavis, Julie and I are praying for you all."

"Thanks Ron." Jack once again heard the click and the dead air.

The Aerospatiale helicopter came in low, struggling with the thin air on Mt. Kilimanjaro. Only its specially modified turbo jets enabled it to fly where most helicopters couldn't go. Usually only high-altitude military choppers could reach that altitude.

"Mr. Hansen," Billy spoke into the radio.

"Go ahead," Mr. Hansen said.

"We've been ordered to start the transport before dark. There's a snowstorm forming on the mountain. We could be frozen in by midnight," Billy said.

"But I just talked to Mr. Big, as you call him," Hansen replied quickly.

"Mr. Big doesn't control the shots, Mr. Hansen. His boss said start now. That's who I have worked for all along. Hook me up to the first container. There will be four more choppers here in a few minutes. We should have them all moved by midnight."

"OK. I hope you know what you're doing. You could get us both killed," Mr. Hansen said.

"Only if you don't do what I tell you to do," Billy replied.

Heather and Rebecca lay huddled on the cold ground. Only a small stream of light from the gray sky leaked in through the broken door.

The Iridium telephone started beeping.

"Ron," Jack said quickly. His anxiety was building. Mavis held onto his right arm.

"That's me. And I've got some coordinates for you. Are you ready?"

"Yes." Jack had retrieved a pen and a soiled piece of paper from his nasty dirty satchel. "Go ahead."

"My analysts tell me there are at least thirty signals from the Serengeti region alone. But there are only four to the southeast of your location closer to the coordinates you gave us. One is at a place called Tsavo, two at Lake Amboseli, and another near the summit of Mt. Kilimanjaro. I can't tell you how I know this, but the Tsavo signal is coming from the train depot. Then there are two boats sitting on Lake Amboseli. The Kilimanjaro location is a camp of some kind. Jack?"

"Yes, Ron."

"One of my mission specialists has two teenage girls and a son in college. She took this a little further than you asked. Call it a mom's prerogative. She says that there are three or four dozen storage containers, a toolshed, and a truck on ground right now. Some of the containers have what looks like long curved sticks in them." Jack raised his eyebrows at the detail he was getting. There was more to this space shuttle mission than just another defense satellite. "The spooks, I mean analysts, also picked up the heat signature of a large helicopter, either military or a civilian like a Sikorsky or modified Aerospatiale. Langley says there are two more trucks headed up the road toward the summit. They estimated about six or eight men. They are carrying weapons, Jack."

Jack's heart leaped.

"That's it. It's Mt. Kilimanjaro. What's the exact location?"

"It's the eastern slope, about five thousand feet from the summit. The road winds down the gradual slope all the way to the base. There's a village at the base. I hope this helps buddy," Ron said in a positive tone.

"You just don't know how much. We're on our way now. I love you man." Jack started to click off the telephone but heard Ron's voice.

"Go get 'em, Jack. I'm just wishing this was my old F-14 Tomcat I was flying, and I would take care of them for you."

"Thanks for the thought. See ya." Jack clicked off the Iridium telephone.

One hundred forty-five miles above the earth Colonel Ron Springer flipped the toggle switch on the massive console. Looking through the window in front of him, he could see the Indian Ocean ahead as the great dark continent, Africa, passed under his wings. He said a prayer as the space shuttle Atlantis sped toward Australia just twenty minutes and ten seconds away.

# 17

# Chris

"Dr. MacGregor, it's my turn to help." The general walked over to them. "My helicopters are all equipped to reach the summit of Kilimanjaro. I can send one to the top and the other two can start at the village and fly up the road." Jack limped around thinking.

"Thanks, General. All right, this is the plan. Daniel, you go to the top. I can't walk fast, and I would just be in the way. Mavis and R.O. will start at 8,000 feet and fly up the road. I will fly up the road from the base of Kilimanjaro. Let's do it." As they all walked toward the helicopters, Jack stopped.

"Daniel. Take your .375 double rifle along with you. I have a hunch you may encounter someone first," Jack said.

"Already loaded, with plenty of spare ammunition," Daniel said.

They were soon divided up except for the pilot of the Bell Jet Ranger. Another Wildlife Service helicopter was on its way to pick him up. He was too tired to go anywhere.

They all knew that darkness would be their enemy. Only two hours of daylight remained, and the pilots had learned about the storm forming around the summit of Kilimanjaro. Even though it was the middle of July, the storms knew no seasons at the equator. A snowstorm in July might as well have been a snowstorm in December in Colorado. There was only one difference. The warmer air at the lower altitudes would turn the snow to rain that would eventually feed the dry springs and creeks of East Africa.

With an hour of daylight to spare, the Tanzanian Air Force helicopters began to approach the majestic crown jewel of Africa. Not discovered until nearly the 19th century, most explorers doubted that a snowcapped mountain could exist on the equator. Full of superstition and tribal folklore, Kilimanjaro was the remaining sentinel in a row of ancient mountains that at one time dotted the dark continent.

"We're on the road at the base of the mountain, setting down next to the village. Do you copy, Daniel?"

"We read you, Jack. We're pushing higher up the mountain, just passing 10,000 feet. I saw Mavis' chopper peal off at 8,000 feet right on top of the road. The storm is beginning to boil at the summit."

Meanwhile, Mavis and R.O. were in the general's helicopter, which had landed in the middle of the mining road at 8,000 feet. The pilot, the general, and two of his men, all armed with M-16 automatic rifles, jumped out and readied themselves for an assault. Mavis and R.O. walked over to the edge of the road and looked down on the plains below. It was an overwhelming sight.

"We just passed 14,000 feet," Daniel spoke into the radio.

Out of nervousness, Daniel opened the breech on the .375 double rifle and double checked it. He felt in the left pocket of his jacket and counted eight of the ten rounds he had gotten from the pilot of one of the helicopters. He had four more in his right pocket. The pilot was a big game hunter and had a similar gun mounted in the gun rack of the helicopter.

"We're closing at 17,000 feet and sucking a lot of thin air. But we're still going up," the pilot said over the intercom. The two soldiers who sat next to Daniel fixed the magazine of the M-16 and set the switch to automatic. "There's the road. We've got snow coming down."

Daniel could see the road, which was lightly dusted with the white of the snow. It was definitely a weird site for being in equatorial Africa. He felt the butterflies in his stomach. But he kept thinking about his beautiful daughter Rebecca. "Baby, hang tight. I'm coming to get you," he said to himself.

As the helicopter struggled to make a turn around a sharp edge of the mountain, three trucks came into view. Ahead he could see the container camp.

"Got a chopper coming in from the east." The pilot radioed to the general down the mountain. "That's a roger, will pull off and wait."

"No!" shouted Daniel. "You'll put me down there now. My baby's down there. Do you understand me?"

"I have orders, sir."

"I don't care about your orders," Daniel interrupted.

"You'll be on your own," the pilot replied.

"I understand. Just do it!"

The black Tanzanian Air Force chopper pushed harder and went into the camp a full half mile ahead of the trucks, which were now lumbering to the top. Hovering over the ground, Daniel leapt out of the now open side door and held tightly to the double rifle. He slipped on the light snow but caught his balance quickly. As he turned and faced the chopper, one of the soldiers tossed him an automatic rifle. Daniel didn't have time to thank him. He slung the M-16 over his shoulder. He felt better armed with more firepower against a heavily-armed enemy, the elephant killers. He could hear the trucks coming up the road.

The helicopter pulled up and flew over the side of the mountain, disappearing down the barren slope out of sight of the incoming trucks. Just as the trucks entered the camp, Daniel ran behind one of the containers holding ivory. In a couple of minutes over a dozen men were bounding out of the three trucks. They began adjusting the cables and harnesses on the containers. Two huge helicopters appeared over the road and hovered while two containers were hooked to the long cables hanging below them. In a few minutes each helicopter was transporting two containers of ivory and animal carcasses off the mountain.

As they left, two more large Aerospatiale helicopters appeared and began the same routine.

Daniel worked his way from one container to the next until he was up against a solid wall of rock going straight up toward the summit. More snow was falling. He jumped when he heard a voice behind him.

"Daniel," Chris said in a hushed voice.

Daniel turned around brandishing the rifle. He immediately lowered it when he recognized Chris. They hugged quickly.

"Where are the girls?" Daniel had a frantic look on his face.

"They're in the toolshed. I was just trying to figure out a plan when I saw the Tanzanian helicopter. I couldn't tell whether it was friend or foe. Not until I saw you just now," Chris whispered.

"They work fast. At this rate, all of these containers will be gone in a few hours." Daniel looked around.

"Depending on the turn around. I mean, who knows where they are going?"

Chris and Daniel decided to move toward the toolshed. They walked slowly along the stone wall of the cliff until they could see the elephant killers, who were now building a fire in an old oil barrel. One of the men pulled a basket from the back of the truck and started passing around food. It looked like long loaves of bread.

"Look over there," Chris whispered to Daniel.

The snow had accumulated on Daniel's dark hair and given him a white cap. Chris gently dusted the wet particles from his head. Daniel did the same.

"There it is. Let's go while they're eating between helicopter stops."

Slowly they inched their way over to the building until it was only ten feet away. The containers blocked the view of the killers from the building. Chris moved softly and quickly to the broken door. He touched it and the metal creaked. He stopped. The killers looked his direction but soon attributed the noise to the wind. Chris reached out and grabbed the door firmly. Daniel appeared and together they pivoted the door with the single lock acting as a hinge.

The sight in front of them was nearly too much to bear. Heather and Rebecca lay quietly on the floor huddled together and not moving. They had been tied together around their feet and chests to make one bundle.

Daniel rushed over and touched their faces. His hands were freezing but he could still feel some warmth in their faces. Heather opened her eyes and started to speak. Chris arrived just in time to clamp his hand over her mouth. He put his mouth next to her ear.

"Heather. You're safe. But the bad guys are outside. Don't talk."

She nodded her head. Rebecca was coming around. The cold and the lack of food had drained the girls of their energy. Soon they were both coherent and sat up as Daniel took his field knife from his pocket and cut the ropes. As they got to their feet, they heard a noise outside as two of the men walked toward the toolshed. Chris pulled up the rifle just as one of the men stepped through the broken doorway. The man ducked quickly outside and in Swahili shouted a warning to the other elephant killers.

"Out fast." Daniel helped the girls through the doorway and alongside two of the storage containers.

A hail of bullets followed in just a few seconds and ripped hundreds of holes in the metal sheeting of the storage building. Chris led the way as they ran down alongside the rock wall toward the edge of the camp and the side of the mountain. The killers had broken into the shed expecting to find bodies. Instead they were greeted with nothing but holes in the walls.

"Fan out. Find them and kill them," the leader of the group shouted in Swahili.

From the edge of the camp, Daniel, Chris, Heather, and Rebecca regrouped. Heather and Rebecca couldn't stop hugging everyone. Chris held Heather tight and rubbed his hand through her nasty matted hair. The odor was appalling but he didn't care.

"OK. Let's work our way down to the last truck on the road. We will disable the other two and take the last one. They won't know what hit them if we move fast. In ten minutes of moving from behind one container after another, they had reached the clearing. Every minute or so they could hear an automatic rifle pop off at a ghostly target where they once had been standing. The killers were now skulking through the vast expanse of the container camp. The snow continued to fall. Darkness was arriving quickly.

In one swift moment, Daniel ran toward the last truck. The girls, operating on adrenaline, kept up. Chris pulled up the rear, constantly watching for any sign of the killers. They reached the truck in a few seconds. Daniel hoisted Heather and Rebecca into the back and ran to position himself behind the wheel. The keys were still there. He turned over the ignition, and it wound to a start. As the old truck belched out a cloud of blue smoke, Chris could hear the killers shouting to each other in Swahili.

Standing in front of the other two trucks, Chris took aim with the .375 double rifle and fired a round into the gas tank. The rifle kicked hard but he barely noticed it as the huge truck exploded in a ball of fire. The force of the explosion knocked him on his back. Scrambling to his feet, he took aim on the second truck. This time he knelt on the ground as he pulled the trigger. A second explosion ensued.

Chris ran toward the truck that Daniel had started as the first of the killers arrived in the clearing and leveled his automatic weapon to fire. Daniel pointed the M-16 out of the window of the truck and fired. With the truck moving, it was a bad shot. But the noise of the six bullets ricocheting off the metal containers was enough to send the killer diving to the ground. By the time the killer got back up, Chris was hanging onto the running board as the truck disappeared down the hill. Heather and Rebecca crawled through the back window of the truck into the cab. Daniel found the heater button and in less than a mile, the cabin of the truck had begun to warm. They chugged down the snowy slope.

With Chris inside, all seemed well, for now.

# 18

# Angel of Africa

The heavy snowfall coated the road with three inches of snow in one hour. The old truck, which carried Daniel, Rebecca, Chris, and Heather, chugged along at a slow speed until the gas needle read empty. Darkness had seized all of Africa.

"Tango Zulu One calling all Tanzanian Air Force units."

"We read you, General," came the response from the other two helicopters.

"The storm is too great. Bring all aircraft down from the mountain. Meet me at the air depot in Moshi."

"Roger," the pilots radioed back.

After a major scene with Mavis, she and R.O. were dropped off at the base of Kilimanjaro where they met Jack. The helicopters flew on to Moshi to refuel. The general promised they would be back at the first sign of daylight.

The MacGregors, disheartened and distraught, found a small store that stocked an unusual variety of European and local groceries. The snowstorm had turned into a powerful rain in the village. They walked into the store, found a few chairs next to a cooler, and sat down.

Too tired to talk, they simply drank the water and soda Jack bought. They munched on anything that resembled the food they would eat back home. Jack ate some chips and fumbled with his Iridium telephone.

"What did the pilot tell you about dropping Daniel off on the mountain?" Mavis asked for the fourth time.

"The same as I mentioned before, honey. He didn't see anything."

And so went their conversation during the night. The old couple who owned the store let them stay after they locked the doors.

Back on Kilimanjaro, the truck was becoming coated with a layer of snow as it sat in the middle of the road just ten miles from the container camp.

"Out of gas," Daniel said solemnly.

"The snow has picked up so we better sit tight in here till the storm breaks."

The girls cuddled up against their dad and brother. They were happy to be with a member of their family and not alone anymore. The night passed quickly and the cold invaded the once warm cabin. By daybreak, the mountain adventurers were shivering. The cold penetrated their bones, muscles, and joints. Their eyes were droopy from fatigue.

Back at the village at the base of Kilimanjaro, the general had kept his word and appeared with four helicopters . Within a few minutes of the sun's first rays, the MacGregors were loaded up and each helicopter was assigned a grid to check. A huge Sikorsky troop transport helicopter had arrived and was ordered to the container camp to secure the area. Like a big grasshopper with a belly stuffed full of food, it launched and began climbing methodically toward the summit. The twenty Tanzanian marines readied their weapons. But before they got there, the Aerospatiale had already made four early morning trips from the mountain to the cargo ship. Only three containers of ivory remained.

The container operation had begun anew. The remainder of the dead lion carcasses were to be left behind. As Billy cleared the edge of the mountain, he steered the chopper down the mountain slope toward the base. Two containers packed with the tusks of the gentle giants dangled on a steel cable and harness below him. Rock music blared over his CD player. As he reached to change a track on the CD, he jumped from a sudden motion above him and the roar of the twin-engine plane.

"Whew, Daddy," yelled the grizzled old pilot in the Rios boots and Resistol Diamond Horseshoe hat. "I've been waitin' for you to reappear and that you did. Thank you very much," said the old cowboy sporting the World War II aviator wings on his leather vest. He reached out and pushed the button on his CD player. George Strait's voice rang out from the four stereo speakers in the cabin of the Cessna 310 Sky Knight. Making a broad turn in the sky, he knew he had the advantage because of the helicopter's cargo. So he circled overhead out of sight and decided to follow him.

"You old fool," Billy yelled to no avail. Then he lost sight of the Cessna. Scanning the sky and horizon, the twin engine plane was nowhere to be found. He chalked it up to a near collision and turned the music back up.

"Safari 1 to base. Do you copy?"

"We copy, Billy. Bring her on in. The last load's right behind you."

"Roger," Billy replied. After ten minutes of the Indian Ocean beneath him, he spotted the Malaysian cargo ship.

Cruising in smoothly, he hovered over the aft hold as he lowered the cable. The sailors maneuvered the containers into the hold and released the harness. As Billy moved the Aerospatiale out of the way, he could see the other helicopter with the last container coming in over the blue water. In a few minutes the last of the ivory was on board.

"Mission completed," came the voice of Mr. Big over the radio. "Now you two boys head back to Nairobi. Drop the choppers off where they belong and catch the next flight to Delhi."

"We copy," was Billy's reply. He was a bit nervous to separate himself from so much that belonged to him.

"Roger, boss," was the other pilot's response.

But when they reached the coast of Kenya, they had a surprise waiting for them. Fighter jets with markings of the Kenya Air Force screamed by rattling every piece of glass on the choppers.

"Aerospatiale. You are instructed to follow us to Mombasa and land at the airport. Do you copy? Do not take evasive action or you will regret it."

"The heck with you," shouted Billy as the jets screamed by for the second time. He pulled back on the collective, increased the throttle, and pushed forward on the cyclic. At a high rate of speed, the Aerospatiale dropped down to hug the surface of the ocean in a moronic attempt to allude the jets.

Within seconds, an air-to-air missile dropped from the wing of one of the fighters and locked in on the Aerospatiale. Billy never knew what hit him as the helicopter evaporated into millions of tiny pieces.

"I will comply, I will comply," shouted the other helicopter pilot over the radio as he kept a steady altitude and heading for Mombasa.

"*Adios, amigos,*" the old cowboy pilot said as he banked the Cessna 310 back toward Kilimanjaro. "This is High Plains Drifter, go ahead."

"We've got you loud and clear," spoke the general into the radio. "Thanks for the tip on the choppers and the cargo ship. We've handed it over to the Kenya Navy. They're on their way now since the Malaysian ship is out of Tanzanian jurisdiction."

"How can I help you? I've been listening to all the air

traffic about the lost kids on Kilimanjaro," the cowboy pilot said.

"I've got four helos at different spots on the summit road. If you want to pick an area and start looking, then it is much appreciated."

"Roger and out." He had Kilimanjaro dead ahead. He pulled back on the controls and was soon at 14,000 feet. The rocket conversion Cessna 310 Sky Knight bolted across the sky and in a few minutes he was buzzing the container camp. He could see the Tanzanian Marines rounding up the elephant killers. A few of the killers lay dead on the ground. A couple of flashes of light told him a small firefight was still going on. But he knew the Tanzanians would have no problem with these thugs.

Banking wide, he found the summit road and followed it gently spiraling down the mountain. Just as he passed by a small ridge, he could see smoke.

"See, Dad. My lighter has paid off four times in one trip. I've carried it at least a hundred times and never needed it." Rebecca attempted a weak smile. She was weary but her heart was full.

Chris, Daniel, Heather, and Rebecca were warming themselves next to a fire that they had started from the canvas covering on the bed of the truck. A wooden side rail they had torn off the truck added to the heat and the smoke.

As the old cowboy aviator spotted the smoke, he pushed the controls down and passed over their heads at two hundred feet with a loud roar. Dipping his wings right and left, he signaled that he had spotted them. He flipped the toggle switch for the radio on his overhead console and gave the coordinates to the general.

Within twenty minutes a military helicopter was landing on the road to pick up the foursome. It just happened to be the helicopter that Mavis was in.

Again she bounded out of the chopper while the rotor blades were still spinning. R.O. was right behind her. As she reached Heather, Heather felt her back pop as her mother squeezed her.

"Mom. Don't break me in half. I'm glad to see you, too."

Mavis had no more tears. Only a smile from ear to ear greeted her daughter. She turned to R.O. who unexpectedly got all of her attention.

"What?" he said with a surprised look on his face.

"Listen to me carefully because I love you very much." Heather and Chris gave each other a strange look. "We lost Chris in Cayman. We lost Heather and Chris in Africa. So listen up, R.O., I can't take anymore of this. So if you get lost, I'm not coming after you. You got that mister?" Tears flowed from her eyes as all three kids hugged their mom.

Rebecca and her dad were still hugging as they watched the MacGregor reunion.

"Heather. What is that nasty junk in your hair? Whew! It smells dead!" R.O said. He smiled at his sister. "I found one of your scrunchies in my pocket. Do you want it?"

Heather took the yellow scrunchie, the color she preferred, and pulled back her matted hair. It was stiff and sticky. She slipped the scrunchie around the end and pulled it through.

"Thanks R.O." She leaned over and hugged him.

He kissed her on the cheek. Something he never does.

# Epilogue

The French restaurant was situated on a broad avenue. Despite the fact that the stiff-necked British had built the avenue, it resembled a quaint spot on the Rue Mars in Paris. It was the prettiest street in Nairobi with beautiful trees lining both sides. Tourists and the elite of Kenya wandered through quaint shops that had famous labels and big price tags. It was still only a few blocks from the misery of the slums of Africa.

But for now, the MacGregors and the Okeres sat comfortably in heavily padded leather chairs and dined on a variety of French pastries, croissants, and crepes.

Chris, Heather, and Rebecca's rebirth into civilization had occurred two days earlier, but they still hadn't gotten their fill of eating. They vowed never again to put a freeze-dried food to their lips. Daniel, Mavis, R.O., and Jack weren't much better off.

"Heather, I've never seen anyone stuff so much food in their mouth at one time. That is awesome." R.O. goaded his sister.

She just smiled back showing a mouth full of food.

"Cool. Wanta see me do it?"

"No," Mavis said firmly and took a sip of hot tea.

"Here comes Claude Metumbe now," Daniel said. He stood up to greet his superior in the Ranger Service. "Good to see all of you," Metumbe said. He smiled, leaned over and kissed the hands of Mavis and Elizabeth, Daniel's wife. He began to summarize the saga of the past week, filling in the gaps.

"Where do I start?"

"Start with the ivory poaching," Jack said.

"Mr. James Brockman is the undersecretary to the Chairman of the Kenya Wildlife Service. His office is also in charge of the census. The census told us that even though the elephant population was growing, there would be a decline in the growth that we could not explain. It appears from our internal investigation that Brockman has manipulated this for the past couple of years. He then took measures that would conceal the decline from us and protect him while he managed to develop an ivory trading business. With several African nations still selling 'culled' ivory, there remains a strong international market."

"Brockman? Did I meet him, Daniel?" Jack asked.

"Yes. He was the heavy set man. A member of an old colonial family. He definitely liked to eat."

"I remember him. He's the super huge guy who kept eating all the strawberries," R.O. added.

Mavis frowned. R.O. got the message.

"Brockman was able to recruit some pilots and poachers to cull elephant herds in remote areas of Kenya and Tanzania. Most of the men he hired were either right out of prison or veterans of the civil wars to the south. He would manipulate wildlife records from field rangers and would hit areas that were understaffed or were felt secure. It worked. He was able to accumulate millions of dollars worth of ivory, lion and leopard skins, and big cat skulls. The Kenya Navy boarded the cargo ship and confiscated some of the contraband. It is estimated that the carcasses and ivory he left on Kilimanjaro and the ship were just a small part of what actually made it to India. Maybe ten percent."

"What about Brockman?" Jack asked.

"He's in the hospital in Mombasa in a coma. Apparently he resisted arrest and suffered several gunshot wounds. He is not expected to survive."

Heather had had just about enough. She suddenly rose from the table and stood facing everyone. Her face was stern and she had a deep frown on her forehead. Everyone quit talking.

"I'm sorry anyone has to die. That's sad for their family and friends. But I saw what his men did to those elephant families. That's what's really sad. That there are people like that in this world just doesn't make sense. I don't have any tears for the big Mr. Brockman. I don't feel any sadness for predators like him." She looked down at the table and then across to her father. She knew that he had dedicated his whole life to understanding and helping wildlife. "I've saved my tears for the elephant mothers and babies who were slaughtered needlessly." Heather's voice quivered and she began to cry. She put her hands over her face as she sat down and sobbed quietly. Jack got up from the table and walked around to her. He pulled her close to him.

Everyone at the table was quiet. Then Metumbe continued.

"We also learned from Brockman's computer files who was really behind the whole scheme. It's Sir Frederick Henning."

Daniel had a sick feeling in his stomach.

"Sir Frederick Henning was indicted this morning by the Supreme Court of Kenya for high crimes against the state. What we have learned is that as Chairman of the Kenya Wildlife Service, he established an international trade in ivory and rhino horns that covers the globe. It is estimated from the secret records recovered from an underground vault only yesterday that he has accumulated over five hundred million dollars from animal contraband over the last twenty-three years."

"That is sickening," Mavis said and put down her fork.

"Where is he?" Daniel asked knowing the answer before he asked it.

"Whereabouts unknown. Interpol, Scotland Yard, and the FBI have all been notified. I suspect he is somewhere in Russia. His files had extensive records of sales to the former Soviet Union and East Germany. And then after the fall of the Berlin Wall, there were continued sales to Russia, southeast Asia, and some western nations, which I can't name. Our president is contacting the western nations privately to explore the problem. I'm afraid that other issues such as drugs, slavery, and terrorism have been raised as well."

There was a pall of silence around the table.

"I'm sorry to ruin your celebration. But we should be happy it's over. With this scandal reaching so deep into the government, I can't believe it will ever happen again. Now enjoy your dinner. I must go. Our current director has resigned and I've been appointed the new Director of the Kenya Wildlife Service."

"Oh, congratulations," Mavis said and everyone joined in.

Daniel got up and walked around and hugged his old friend.

"I'm going to need a new Deputy Director and Chief of Ranger Operations. Got anyone in mind?" Metumbe winked at Daniel.

"Daddy!" Rebecca shouted with a big smile on her face.

"Daddy sounds good to me," Metumbe said and turned to leave. He stopped and faced Daniel. "Congratulations, Deputy Director Okere."

Everyone at the table applauded. The other patrons of the restaurant stared at the celebration.

"Can I ask you just one more thing?" Mavis said.

"Who was the pilot of the Cessna 310?"

"I was wondering if you were going to ask. He is retired Brigadier General Virgil Miller, United States Air Force. He is a highly decorated World War II, Korea, and Vietnam pilot. His daughter was Dr. Judith Miller, a lowland primate specialist."

"Was?" Mavis asked solemnly.

"Yes. She was murdered by gorilla poachers about five years ago near Lake Victoria. The general came here for her memorial and has stayed ever since. He has played an important role in uncovering several poaching rings. He has proven to be our best secret weapon. When I talked to him this morning, he was fueling his plane and called to say good-bye."

"Where will he go?" R.O. asked.

"I imagine he is going home. Which reminds me I must leave."

R.O. stood up and walked over to Metumbe.

"Sir," he said.

"Yes, Mr. MacGregor." Metumbe looked down at R.O. and smiled.

"I would like to give you something to help keep fighting those criminals who kill the elephants and lions. It's worth a lot of money." R.O. reached into the cargo pocket of his shorts and pulled out one of his mechanical toys. "This is Roger." R.O. handed it to Metumbe.

"Well, I...thank you. But what will I do with Roger?"

"Here, push this button and set him on the table." R.O. pointed to a red button and handed it to Metumbe.

Metumbe looked around at the table and caught Mavis' eye. She shook her head up and down and smiled. Metumbe set Roger on the table and pushed the button. The red and green "Samburu" lights came on, the little lever popped up and down. But after about ten seconds, with everyone thoroughly entertained, Roger

did something brand new. A small trapdoor on the side
of the boat-shaped toy popped open and green shiny
objects rolled out on the table. Everyone was perfectly
still.

Jack got up from his chair slowly and limped over to
where R.O. and Metumbe were standing. He picked up
one of the green objects and held it up in the air so the
natural light of the street passed through. Everyone at
the table followed his every move. Finally he spoke.
R.O. was already smiling from ear to ear.

"It's an emerald."

A collective gasp came from around the table. Chris
gave Heather a high five.

"Little brother, you have outdone yourself." Chris
smiled.

"I can only guess where they came from," Mavis
said. She got up and walked over to Ryan and knelt so
they could be eye to eye.

"Ryan…" She corrected herself. "R.O. Are those
from where I think they're from?"

Ryan shook his head yes.

"Cayman," he said. "When I got to the hospital after
the hurricane, I found them in the pocket of my shorts.
Before the nurses threw the shorts away, I poured them
into one of my machines. When I built Roger, I thought
they would give him some weight and the green would
reflect in the light. It makes a great green, Mom."

Chris and Heather were fighting to hold back their
laughter. They truly felt for their brother.

"I know, hon. We'll have to talk about this and
contact the Inspector of the Royal Cayman Police Service to see what to do with the emeralds."

"But I want the elephants to have them." R.O. looked
deep into his mother's eyes and she knew he meant it.

"If the Inspector says its OK, then we'll give them to
Mr. Metumbe for the elephants. That's the best we can
do."

"I know, Mom. Thanks." R.O. reached out and hugged his mother.

Jack started scooping up the emeralds and poured the rest of them out of Roger onto a linen table napkin. Folding the napkin, he put it in his pocket.

Sensing it was time to leave, Metumbe walked around the table and shook everyone's hands. Daniel's wife gave him a hug.

"Oh, I almost forgot something." He reached into his suit pocket and brought out an envelope. He handed it to Chris. "My office received this e-mail from the U.S. this morning. It's marked 'urgent.' Good-bye." Soon he was out the door.

All eyes were on Chris. Slowly he opened it, peeled out the piece of paper and read it. He slid it back into the envelope.

"No you don't, mister. Either read it out loud or I will. There are no secrets in this family today!" Mavis said.

Chris carefully opened the paper again and scanned the table, making eye contact with everyone. He knew it would be better if he read it.

> "Dear Chris: I've got great news. I've been selected as one of the economic interns for the United States delegation for the Environmental Summit next month in Cairo. I can hardly wait to see you. I know that you and your family must be having a fabulous time in East Africa. I can only imagine the calm and serene days of watching beautiful wildlife. And the idea of sleeping peacefully under the stars only to wake up to a rich camp breakfast cooked by safari chefs is just awesome. What a life! Sorry I missed the fun.
>
> Love, Natalie."

Chris sat quietly and then looked up. Everyone had absolutely no expression on their faces. Suddenly R.O. chuckled and everyone burst out laughing at the same time. They laughed and then laughed even more.

The MacGregors and the Okeres forced themselves back into the rich French cuisine. Heather and Rebecca loosened their shorts and tried to eat more. R.O. played with his eight-inch tall soufflé long enough to watch it drop to the size of a pancake.

Chris sat and talked to his mother. He was excited about going to Egypt, their next stop. He had always wanted to visit the Egyptian museum and see Luxor and the Valley of the Kings. And to see Natalie would be just incredible as far as he was concerned.

"I can't wait to see her either," Mavis said.

The party continued on while forty miles away the Cessna 310 climbed to a cruising altitude. Brigadier General Virgil Miller received air traffic clearance to Addis Abbaba, the capital of Ethiopia. There he would hopscotch over to the Red Sea and follow it all the way to Cairo. He had mapped out a flight plan to Cairo, Rome, Paris, and London. Then there would be a long jump to Iceland, then to Nova Scotia. It would be an easy flight back to the Midwest from there. As the Cessna acquired altitude, the general reached over to the control panel and lifted up the picture of his daughter Judith.

"Well, honey, it's time to go home." He rubbed his thumb across the well worn picture and put it back in its place.

As the sun began to set on the Serengeti, a mother elephant rubbed her trunk across the body of her baby as he splashed water from the small temporary lake brought on by the very late summer rains. She was happy that they were together, but the stains around her eyes gave her the appearance of a strange looking mask that reached from ear to ear across the breadth of her face. They were the dark stains of tears. Tears from missing her lifelong friends, her companions, her family that had been killed.

No human on earth could understand her pain or feel her loneliness. For in Africa, it is only the wild animals who really understand each other. And at this moment in time, it was only the other elephants who could understand her elephant tears.

Richard Trout, the author of this action/adventure series of novels about the MacGregor family, is an environmental biologist and college professor. He is a strong advocate for the protection of threatened and endangered species and believes that education is the key.

Trout speaks to classes in elementary, middle schools, high schools, and college on the following topics:

How to Write Action/Adventure Fiction
What Makes a Novel a Techno-thriller
Taking a Novel from Concept to Bookstore
Environmental Problems of the Day
Diving the Cayman Wall
Sharks of the California Straits
East African Wildlife and Their Habitats
Reef Ecology
The Secrets of Ancient Egypt
Marinelife of the Red Sea

For more information, contact LangMarc Publishing
1-800-864-1648

# GLOSSARY

## Marrakech Stew
### From Chapter Six "Tastes Like Kudu"

1-1/2 cups of chopped onion
1 cup of sliced celery
1 medium sweet red pepper, sliced
4 cloves garlic, minced
1 tbsp. all-purpose flour
1 tsp. ground cinnamon
1/2 tsp. curry powder
1/4 tsp. cumin
1/4 tsp. ground cloves
1/4 tsp. turmeric
1 tsp. chili powder
1/4 tsp. ground red pepper
1/2 medium butternut squash, peeled and cubed
1 can diced tomatoes
1/2 cup chicken or vegetable broth
8 oz. fresh or frozen and thawed chopped okra
1 can (16 oz.) chick-peas, rinsed and drained
1/4 cup raisins
1-1/2 lbs. trimmed and cubed kudu (sirloin steak)
Salt and freshly ground pepper
3 tbsp. Olive Oil

Pour two tablespoons olive oil in a Dutch oven. Warm over medium heat until hot. Add the onions, celery, and sweet red peppers. Saute' for five minutes, or until vegetables are tender. Stir in the flour, cinnamon, curry powder, cumin, cloves, turmeric, chili powder, and ground pepper. Cook and stir over medium-low heat for two minutes. Add the garlic and stir. As soon as you smell the garlic cooking, add the broth. Stir in the squash, tomatoes and bring to a boil over high heat. While stew is simmering, pour remaining tablespoon of olive oil into a skillet. Warm over medium heat until hot. Add cubed beef that has been lightly salted and peppered. Stir occasionally until browned thoroughly, about ten minutes. Remove from heat and add to the stew. Stir in the okra, chick-peas, and raisins and simmer for ten to fifteen minutes, or until the okra is tender. Season with salt and freshly ground pepper. Serve with thick, crusty bread. Serves six. Variation: Any lean wild meat such as venison is wonderful with this recipe. Used by permission. © 2000 by Stephen C. Funk

# Wild Animals of East Africa
## Mentioned in *Elephant Tears*

Each animal mentioned in *Elephant Tears* has a common name and a scientific name. The scientific name is derived from Latin words that describe the animal's shape, color, unique characteristic, or some type of behavior. The scientific name may also include the name of the scientist who discovered the animal. The scientific name has two parts. The first word listed is called the genus and should always have a capitalized first letter. The second word is called the species and should have a lower case first letter. Both words should be underlined or printed in italics whenever they are used.

Sometimes only the genus is listed. This may mean that the exact species is not known or that there are too many species to list. In that case, the scientist will write the genus and then follow it with sp. The specialty in biology dedicated to studying the naming of animals is called taxonomy.

| | |
|---|---|
| Agama lizard | *Agama sp.* |
| Baboon | *Papio sp.* |
| Cheetah | *Acinonyx jubatus* |
| Duiker | *Sylvicapra grimmia* |
| Elephant | *Loxodonta africana* |
| Gemsbok | *Oryx gazella* |
| Giraffe | *Giraffa cemelopardalis* |
| Guinea fowl | *Numididae meleagris* |
| Hyena | *Crocuta crocuta* |
| Impala | *Aepyceros melampus* |
| Kudu | *Tragelaphus strepsiceros* |
| Lion | *Panthera leo* |
| Mamba | *Dendroaspic sp.* |
| Monkey, vervet | *Cercopithecus pygerythrus* |
| Secretary bird | *Sagitarius serpentarius* |
| Warthog | *Phacochoerus aethiopicus* |
| Wild dog | *Lycaon pictus* |
| Zebra | *Equus burchelli* |

# Rebecca Teaches Heather
# to Count to Ten in Swahili

| | |
|---|---|
| One | *Moja* |
| Two | *Mbili* |
| Three | *Tatu* |
| Four | *Nne* |
| Five | *Tano* |
| Six | *Sita* |
| Seven | *Saba* |
| Eight | *Nane* |
| Nine | *Tisa* |
| Ten | *Kumi* |

If you wish to count from ten to twenty, simply add the connective word "na" between the word for ten and the number you desire.

| Example: | | |
|---|---|---|
| | Eleven | *Kumi na moja* |
| | Fourteen | *Kumi na Nne* |
| | Twenty | *Ishirini* |
| | Twenty-three | *Ishirini na Tatu* |

# Library and Internet Activities

East African Wildlife
Serengeti Game Park
Amboseli Game Park
Tsavo Game Park
Masai Mara Game Park
Nairobi, the capitol of Kenya
Kenya
Tanzania
Elephant Poaching
CITIES (Congress on the International Trade in Endangered
      Species)
Samburu Tribe
Kikuyu Tribe
Masai Tribe
Portuguese Exploration of Africa
Mombasa to Nairobi Railroad
*Cry of the Kalahari* by Delia and Mark Owens
*The Eye of the Elephant* by Delia and Mark Owens
Owens Foundation for Wildlife Conservation, Inc.
*Out of Africa* by Karen Blixen
*The Green Hills of Africa* by Ernest Hemingway
Jane Goodall and Chimpanzee Research
Diane Fossey and Gorilla Research
How Zoos Protect the DNA of Endangered Species
Bell Helicopters
Aerospatiale Helicopters
Big Game Hunting in Africa
Hunting as a Means of Wildlife Conservation
*Born Free* by Joy Adamson
*My African Journey* by Winston Churchill

# Cayman Gold: Lost Treasure of Devils Grotto

Book 1 of MacGregor Family Series

"Children's Bookwatch" • *Midwest Book Review*

"...*Cayman Gold* is a well-crafted adventure with meticulous attention to accuracy in detail and highly recommended reading for teens and young adults." James Cox, Editor-in-Chief

"Kids Books" • *Northwest Metro Times*

"This riveting story combines historical events, hurricanes, daring escapades and some nasty bad guys and puts them all together in a way that will keep you on the edge of your seat until the final page. Enjoy *Cayman Gold*."—Dale Knowles

"Book Briefs" • The Sunday *Oklahoman*

"...This adventure story offers suspense and some good lessons in conservation."—Kay Dye

"I am thrilled to see fresh, quality literature! While *Cayman Gold* is written primarily for young people, I believe the entire family will enjoy reading this exciting adventure."—Dr. Fred Rhodes, Putnam City Schools, OK City.

"I was quickly drawn into the story and thoroughly enjoyed *Cayman Gold*. I know for my students this is a book they will enjoy."—Ginna Bloom, Library/Media Specialist

"The word that comes to mind when I think of *Cayman Gold* is WOW! ...a wonderful book for people of all ages. My whole family has read and enjoyed it. The attention to detail is great...I can't wait until Mr. Trout's next book!"
—Bryan Luff, Oklahoma City, OK.

"I enjoyed *Cayman Gold* so much. I love hearing about the tropics. The descriptions were so intense, I could almost feel the warm Caribbean breeze."—Jamie Guthrie, Yukon, OK.

"*Cayman Gold* is an exciting adventure story...I learned a lot about the Cayman Islands and scuba diving. I liked it so much I gave a copy to a friend."—Joshua Chesnut, Jenks, OK.

"*Cayman Gold* was so exciting, I didn't want to put it down. Can't wait until the next adventure comes out."—Drew Nevius, Edmond, OK.

# To Order Copies

If unavailable at your local bookstores, LangMarc Publishing will fill your order within 24 hours.

Postal Orders: LangMarc Publishing
P.O. Box 33817 • San Antonio, Texas 78265-3817

*Elephant Tears: Mask of the Elephant*
$9.95 + $1.50 shipping 1 or 2 books
*Cayman Gold: Lost Treasure of Devils Grotto*
$9.95 + $1.50 shipping 1 or 2 books

Call for quantity discounts for classrooms
and UPS charges on quantity orders.
1-800-864-1648

Please send payment with order:
_____ Copies of *Elephant Tears* @ $9.95 _____
_____ Copies of *Cayman Gold* @ $9.95 _____
Sales tax (Texas only)
Shipping _____
Check enclosed: _____

Or your Mastercard, Visa, Discover, American Express Card number and expiration date.

Expires: _____
Your Name: _____

Address: _____

_____

Telephone Number: _____